THE BOSS

MANHATTAN RECORDS

M. S. PARKER

BELMONTE PUBLISHING, LLC

Copyright © 2019 Belmonte Publishing LLC

Published by Belmonte Publishing LLC

ONE

NATE

"As always, the room is paid through the weekend," I said as I reached for my suit jacket. "You're welcome to stay, and I encourage you to do so as this will be your last opportunity."

Roma straightened, her robe opening far enough for me to see one swollen nipple. "What does that mean?"

"Tonight was our swan song," I said evenly. "Our final scene."

"I know what *swan song* means," she snapped, her expression twisting into something ugly. "What I'm asking is what the hell you think you're doing."

I raised an eyebrow. Her anger wasn't surprising. One of the things that had appealed to me about Roma was seeing someone with such a temper submitting to me, even when I infuriated her. It had been exciting at first. At present, it was just annoying.

"I'm ending this arrangement," I said. "I was trying to be

polite about it, but since you seem determined to make me be blunt, I will. We're done."

"No." She stood up, not appearing to notice that her robe was hanging open, exposing the red lines the robes had made, the bruised flesh from the clamps. "You don't end this until we both say we're done."

I turned to face her, sliding my hands into my pockets to keep the image of the calm, unruffled Dom. "The arrangement was, either one of us could end things at any point. This is me, ending the arrangement. Now. Tonight."

She shook her head, cheeks coloring even as the finger she pointed at me shook. "No. No! After all the shit I've done for you and let you do to me, you *owe* me. That's what this arrangement was about, asshole! I play your little fucktoy, and you get me what I want."

I inhaled slowly and then let out the breath just as slowly. This had happened to me before, but it didn't make it any more pleasant. "You understood exactly what this was when you agreed to it. We fucked, and you enjoyed it because you like men fawning all over you. Wasn't that your fantasy tonight? To have more than one man fuck you while I watched? So I could see how they all want you?"

"Fuck you!" She had tears in her eyes, but they weren't because she was hurt. She was furious. Or she was trying to manipulate me. Either one didn't do anything but confirm that I was making the right choice.

"It's not my fault you got more involved than you should have," I started toward the door. "You knew the score going into this. You got great sex and got to be seen on my arm at big events, meet all of my connections. I was supposed to get a sub without all this drama. If anyone should be pissed, it's me."

A glass hit the wall next to the door, shattering all over the carpet.

"Don't you dare walk away from me, you fucking bastard!"

I paused but didn't turn. I kept my voice calm, even though I was seething inside. She was going too far. "Roma, I will call security to throw you out on your ass if you can't behave like an adult."

"You're a real son of a bitch, you know that?"

"Yes, well, you're a bitch, so I guess we're about even."

I left before she could throw something else at me. I'd pay for the damage that'd happened before I walked out, but if she trashed the hotel room, I'd have her ass arrested and held accountable for the rest of it. She could be as pissed at me as she wanted, but she was acting like a child. If I'd known she'd come with that much drama, I wouldn't have even bothered.

The sex hadn't been *that* good.

TWO

ASHLEE

"DAMMIT!" I SPUN AROUND, SOCKS SLIPPING ON THE linoleum floor as I attempted to stop my forward momentum. I caught myself on the edge of the counter and managed to yank open the microwave door before disaster struck.

I removed the fork from the plastic bowl of popcorn and tossed it into the sink. I sighed, closing my eyes for a moment. That could have been disastrous, and the worst part was, it wasn't the first time I'd nearly blown up my microwave because I'd forgotten to remove a metal utensil from something I was heating up. I didn't even have a good excuse this time. Other times I'd done stuff this absent-minded, I'd at least been able to claim that I had something more important on my mind. A doctor's trip with Mom. A final I wasn't sure I could pass. A job interview.

Tonight, I'd been dancing around my kitchen to a song I'd heard at work. It was a brand-new single from Unraveling, and it'd been playing all over the place. I generally only liked Unraveling's older stuff, back from when they'd first been

5

signed, but this felt more like that rather than their last album. I may only have been a runner at Manhattan Records when "Threads of My Mind" had been released, but even I'd known how unhappy everyone had been about its performance.

I shook my popcorn bowl, even though the butter and salt hadn't had much time to settle, then double-checked to make sure I hadn't left anything else behind before turning the microwave back on. While I waited for my snack, I washed the fork, dried it, and put it away, my thoughts wandering as I did the mundane task.

What was it about "Fire and Light" that made it so much better than anything Unraveling had done the last time? One of the things I enjoyed about working at Manhattan Records was getting to better understand the intricacies of how it all worked. Not only how an album came together, but all of the different roles people played in the process. Being in the A&R department – Artists and Repertoire – I would eventually get to see all sorts of aspects of the music industry as I continued my rise in the company.

As much as I liked my work, I wasn't the sort of person who took it home with me, but this song just wouldn't get out of my head, which made it hard to stop thinking about work. I'd even had music streaming while I'd cleaned today, but I'd caught myself humming the song in the shower.

The microwave dinged, and I retrieved my popcorn, carrying it the short distance to the other side of the room where my second-hand couch sat across from a small, but more than serviceable, television. My place wasn't big, and my things weren't new, but I didn't mind. I was twenty-three years old, and I had my own apartment. I'd started as an intern at Manhattan Records when I was barely twenty, moved up to runner shortly after I graduated from NYU, and three months ago, I'd gotten a promotion.

Life was good.

It hadn't always been that way, but if I'd learned anything, it'd been to appreciate what I had when I had it.

I pulled my feet up under me, wrapped an arm around my popcorn bowl, and picked up my remote. I'd been waiting all week to binge the second season of my newest guilty pleasure. A fictional show about a reality show. I'd stumbled on the first season a couple weeks ago and finished it up last Sunday afternoon, but this past week had been too busy for me to be able to watch more than an episode or two a night, so I'd decided to give myself a little reward for hard work well done and spend my Saturday night watching TV while snacking to my heart's content.

I shifted, frowning as I couldn't quite get comfortable. Something was lumpy right against the middle of my back, and it took me a moment to realize it was my hair. It hung nearly to my waist, and I hadn't felt like taking the time to completely dry it after my shower, which meant the only way to keep it from becoming a tangled mess was to braid it.

The door across the hall slammed, and I heard a burst of laughter as my neighbors headed out for the night. I'd lived here for a couple months and had met them a day or two after I'd moved in. Perry and Gary. Nice guys. About my age and fellow NYU graduates. They hadn't been in the communications program, but we'd shared a couple of the same teachers, though not at the same time.

We'd talked a few times, whenever we happened to run into each other in the hall or at the mailboxes. Once, I'd been downstairs doing my laundry, and they'd come down and spent an hour with me. Gary was a flirt, but he never took things too far, and I definitely wasn't Perry's type considering he was gay. I hadn't been worried about moving to Lower Manhattan on my own, but Mom hadn't been thrilled. When I told her about Perry and Gary, she'd felt much better.

I may have exaggerated my 'friendship' with them, but if it made her worry less, the little white lie was worth it. Besides, I had a feeling they were the sort of neighbors who'd at least keep an eye out for anything suspicious. We'd had a couple of those in the Staten Island neighborhood where I'd grown up.

As if the thought of her had prompted it, Mom's text tone went off on my phone. I went to my favorite streaming app, then leaned forward to pick up my phone.

Did you see last night's Murder Mysteries? *I think that suspect looks like Lauren Lopez's Uncle Mauro.*

I laughed and shook my head. Mom's newest obsession was anything about unsolved murders. She was convinced she was going to solve one of the cold cases, and every so often, she'd send me a text with her thoughts on a specific episode. Sometimes I watched them, sometimes I didn't, but I always listened to her theories. She was never actually serious, but it was a thing of ours. We'd always made a point of having something we could talk about that had nothing to do with real life. It had been our way of dealing with things when they'd gotten bad, and we'd continued it even as life had gotten better.

Last year, we'd discussed bird watching. The year before that, it'd been musicals. Whenever an Olympic year came around, we'd share tidbits about athletes and countries and cultures.

Was Uncle Mauro the one with the limp or the one who was missing the tip of his left pinky finger?

Two mouthfuls of popcorn later, Mom's response came through.

Dammit. I guess that would discount him since they had a set of full fingerprints and he was reported running away from the scene.

I started the first episode, fully aware that I would probably continue to have minor interruptions for the next couple hours until Mom decided it was time for her to go to bed. I wouldn't trade it for the world, though. We still lived in the same city, but I didn't get home to visit as much as I wanted. This was a good way for me to stay in touch as my schedule grew busier and busier.

I never wanted to be too busy for her. She'd never been too busy for me, no matter what was going on in the rest of her life. I was always her top priority, and she'd always be mine.

Anything exciting at work? Possible serial killers? Romantic possibilities? Hopefully not the same person.

I coughed as a dry bit of popcorn got stuck. Leave it to Mom to bring up my dating life – or lack thereof – in a creative way.

THREE
ASHLEE

Artists and Repertoire in the music industry referred to the department that was responsible for the broad concepts of talent scouting and overseeing artistic development. At least, that was how it'd been explained to me when I'd first applied for an internship at Manhattan Records. I had a degree in communications, but that had covered so many different possibilities that it'd been impossible to remember all of the definitions for every department in every field.

When I'd first applied to be an intern, I hadn't known where I wanted to work, but as a runner, I'd had the chance to see for myself who did what and how and where. After six months or so, I'd been moved to run for primarily A&R, and that's how I'd decided this was where I wanted to be.

At least, that was the story I kept telling myself.

Not because I disliked my job. I liked it well enough. And I was pretty good at it. More than pretty good, as I'd discovered three months ago when I'd gotten a promotion from runner to personal assistant.

Speaking of...

I held out a cup of Salted Caramel Mocha Coffee as the elevator door opened, and my boss stepped out. Stu Hancock had been with Manhattan Records almost since the beginning, even though he barely looked old enough to vote. I was pretty sure I actually looked older than Mr. Hancock.

"Good morning," I said as I fell in step with him. "I put your mail on your desk, but most of it looks like junk. I confirmed your first appointment of the day and will start working my way through the rest of your schedule first thing."

"You know, Miss Webb, you aren't required to get me coffee each morning," he said with a smile. "I appreciate it, don't get me wrong, but it's not really necessary."

I shrugged. "I figured if I was already stopping to get my own, I might as well pick up yours and Ms. Lamas's while I'm there. No point in either of you needing to stop on your way in or send Flora or me out again."

"Well, thank you."

One of the things I appreciated the most about working under Mr. Hancock and Suzie Lamas was how well they managed to balance having a department that was both professional and casual. They didn't always take the time to thank us for doing something that was our actual job, but any time we went above and beyond, they made a point of expressing their gratitude.

"There's a voicemail about the event this weekend. I

believe it's Zed Hipwood inquiring about perks for Unraveling's appearance."

A shadow passed across Mr. Hancock's usually clear blue eyes. It wasn't there long, but it was enough for me to know that he wasn't fond of one of Manhattan Records' biggest stars. I'd heard conflicting stories about Hipwood over the past couple years, and there'd been all sorts of stories about him since the band had first appeared on the scene.

"Was he sober?"

I didn't answer right away, thinking carefully about the message I'd listened to. I didn't want to make an assumption and possibly cause an issue between the company and Unraveling's frontman. Mr. Hancock didn't rush me, which I appreciated. He and Ms. Lamas didn't ask rhetorical questions, and they didn't ask questions they didn't want answers to. If anything, they seemed to appreciate it when we took the time to come up with a clear and honest answer.

"It was hard to tell," I said finally. "He wasn't slurring his words, and his statements were understandable, but I know that people who are used to drinking a lot don't always have the same noticeable signs of being drunk that most people think of."

"True," Mr. Hancock said as I followed him into his office. He sat down behind his desk and sighed. "And Zed's definitely no stranger to alcohol."

"I've...guessed as much."

He pinched the bridge of his nose, and for once, he actually looked like he was in his early forties. "What did he want?"

I'd had to listen to the message three times to get it all, but

I was confident I'd managed to record everything. I pulled out my notebook and opened to the page for today. I transcribed notes into my phone at the end of every day, but I liked to have a hard copy too, especially if I was trying to take notes while I was on the phone. I found it simpler to do it that way.

"The event this weekend is to promote the summer releases and concert tours," I said. I'd double-checked that Hipwood had been correct about the point of the event. "He wants Unraveling to have the first announcement, both for the release and the tour."

Mr. Hancock nodded. "All right. What else?"

"He wants the band to have a private green room where they can go whenever they 'get bored.'" It might've been a little immature of me to include the air quotes, but I wasn't going to claim those words as my own. And I intended to continue making sure my boss knew what I had and hadn't said. "In said green room, he wants a specific selection of alcoholic beverages, of which I have a list, enough for each of 'his boys' to 'chill.' He's also asking for ten 'hot bitches' to be dancing in the room at all times."

Hancock leaned forward, his eyes closed and rubbed his temples. "He does have a way with words, doesn't he?" He didn't even bother to hide his sarcasm.

"Quite the gentleman." The words popped out of my mouth before I could think about the wisdom of actually saying them. "Sorry."

Hancock shook his head. "Don't worry about it. What else was there?"

"He wants Starburst Jellybeans, but only the yellow and green ones."

"He has a thing about red dye," Hancock said. "Not an allergy. He just hates it."

I nodded. "I actually remember reading that a few years ago."

"You're an Unraveling fan, then?"

I held up a hand and wiggled it back and forth. "If I'm going to be completely honest, I liked most of their first album, but only a song or two off every album since."

One side of Hancock's mouth tipped up in a half-smile. "They still manage to sell out stadiums all over the country."

I shrugged. "I didn't say *other* people didn't still like their music."

"Good point." Hancock leaned back. "Continue. Because I know there's more."

I blew out a breath. "You're right. There's also a list of half a dozen other snacks, including mini sliders, burritos, and organic kale."

"The new bass player only eats organic," Hancock explained. "I'm actually a little surprised that Hipwood even knows that."

I hesitated, then said, "I'm pretty sure the new organic bass player has a couple friends Hipwood likes a lot."

"Are we talking female friends we'll probably have to add to the backstage pass list until Hipwood gets tired of them, or either gender friends who are supplying Unraveling with things that are less than legal?"

I lifted a shoulder. "I think the former, but it might be the latter."

Hancock nodded. "All right. I'll make sure I let Nate know about that possible problem."

Nate.

That would be Nate Lexington. CEO and co-owner of Manhattan Records. The face of the company. Everyone's boss of bosses.

I'd seen him from a distance a few times but hadn't ever actually spoken to him, and I was fine with that. I'd put everything I had into a nice, neat package and give it to Mr. Hancock to use as he saw fit. Anything other than information gathering and doing whatever my immediate boss in the A&R department told me was well above my pay grade.

FOUR
NATE

WHEN THE PHONE IN MY DESK BUZZED AGAIN, I SIGHED and pulled out the phone. It'd been going off at least once an hour since I'd gotten up this morning and I didn't need to look at it to know it was Roma. I had two phones. One for women and the other for everything else. It made things much simpler to keep sex and my actual life separate.

Occasionally, the women I dumped would try to cling to me, calling, texting, that sort of thing, but ignoring them generally got the point across. A day or two of a few tearful voicemails or angry text messages and then it was done. At least I assumed the voicemails were tearful. I never listened to them. The only reason I didn't delete and block numbers immediately after ending an arrangement was because I'd learned early on that some women, if provoked too much, would go that extra mile to find my personal number or harass me at work.

Hudson MacIntosh.

I'd learned a lot about how to handle women from that

nutcase. Ghosting her had pissed her off but blocking her number had been the last straw. She'd showed up at my place, pounding on my door and making an embarrassment of herself. When that hadn't gotten her anything but a police escort back to her car, she'd come into work and stood in the lobby when security wouldn't let her upstairs. Manhattan Records had just been getting their feet underneath them at the time, and it'd been a headache I hadn't needed. Eventually, strings had been pulled, and I'd been able to quietly take out a restraining order against her.

I opened my messages and scrolled to the bottom, not bothering to read the litany of insults and curses being hurled my way. The other benefit of having a separate phone for all communication with my 'girlfriends' was that I had everything readily available should I need to take legal action.

Again, Hudson MacIntosh.

She'd followed the restraining order and stayed away, but that hadn't prevented her from going to a tabloid with stories of our bedroom exploits. Fortunately for me, that'd backfired on her. She hadn't realized that telling people I'd used handcuffs and blindfolds had reflected on her more than me.

Sexist, sure, but that wasn't my fault. I couldn't make society think the same way about a man with certain kinks as they did about a woman who had them too. Just like those anonymous pictures of her on her knees, sucking me off while I watched the NFL draft had sent her back to Nebraska with her tail between her legs while I'd pretty much just gotten a headshake and eye roll.

At least she hadn't tried to say it hadn't been consensual. I still had the footage the pictures had come from, and there'd be absolutely no doubt in anyone's mind that she'd consented if I released that tape. I hadn't done it, of course, because she'd backed off, but I would've.

That was the whole point of me getting permission to record everything. The women I was with knew that no matter where we were or what we were doing, chances were high that I was recording every movement in some way. I'd worked too fucking hard to get where I was to have some bitch lie about me and steal it all. Most of them thought I liked to watch it later and jerk off to it, but the truth was, everything was stored away in case I needed it for some legal reason.

I didn't do re-runs.

Speaking of which...

There's no further discussion warranted. You agreed to all terms prior to entering into our agreement. Don't contact me again.

As I sent the message, I wondered if perhaps I should start drawing up actual contracts. I hadn't wanted to go that far since I'd most likely need to bring an actual lawyer into it to make them binding. I had a business degree from NYU and could find my way around a record contract, but something like this would need more than that little bit of knowledge to make it worth the effort. A poorly written contract could fuck me up worse than not having one at all.

Since I hadn't yet replaced Roma, I turned the phone off and returned it to my desk. Work was going to be my only focus for a while. I'd had enough of women for at least a couple weeks.

I'd barely started going through my email when someone

knocked on the door. A wave of relief went through me when I looked up to see my partner, Finley Kordell, standing in the doorway. I waved him in.

Finley was eleven years older than me and actually resembled me enough for people to occasionally wonder if we were brothers. His hair was a rusty, cinnamon sort of color rather than nearly white-blond like mine, and my eyes were dark brown while his were blue, but we were both tall, with broad shoulders and square jaws. I was a couple inches taller, but for a guy heading toward fifty, Finley probably could've knocked me on my ass if he really tried. I always thought it was something about the eyes.

Luckily for me, he was laid-back enough that in the ten-plus years we'd known each other, we'd never once come to any sort of physical altercation. In fact, Finley was one of the few people who could call me on my shit and get away with it.

Judging by the expression on his face at the moment, he was about to do just that.

"I'm hearing rumors that Zed is being a pain in the ass again."

"I wasn't aware that he'd ever stopped," I said dryly. "Tell me something I don't know."

"He's harassing A&R about special perks for the event this weekend." Finley sat on the couch against the far wall rather than in the chair across from me.

"Suzie came to you?"

He shook his head. "I happened to overhear Stu's assistant telling him about the call. I didn't stick around to find out details since we both know he'll come to us if it's something we need to know."

"How did Stu's assistant get the call?" I asked. I vaguely remembered something about hiring a second assistant for A&R so Stu and Suzie could each have their own, but I didn't recall having met the person.

"She's always here half an hour before Stu, going through email and voicemail to weed out the stuff he doesn't need to bother himself with." Finley sent a pointed look at the stack of unopened mail next to my computer. "It's why I suggested you get an assistant yourself."

"And I told you that it wouldn't be worth it since I'd have to waste my time showing him or her how I liked things done, only to have them quit in a couple weeks either because I was too mean or because I wouldn't fuck them. Possibly both."

He didn't even blink. "Your humility never ceases to amaze me."

I tipped him a sarcastic salute. "I've never claimed to lack confidence."

"No, you have not," he admitted. "On a different note, have you decided if you want Ollie Chandler sitting next to you or Roma during the dinner? Apparently, it'll make a difference in the optics."

"Shit."

Finley sighed. "What did you do?"

I tapped my pen on the desk. "I forgot that I'd included her on the guest list."

"And you've dumped her."

"She was getting too clingy," I said. "And I was bored."

Finley leaned forward, resting his elbows on his knees. "Have you ever met anyone who hasn't bored you?"

"Only you," I answered with a grin. When he didn't smile back, I cleared my throat. "Look, we both know Roma was only with me to meet people who could further her career. She knew that I was only with her for the sex. We both got what we wanted until it wasn't working anymore."

"And did she feel the same when you informed her that you didn't want her anymore?"

I narrowed my eyes. "It's not my fault she wanted more than I'm willing to give."

"Do you really think it's unusual for a woman to believe that a man may wish to spend time with her for reasons other than sex?"

"If she's with me, it should be unusual. I don't lead these women on, Finley, you know that."

"I know, but I'm a little tired of ending up your plus one because you keep breaking up with your women before events."

I grinned at him. "Come on, Finley. We make a cute couple."

He laughed, and I knew his annoyance at me would fade. He'd never hidden the fact that he was gay, but it wasn't something he advertised either. He was a discreet man about all aspects of his life, personal and professional. It was why we worked so well together. He liked doing the behind-the-scenes things, and I liked being the public face of the company. I might not always like socializing, but I liked the prestige and attention that came with running a company like Manhattan Records.

There were always the assholes who liked to make inferences – or flat-out statements – that Finley and I were lovers, but neither one of us let those sorts of things get to us. Once Finley realized that he wouldn't lose my friendship because some homophobic jackoffs liked to run their mouths, it'd become a joke between us.

"I mean it this time, Nate. I've got plans this weekend, so unless you want the table number to be uneven, you better figure out someone to take." He leaned back again and crossed his legs. "Now, what are we going to do about our star asshole?"

FIVE

ASHLEE

WHEN I GOT BACK FROM LUNCH, MR. HANCOCK WAS still out at his business meeting slash lunch, so I headed over to Ms. Lamas's office to ask if there was anything I could do for her. I liked her as much as I liked Mr. Hancock, but she definitely wasn't as easy-going about things. It was a completely different learning experience. One I appreciated, but sometimes, she scared the shit out of me.

"Anything I can help you with?" I asked after she called me into her office.

"Stu still at lunch?"

"Yes, ma'am."

"I told Nate if he put Stu in charge of wining and dining, he'd lose an entire afternoon." Despite the words, her tone was affectionate. She and Stu had a strange sort of relationship, something like I'd always imagined a sibling would be. She sighed. "But he's good at what he does. I'd be too busy looking at my phone and thinking about getting back to the office. He enjoys his role, and I enjoy mine."

That was probably the longest speech I'd ever heard her give. Generally, she was more of an action person than a talking person.

"Do you need his approval for any of the tasks you've completed?" she asked briskly. "Anything you're waiting on?"

"No. Once I finished my list, I left it on his desk to review. He'd already given me permission to look into all of the requests..." I paused, realizing I was saying too much. "Sorry, ma'am. You didn't ask for details. The answer's no, I'm not waiting on his approval for anything."

"What did he have you working on?"

"Seeing how many of Unraveling's requested perks are feasible." I kept my answer concise.

She gave me a searching look. "How long have you been his assistant?"

"Three months, ma'am."

A long pause, and then she nodded as if she'd decided something. "I have something I'd like you and Flora to do."

I listened as she explained the task, asked two clarifying questions, and then went out to find Flora. The two of us knew each other, of course, and we'd talked in passing as well as when we were waiting on our bosses. We'd even both worked on the same project, but we'd had our own individual tasks and had barely interacted. I didn't think she was the kind of person I'd ever really be good friends with, but I figured we could work together without a problem.

"She wants us to do what?" Flora asked.

She was pretty, with fashionably-short caramel-colored curls and the type of slender figure that she enjoyed flaunting. She wasn't like the catty girls I'd gone to school with, but she did seem to enjoy the attention.

"We're supposed to check out whatever musical acts that are going viral," I repeated, "and make notes. She wants to know a summary of the comments, both positive and negative. We're also to make suggestions for possible ways to market each act, as well as what we think are their biggest strengths and weaknesses."

"Is that really an assistant's job?" Flora asked as she perched on the edge of my desk. "I mean, I get that's what A&R does, but doesn't it seem weird to you?"

I shrugged. "Not really. I mean, as assistants, isn't it our job to do what our bosses tell us?"

Flora leaned closer, a gleam in her cyan eyes. "I like Ms. Lamas and Mr. Hancock as bosses, but you have to admit, wouldn't it be amazing to work under the *big* boss?"

She didn't have to say his name because, even though, technically, Manhattan Records was owned by both Nate Lexington and Finley Kordell, everyone knew that Mr. Lexington was 'the big boss.' And I had a feeling this particular conversation wasn't going to go anywhere good.

"Could you imagine what it would be like to be *under* him?" She wiggled her eyebrows.

I rolled my eyes. "Really? That's the innuendo you're going with?"

"I can do a lot better than that," she said with a grin. "He can boss me around anytime, especially if it means I get to find out just how *big* the boss is."

"You do realize that's not innuendo, right? There's no

subtext there. Just text." I clicked on a popular video, then cursed under my breath as it tried to load.

I needed to call IT to check the network. Something had been making the connection screwy for the past two weeks, and everyone was tired of it, but the only thing any of us could do was call IT and wait for them to do whatever it was they did and hope it worked.

Personally, I had a theory that they were messing with us as some sort of massive practical joke that was going to get the entire department fired soon. In all honesty, I didn't understand how they hadn't been fired already. Mr. Lexington wasn't known for being the most understanding of bosses. He wasn't a monster or anything, but he expected his employees to do their jobs and do them well.

Maybe it was Mr. Kordell who was keeping the IT guys around. Since he was the co-owner, he might've used his position to prevent Mr. Lexington from doing a mass firing. He was probably that sort of guy. I'd never met him, but I'd heard good things. He'd been the original financial backer, taking a chance partnering with Mr. Lexington, but didn't want to be in the public eye. He came to the company Christmas party every year, but mostly kept to himself. I didn't think it was out of a dislike of people but what did I know?

"You've got it bad, girl." Flora pushed my shoulder.

"What?" I blinked up at her. "What do I have?"

She leaned closer to me and put her hand to her mouth as if she intended to tell me something private. "You were thinking about how big Nate's cock is."

"Flora!" Heat flooded my face. "You can't talk like that about our boss!"

She shrugged and smoothed down her skirt. "Come on, Ash. You can't tell me you haven't fantasized about him."

"Ashlee," I corrected her for what felt like the thousandth time. "And no. I leave work at work."

A lie, but a little white one and not something that had anything at all to do with Nate Lexington. I figured that meant it didn't really count.

"Not even with those rumors?"

I frowned. "We really shouldn't be talking about this. It's completely inappropriate."

"Heaven forbid we do anything inappropriate." She rolled her eyes and then ran her pinky finger along her bottom lip, as if she needed to smooth out her burgundy lipstick. "You don't really want to sit here staring at videos of people desperate for attention and then have to write some massive report like we're in high school. I've got some seriously juicy gossip. It confirms a lot of what people say about him."

I ignored her and opened my desk drawer to get my earbuds. Ms. Lamas had given us both this task, but if Flora wasn't going to take it seriously, I'd have to do it myself.

Unfortunately, my earbuds weren't in my right drawer, which meant they were in the left one, and Flora was in front of it. I'd just have to try to block her out. That, however, was easier said than done.

"My best friend, Naima, is cousins with this girl who dated Nate for a few weeks last summer, and the things she told Naima about what Nate likes in the bedroom...it's like something straight out of one of those kinky erotic novels."

She said it with disgust, like she didn't have one of those

novels in the bottom left drawer of her desk. If she wasn't gossiping with her friends when she was supposed to be working, she was reading.

"Naima said it's not just like handcuffs and blindfolds either. I guess he tied her cousin up with ropes until she couldn't move, and then he did all sorts of things to her. He even made her give him a blowjob in a restaurant."

I stared harder at the screen and pretended that my entire face wasn't burning with embarrassment. I wasn't a prude, but this wasn't workplace conversation. Besides, I didn't want to think about my boss that way. Sure, he was gorgeous, but I'd have needed to be blind or dead not to realize that.

Out of the corner of my eye, I saw Flora watching me and wondered if the entertainment had turned from her gossiping to her trying to see how far she could push me. She was going to be disappointed. I wasn't a combative person. I'd told her I didn't think the conversation was appropriate, and now I was going to ignore her. If she couldn't get a rise out of me, she'd most likely stop.

"Could you imagine it? Being at a restaurant with him, and then he tells you to pretend you dropped something under the table, get down on your knees, and go down on him right there?" She sighed. "I get horny just thinking about it..."

Her voice trailed off on the last word, and I raised my head, assuming that she'd decided that we needed to get our work done.

That wasn't it at all.

The reason Flora had stopped was the glowering man in the expensive Italian suit.

Shit.

"You two. My office. Now."

Fuck my life.

SIX

NATE

I never pretended to be the boss everyone loved, and I certainly wasn't the boss known for having close, personal relationships with his employees. I didn't ask for ass-kissing, and I quite frankly didn't want it, but I did believe in respect.

And what I'd just heard wasn't even close to respectful.

"You two. My office. Now."

I didn't wait to see if they would follow me because, if they didn't, they wouldn't even get the chance to try to save their jobs. Not that they had much of one anyway, but any chance was better than no chance.

"Shut the door," I said as I walked around my desk and sank into my chair.

I left them standing as I gave them both hard looks. The short one with the long, henna-red hair looked mortified, her eyes darting everywhere around me but never actually looking directly at me. Her friend's face was red, but there was a defiant jut to her chin that told me she wouldn't go easily.

"Names?"

"Flora Watts," the taller one said, folding her arms.

"Ashlee Webb." The redhead's voice was soft.

Their names were enough to confirm that it had been the first young woman who'd been speaking. I hadn't heard the other one speak at all, not even to tell her friend to be quiet. She could have been speaking before I'd gotten there.

"That was quite an interesting conversation I walked into." I started in without asking either of them to sit down. "Would either of you like to explain? Or perhaps just give me a reason why I shouldn't fire both of you right now?"

Flora didn't wait more than a few seconds to start talking. "I don't know what you think you heard, Mr. Lexington, but Ashlee and I here were just talking about this book she was reading about this employee sleeping with her boss."

Ashlee's head snapped up, eyes wide enough for me to be able to identify the color of her irises as turquoise. "I–I–"

"Maybe the subject matter wasn't entirely workplace appropriate," Flora continued, "but how is discussing literature a firing offense? There's nothing in the company's policies about not talking about books."

"I wasn't reading a book!" Ashlee blurted out. Her cheeks colored.

Flora shot her one of the dirtiest looks I'd ever seen, and if the attitude she'd been showing hadn't already been convincing me that she was full of shit, that would've done it right there. Still, I waited to see if Ashlee would clarify her statement, but she said nothing.

"What about it, Miss Watts?" I asked dryly. "Were the two of you discussing a book, or is there something you would like to amend about your statement?"

Flora's mouth twisted into a scowl. "It's not like I was saying anything mean."

I raised an eyebrow. "I think I've heard enough. You're suspended for the remainder of the week. I'll be speaking with Stu and Suzie regarding your usual work to determine if you'll be on probation when you return."

She opened her mouth, then snapped it shut again.

Wise move.

"Out. Now."

Flora scurried away, leaving Ashlee standing in my office, looking like she wanted to be anywhere but here.

"What about you?" I asked, leaning forward and putting my elbows on my desk. "What do you have to say about what I overheard?"

To my surprise, she finally looked at me, her expression smoothed out and blank. Her cheeks were still red but seemed to be completely under control now. No more impromptu statements from her.

"I was working on the assignment Ms. Lamas gave me."

I wondered if I could get under her skin again, enough to get a genuine reaction rather than something thought out and calculated.

I raised an eyebrow. "And...?"

She shook her head. "And nothing. I was working."

"Which means your friend was the one running her mouth about things she had no business talking about."

Even though I didn't need her to tell me that Flora had

been the one talking about me, having a witness would make things easier if Flora decided not to take her punishment quietly. While I didn't like hearing anyone talk about me, I knew that plenty of people suspected the sort of person I was like in private. If Flora wanted to lie, she could make my life extremely difficult.

"I asked a question, Miss Webb."

"Actually, no, you didn't."

Okay, not as soft-spoken as I'd thought. She wasn't talking loudly, but there was nothing soft about her resolve.

I rephrased. "Was your friend the one running her mouth about things she had no business talking about?"

Nothing.

"Are you going to claim I didn't ask a question this time?"

"No, sir."

Her quiet words hit me with a punch of lust. I took another look at her, this time letting myself see her as someone other than an employee.

She was more than a foot shorter than me, with fine features that could have made her look delicate if they'd been paired with a slender body. Instead, she had curves that my hands itched to explore. Normally, my women were thin, brittle in ways that went beyond physical.

Not that she was my woman.

Nothing even close to that.

And yet...

I stood up and came around to stand in front of her, leaving barely enough room between us to be appropriate for employer / employee.

"Are you going to answer my question?"

She didn't look up at me, but she didn't look down either. Instead, she stared at the center of my chest. "No, sir. I am not."

I took a half-step forward, crossing into almost-inappropriate territory. I was toeing a line here, and I knew it. I had grounds to fire Flora for the way she was talking, but I'd only suspended her. If I suspended Ashlee without cause, and she reported it to HR, she might have a case for wrongful dismissal, especially if I kept going the way I was going.

But I wasn't done with her yet.

"What about what you were doing? Will you tell me that?"

"I was working on the assignment Ms. Lamas gave me."

"Which was?"

Her eyes flicked up, then back down. "Find viral videos online and make notes. Basically."

That sounded plausible. Part of A&R was finding new talent. It made sense that Stu and Suzie would have their assistants searching the internet. I'd never required them to do their work any specific way.

"So, you were doing your work, but your friend was talking about me?" I made an educated guess and took her silence as affirmation.

She wasn't intimidated by me.

I'd never met anyone like her before, and it intrigued me. It'd been a long time since I'd been curious about anyone, especially a woman. It made me uncharacteristically reckless.

"Do you know anything about an event we're having this weekend?"

Her head came up, confusion written on her face. "Yes. I

handed off Unraveling's requests to Mr. Hancock this morning."

I remembered Finley saying something about Zed and perks. "Unraveling had requests?"

She seemed relieved that we were veering away from the original topic. "Yes, Mr. Lexington. There was a message left for A&R last night."

Curious to know how well she did her job, I asked the question even though I already knew the answer. "Who left the message?"

"Mr. Hipwood," she said. "Mr. Hancock said he planned to speak with you about it."

I nodded. Stu was a good employee. If he said he'd talk to me about it, he'd do it. I didn't need to worry about it. I could turn my attention to something else.

"I have a...proposition," I began. "I...lost my plus one for the event, and I need someone to accompany me. If you do that, I'll forget that you were a part of a conversation that caused one of your co-workers to be suspended."

Her jaw dropped. "I wasn't part of that conversation."

I shrugged. "I don't care."

SEVEN

ASHLEE

WAS MY BOSS SERIOUSLY BLACKMAILING ME INTO GOING on a date with him? I had to be misunderstanding him, right? Because this was Nate Lexington, millionaire CEO and co-owner of Manhattan Records. The man who routinely dated the hottest women in the world, discarding them one right after the other.

He could literally walk into anywhere, snap his fingers, and have a dozen beautiful women ready and willing to do whatever he wanted.

Why me, and why like this?

My confusion was only part of what I was feeling. The rest was anger.

Who the *hell* did he think he was? That sort of thing might've been the way things worked as little as a couple years ago, but the age of free-for-all sexual harassment and manipulation was over. People who did things like that didn't get a free pass anymore. Even if the HR department here wouldn't listen to me, I had options. If nothing else, I could take to social media.

But if I did any of those things, I'd lose my job.

If I refused him, I'd probably only get suspended, but I had no doubt that if I caused problems for him, he'd do whatever he could to get me out of his company.

And I couldn't let that happen. I needed to stay at Manhattan Records, even if it meant letting my boss think he could force me to go on a date with him.

Besides, it wasn't like this was some private function where he could manhandle me. Mr. Hancock and Ms. Lamas would even be there. I could approach this as a learning experience, seeing first-hand what A&R did at events like this. After all, I'd already been working on it. For all I knew, I would've been invited anyway.

I was justifying it to myself, and I knew it, but when I weighed my options, this was the comparatively better answer.

"I'll go," I said. I held his gaze for a moment, then dropped my eyes. "May I go back to work now? If I'm the only one doing the assignment, it will take me twice as long to finish it."

I made my voice as flat as possible. If he took that to mean that I disapproved of his methods, I hoped he'd feel bad about it, but I doubted it. The sort of man who'd blackmail an innocent person by accusing them of something they didn't do wasn't exactly the kind of man who'd care about the approval of a subordinate.

"Go ahead," he said. "I'll get you the details about this weekend."

I didn't bother to acknowledge the last statement as I left the office and headed back down to A&R and my desk. I had no doubt I'd have to be the one to eventually explain to Mr. Hancock and Ms. Lamas what'd happened since neither Flora nor Nate would do it, but if I had at least some of the work done by then, they'd hopefully see that I didn't intend to slack off just because I was the only one left.

To my surprise, Flora was standing by my desk when I arrived, but I wasn't even going to bother hoping that she wanted us to talk to our bosses together. The expression on her face was mutinous, to say the least.

"I figured we could walk out together," she said. "Strength in numbers, you know."

Shit.

I licked my dry lips. "I—"

"I can't believe he suspended us for a whole week just because we were talking about the same rumors that everyone else here talks about. It wasn't like we were insulting him or anything."

It was on the tip of my tongue to remind her that *we* hadn't said anything at all, but when I considered that she hadn't even bothered to apologize for lying about the conversation being about a book I was reading, I knew it wouldn't do anything but make matters worse. Especially since I had the feeling there wasn't any way I could get out of telling her that I hadn't been suspended at all.

"Come on," she said. "Let's get shit-faced. It's not like we have to work tomorrow. You're buying the first round since I had to wait for you."

"I can't," I said, mentally crossing my fingers that she'd let it go at that.

She rolled her eyes. "Yes, you can. That's what people do when they have a shitty day at work. They get drunk and maybe even get laid." She reached for the bottom drawer of my desk. "Where's your purse? If we make it out without being seen, he'll have to tell Hancock and Lamas himself. I can't believe I was actually thinking about how much I'd like to fuck him. Douchebag—"

"Flora," I cut in. As I'd learned not too long ago, she wouldn't stop unless I interrupted. "I can't leave. I still have to work."

Her eyes narrowed. "He put off your suspension until tomorrow?"

I shook my head, wishing there was an easier way to do this. "I wasn't suspended." Her mouth dropped opened, and I seized the opportunity to spin a little white lie. "Because he didn't hear me say anything, he couldn't suspend me without risking me going to HR."

Okay, not exactly a *little* lie, but it was a necessary one.

"Right," she sneered. "I'm sure as soon as I left the room, you told him *all* about our conversation. Probably threw in a few extras too, right? Maybe embellished some of the things I said."

I shook my head, but she didn't give me a chance to tell her that it hadn't been like that.

"Or maybe you didn't *say* anything. You weren't up there long, but maybe he doesn't have the stamina that rumors claim."

Her voice kept getting louder, and I looked around, fully

expecting people to be staring at us. Fortunately, she wasn't as loud as it seemed.

"Was that it, Ashlee? Did you offer to blow him right there in his office or did he want you to meet him after work? How long do you have to fuck him to make up for him not suspending you?"

"Enough!" I snapped. "I get that you're pissed about what happened, but it's not my fault. You should probably go before Mr. Lexington realizes you're still here and calls security. I'm sure you don't want to be escorted out."

A flicker of fear within the anger told me I was on the right track. If she was the one in charge of making the scene, she was okay with that, but she didn't want to be embarrassed by losing that control. She glared at me for one more moment, then spun around and stomped away.

I breathed a sigh of relief as I slumped into my chair, but it was short-lived. I now knew for certain that I had to find some way out of my 'date' this weekend. If Flora was already assuming that I'd traded sexual favors for not being suspended, everyone would believe I was sleeping with the boss if I showed up at an event on his arm.

That was not the sort of reputation I wanted in the industry, or in my personal life for that matter. Even if it wasn't true, people would think it was. I'd never get past it. And it wouldn't end at this company. People in the industry knew Mr. Lexington and his reputation. Even if they didn't hear the rumors, they'd made the same assumptions Flora had, with or without knowing about this particular incident.

I didn't usually care what people thought about me, but there were a couple people who were important to me, and I didn't want them to think that I'd gotten my most recent promotion because I'd had sex with Mr. Lexington. Or that I'd gotten *anything* from him for any sort of favors at all. I'd never taken the easy way, and it irked me to think that people would think I had simply because Flora hadn't taken responsibility for her behavior and told Mr. Lexington that I was innocent.

This was *not* the way I'd wanted to start this week.

EIGHT

NATE

THIS WAS NOT HOW I'D EXPECTED MY DAY TO GO. THE discussion with Finley hadn't been too out of the ordinary, but when I'd headed for the A&R department to speak with Suzie, I hadn't expected to hear two women talking about my sexual preferences. And I *certainly* hadn't expected to be so interested in one of those women.

Granted, I hadn't specifically heard that one talking about me, but she hadn't told Flora to stop. Still, I knew making her go this Friday in exchange for not being suspended could get me in some serious trouble with HR. I didn't intend to take things any further than that, especially since I wasn't going to force her into any sort of physical contact. A date was one thing. Anything else would be wrong.

Well, *completely* wrong instead of just a little gray area sort of wrong.

That didn't, however, mean that I was going to try to get her to agree to some physical contact.

I could still picture the way she'd looked at me, that combination of submission and defiance. She'd wanted to argue with me, but she'd held back. I hadn't seen fear, though. It'd been more like watching someone think through a list of pros and cons before making a decision. But she hadn't held onto that insolence though, not like Flora had. The way she'd looked down after meeting my eyes. How she'd held back her arguments even when I'd pushed her.

When she'd left, I'd waited until she disappeared to give in to all of the possibilities that had flooded my mind. And there'd been a lot of them. Possibilities and fantasies galore.

The curvy red-head tied up in my bed – *a* bed.

Pale lace lingerie that enticed.

Her eyes nearly black with desire.

Those legs wrapped around my waist.

Lips swollen and begging.

It had been that last one that had gotten me out of my chair and into the private bathroom connected to my office. Despite the thoughts that had just raced through my mind, thinking about sex during work wasn't my thing. Usually. I didn't seem to be doing anything my usual way today.

Including the fact that I was getting a massive erection in the middle of a workday thanks to intimidating an employee into going on a date with me.

As much as I tried to shame myself into losing my hard-on, it didn't appear to be working. Probably because I couldn't stop thinking about Ashlee. She was an assistant in the A&R department, which meant she had to have been here for a while, but I had no recollection of seeing her before, let alone meeting her. If I had, I probably would have already pulled up her employee file and learned everything I could about her.

I leaned down and splashed cold water on my face. Refreshing. Did jack-shit to stop the stream of pornographic images starring a certain curvy employee of mine.

Baseball statistics.

Mud.

Nothing.

Okay, maybe I needed something that wasn't just unsexy. I needed something gross.

Hairy, obese men in towels.

Oozing open wounds.

Blood-soaked bandages.

That stuff turned my stomach, but my cock was standing strong. Impressive, even for me.

I supposed that left only one option.

I didn't do this at work. Ever. But since I was breaking all sorts of rules today, what was one more? I needed to make this quick and efficient. It wasn't about pleasure, or even about getting out of my head for a while, but rather about me taking care of a physical necessity so I could get back to work.

Deliberately, I pushed aside the thoughts of my employee and called up a random image from a past encounter. Not Roma, but a svelte blonde flight attendant I'd gotten to know better during a cross-country flight for business.

Robin. That had been her name. Or close enough anyway.

I let the memory fill my mind as I unzipped my pants and pushed them down far enough to free my cock. As I wrapped my fist around the base, I closed my eyes to better call up the visual.

Robin's pert little ass swayed from side-to-side as I followed her to the bathroom. Other passengers watched us as we both went inside, knowing what we'd be doing in there. Neither one of us said a word as she leaned against the sink, her heels putting her at exactly the right height for what came next.

I pushed her skirt up and her panties down, using my foot to move her feet farther apart. She glanced over her shoulder and asked if I could fuck her ass. She and her boyfriend had an open relationship, and he liked to hear about the men she fucked, but her pussy was off-limits. I shrugged. A hole was a hole...

But apparently, a fantasy wasn't just a fantasy. I let out a groan of frustration. My erection hadn't gone away, but it'd softened enough for me to know that thinking about how I'd fucked Robin so hard she'd been walking funny when we came out of the bathroom wasn't going to get me off.

I didn't bother trying to think of anything or anyone else. I'd already known that only fantasizing about Ashlee would work. Now, I had to accept and move on with it. My hand moved over my cock as a scene played out in my mind.

Ashlee walked into my office wearing only a long black coat. Without a word, she undid the buttons and let it fall. Beneath, she wore only the skimpiest of sheer triangles over each of her nipples and another between her legs. They served more as friction for sensitive skin than any real purpose. She kept her head down as she waited for her instructions.

"Here."

She came toward me with small, delicate steps, her natural stride hampered by her heels. She hated wearing them, and her obedience despite this was one of the many reasons she'd lasted so long.

"Kneel."

She went to the ground in front of me and clasped her hands behind her back. I reached for the slim silver chain that hung from her collar and used it to drag her into the space between my legs.

"Lick."

She obediently opened her mouth and stuck out her tongue. It had taken her days of practice to be able to keep her balance without her hands, but now she was able to focus solely on the soft little licks she made up and down my throbbing cock. Her face held such wonderful expressions that I required her to wear her hair back unless told otherwise. It had the added benefit of allowing me to watch that talented pink tongue of hers as she laved over every inch of me.

"Suck."

She moved up to give herself the leverage she needed to take my cock into her mouth without using her hands. She took the tip between her lips first, then lowered her head slowly, letting me enjoy the sensation of sliding over her tongue on my way to the back of her throat. Her body stiffened for a moment when the head of my dick reached the back of her mouth, but she didn't struggle.

"Good girl."

I put a hand on her head, keeping steady pressure there as she continued descending. When her lips were stretched tight around the base of my cock, saliva dribbling down her chin and onto my balls, I held her there. Her throat muscles convulsively squeezed, and I could feel the tension in her body as she fought against her own instincts. She wouldn't tap out, though. She enjoyed this as much as I did, or she wouldn't keep coming back.

I yanked out her ponytail and grabbed two fistfuls of her hair. I gave her a few seconds to process what was coming, and then I raised her up just enough to give me room to thrust. I held her head steady and pistoned my hips, slamming into her face over and over. I'd come down her throat and then have her lick my balls and ass until I was hard again. After that...

I bit back a curse as I came and slammed my free hand on the cold marble counter, my other hand rapidly fisting over my cock as I drained out every last drop. Maybe once I cleaned up, I'd finally be able to concentrate on work.

And maybe I needed to reconsider taking Ashlee on Friday. If one conversation with her could fuck with my head that much, who knew what several hours with her would do.

NINE
ASHLEE

I HAD A VERY NARROW WINDOW IN WHICH TO PREVENT the damage that was coming. Flora and I being called into the CEO's office, that had made it out of the A&R department before I'd even gotten back. That meant people had been paying attention when Flora and I had come back, and at least a few had heard the things she'd been shouting at me. Now, those were just accusations, and I'd never done anything that would support the things she'd said, but it was something interesting, and people were going to spread anything that hinted at gossip. If nothing else new or unusual happened, however, the rumors would die.

But if I showed up to an event on his arm, things would explode.

I wouldn't be able to take that back, and no one would believe for a moment that I hadn't been performing sexual favors for Mr. Lexington, maybe for years.

Which meant I needed to fix this *before* I went home for the day. Flora would be on the phone to her friends as soon as they got off – if she hadn't been talking to them already – but if they came in tomorrow and saw that everything was the same, her accusations would lose steam. By the end of the week, they would have lost all their firepower. When she came back on Monday and found that the only thing I'd done differently this week was take care of her job, too, she might even give it up.

Some people would always believe the negative, and I couldn't help that any more than I could help any of the other shit people had believed about me over the years. What I could control, however, was how much I let it bother me.

And I could do whatever possible to nip things in the bud.

Which was why I was sitting in the lobby of Manhattan Records nearly two hours after everyone else had gone home. I'd brought my work laptop with me after promising Mr. Hancock that I'd do some extra work at home, and I'd been using it while I waited for Mr. Lexington to come downstairs.

Except I was starting to think that Mr. Lexington wouldn't be coming anytime soon. I knew he worked a lot, but I'd thought a couple extra hours here and there, with the occasional weekend. Apparently, I'd underestimated him by assuming that his reputation as a playboy meant that he spent time at bars and parties.

For the first time, I wondered if I'd been listening to rumors about him the way people would listen to rumors about me.

Still, that bit of guilt I felt wasn't enough to keep my 'date' this weekend.

I sighed as I looked at the clock again. I hadn't had much

in the way of lunch, and I was starting to get hungry. If I had to wait here much longer, I wasn't going to take responsibility for anything I said or did. Being weak and loopy from hunger was a genuine defense for stupid behavior.

Or I could take the initiative and do something rather than passively waiting to react.

I put my laptop in my bag, took a fortifying breath, and headed for the CEO's office. The entire floor was down to evening lighting, and eerie shadows lingered in the corners. My heels made strange sounds on the carpet, something I hadn't noticed until now when I went down the hall to Mr. Lexington's office, reminding me I was far more alone than I had been earlier today. No receptionist. No bosses expecting to see me. No co-workers.

I wasn't afraid of him, exactly, but I'd have been lying if I said the idea of being so completely alone with Mr. Lexington didn't make my heart beat faster.

The door was closed, and for a moment, I wondered if I'd missed him leaving. Perhaps he'd gone home – or wherever – while I'd been watching one of the dozens of videos I'd watched today. I wasn't about to leave without at least seeing this through.

I knocked, then waited. When I didn't hear anything after a minute, I raised my hand to knock again...and almost hit my boss right in his firm-looking chest.

I managed to stop my hand, but not my surprised exclamation. "Oh!"

He looked equally surprised but managed to hide it much quicker than I did. "Miss Webb, I thought you'd gone home for the day."

"Are you keeping tabs on me?" I asked, startled enough to forget why I'd come in the first place.

One side of his mouth tipped up in a half-smile, and for the first time, I noticed how warm his mocha brown eyes could be. "I just meant that I'm usually the only one left by this time. Come in."

He stepped out of the way as he issued his invitation, his behavior a complete one-eighty from when he'd ordered me here earlier. Granted, earlier, he'd had a reason to think I'd done something wrong, but the change left my head spinning.

I followed him inside, this time leaving the door open and walking over to his desk with him. He leaned against it, and I kept a chair between us, but I was still closer than I'd been before.

"I spoke with Mr. Hancock and Ms. Lamas," he said. "They both speak highly of you."

I blushed, half from embarrassment, half from pride. "I've enjoyed working for them. It's been a real learning experience."

"Is that where you see yourself in the future?" he asked. "In their positions? Heading up A&R?"

I shrugged. "Maybe. When I was a runner, it was the department that I was most interested in."

He leaned on his desk, loosely lacing his fingers together in front of him. "I'm guessing you didn't come here to tell me about how much you've enjoyed working in the A&R department. How can I help you, Miss Webb?"

There wasn't really another way to say this other than to just come out with it. "I can't go with you this Friday."

He raised an eyebrow but didn't yell. "Why is that?"

"Because people will think we're sleeping together."

"Is that so?" He seemed amused. "Or perhaps they'll simply think that a member of the A&R department is sitting with the CEO to provide him with information during an event."

I was shaking my head before he'd finished. "That's not what they'll think."

"It will be if that's what I tell them to think."

I gave him a puzzled look. "I'm not sure if you've noticed, but gossip doesn't usually do what it's told."

His mouth tightened. "I'm aware of that, Miss Webb."

"Then you should know that it won't matter what you tell people. They're going to see a wealthy, powerful man with a young woman who works for him. We both know what people will automatically assume."

He stood up straight and stuck his hands in his pockets. "Do you care what people assume?"

"There's a difference between rumors without any substance and feeding what people are already saying," I countered.

"What are people already saying?"

I looked away, unable to meet the intensity of his gaze. "They're saying that because Flora was suspended and I wasn't, I must've...done something to earn a reprieve."

His eyes narrowed. "Excuse me?"

"You know what I mean." I forced my gaze to stay on his. "But if you really want me to spell it out, it's pretty simple. People think I slept with you so you wouldn't suspend me."

"And how did *that* particular rumor get started?"

At the accusation in his voice, my head snapped back in his direction. "I certainly didn't start it."

He gave me a hard look, but then nodded. "I believe you."

"Thanks?" I couldn't stop from making the word sound like a question.

"Who started the rumor?" he repeated.

I shook my head. "I'm not going to add to it."

Before he could argue, someone else knocked on the door. We both turned to see a nervous-looking teenager with a plastic bag full of what – based on the amazing smell – I assumed was take-out.

"I buzzed the door, but no one answered so I tried the door, and it was open." He held up the bag. "The note on the receipt gave the floor and–"

"Thank you," Mr. Lexington said as he crossed over to the delivery guy. He handed over a bill with one hand and took the bag with the other. "Keep the change."

"Thanks." The delivery guy headed back down the hall, and Mr. Lexington watched him go.

When the kid was out of earshot, Mr. Lexington said, "Whoever's on security tonight is getting fired."

At least now I knew that he wasn't sexist when it came to firing people for doing things on the job that they shouldn't.

"But first, dinner." He turned and held up the bag. "Sit. You're eating with me."

That didn't sound like a request, and I doubted I could refuse what I knew was an order.

Dammit.

TEN

NATE

I'D INTENDED TO STOP AT MISS WEBB'S DESK Wednesday or Thursday to remind her of our date, but I hadn't expected anything that had happened within the last few minutes. She'd come to me. To change her mind and decline the invitation.

I'd never had that happen before. Not someone turning me down. Not someone surprising me. And certainly not both from the same person.

Which meant I wanted to talk to her now more than ever. I needed to figure out what made her tick. When my dinner showed up, I seized the opportunity and asked her to stay and eat with me. Well, I supposed the asking was less a question and more a statement, but making requests wasn't really my style.

"You eat take-out?" she asked without moving from where she stood.

"What New Yorker doesn't?" My attempt at charming her fell flat.

"I'd guess most New Yorkers with your bank account don't." Heat flooded her face. "I apologize. That was completely out of line."

"You can make it up to me by eating dinner with me."

For the second time, I was resorting to blackmail to get what I wanted, and it grated on my nerves. From the expression she was trying to hide, it bothered her too.

"And if I decline the invitation?"

"Then we both eat alone." I waited for her to tell me that she wouldn't be eating alone, that she had a boyfriend or a girlfriend waiting for her. The quick conversations I'd had with Stu and Suzie hadn't been about anything personal, but it wouldn't surprise me to find out she was taken.

"Somehow, I doubt it's difficult for you to find a dinner date," she said dryly.

"Eat with me," I said again. "After the way you and your friend were talking about me, it only seems fair."

After a moment, Ashlee sighed. "All right."

I smiled and was surprised to find that it was completely genuine. I walked over to the short couch that sat against the far wall and took my usual seat. I set the bag of food on the low table, and by the time I'd taken out all of the containers, Ashlee was perched on the other end of the couch, looking more like she was poised to run than ready to eat a meal. I wondered if she was scared of me. The size difference alone would be intimidating, I supposed.

"You can relax," I said. "Help yourself to anything."

"Do you always order so much?" she asked as she picked up one of the containers, examined it, and then swapped it out for pineapple curry.

I shrugged. "I don't mind leftovers."

She gave me a puzzled look. "Don't you have a personal chef or something like that?"

I opened one of the containers and took a bite of lemongrass garlic chicken. I chewed slowly, savoring my favorite Thai dish as I thought about how I wanted to answer her question. If I offered too much personal information, she might think that gave her carte blanche to ask all sorts of prying questions. However, it could also get her to open up more.

"I like good food as much as the next person," I said, "but I've never seen the point of hiring someone to cook just for me."

"Makes sense."

I watched her as we both ate in silence. Her focus seemed to be on her food, but the color in her cheeks told me that she was aware of my attention. I couldn't remember the last time I'd seen a woman blush with anything but arousal or anger. Sometimes both.

Ashlee, I gathered, wasn't accustomed to having people look at her. For someone in the A&R department, that was a good thing. It told me she wasn't here to rub elbows with the rich and famous, and that she wouldn't try to steal the limelight from our artists.

"I didn't read your file," I said. The surprise on her face made me smile. "You thought I would."

She shrugged. "It would make sense. You talked to Mr. Hancock and Ms. Lamas to find out what sort of employee I am."

"True, I did. Your file's only going to tell me your education and employment history. I'd much rather talk to you to find out what you're like." It sounded like a line, and it was one I probably would've used at some point in time, but with her, I actually meant it.

"Does that line usually work when you hit on your employees?"

I scowled at her, but then I saw a hint of humor in her eyes, and it blunted the annoyance. "I don't hit on my employees."

She raised her eyebrows but didn't say anything as she took another bite.

I changed the subject. "Did you grow up in New York?"

"Staten Island," she said. "I already know you grew up in the Bronx."

"I did." I leaned back. "Does this mean you read my biography?"

"I may have done some research before coming to work here," she admitted.

"I think it's only fair that I know as much about you as you do about me," I countered. "Only child or one of many?"

"Only child," she said. "And I have a communications degree from NYU. Now you know as much about me as I do about you."

"Somehow, I doubt that." I picked up another container and took a bite. "What made you choose Manhattan Records?"

She blinked, but I wasn't sure why that question surprised her. It should've been expected. It was a safe thing to talk about, even between employee and employer.

"I was still in college when I saw an advertisement for an

internship here. I figured it'd give me an idea of what I wanted to do with my degree."

"You didn't know that you wanted to work in the music industry?" I asked.

"I wasn't one of those kids who always knew exactly what I wanted to do with my life," she answered. "But I'm glad I ended up here. I'm really enjoying working in A&R."

"Did you ever consider becoming a musician?"

She laughed, a soft sound that automatically made me smile. "Mr. Lexington, if you'd ever heard me sing, you wouldn't ask that question."

"You could play an instrument." I stabbed another bite of my meal. "And call me Nate. I feel like a dirty old man when you call me Mr. Lexington."

Her smile fell. "I'm not sure that's a good idea."

I considered her for a moment. "At least when we're outside work hours, then."

The fact that she genuinely seemed reluctant to call me by my first name made me even more certain that she wasn't the sort of woman who would use who I was to get something. If one thing could have made me more curious about her, that was it.

"Okay," she said quietly. She turned her attention back to her food, and the conversation stalled.

"Did you find anything interesting?" I changed the subject. "Any acts you think we should take a look at?"

"There are a couple that sound interesting," she said, the relief in her voice obvious. "I recorded all of the information that Ms. Lamas asked for if you'd like me to get it."

I shook my head. "That's quite all right. If they're good

enough for A&R to get involved, I'll hear about them eventually. That's the point of hiring people I can trust."

I managed not to wince when I said the last word, which was impressive since trust wasn't something I really had with anyone. Finley was pretty much it, though I did trust Stu and Suzie to do their jobs, if only because they were professionals. I supposed that meant it counted in this particular instance.

"You signed Unraveling, right?" she asked.

I drank a quarter of my bottle of water and then managed a tight smile. "I did. As well as Gorgon Poison, Felix Bower, and Rya Flowers."

Her eyes widened slightly. "Those are the four biggest act Manhattan Records ever signed."

I nodded. "They made the company." I leaned closer to her. "Is that what you want to do, Ashlee? Find the next Unraveling or Rya Flowers?"

"Maybe," she said. "I wouldn't hate it."

She didn't tell me not to call her Ashlee, which I hoped meant she was okay with it. I liked this feeling of informality between us. Probably more than I should. But I didn't like the idea of us going into the event on Friday and have her calling me Mr. Lexington.

That could end up being a problem.

ELEVEN

ASHLEE

TODAY WAS A WEIRD DAY ALL THE WAY AROUND. WEIRD enough that eating take-out with my bosses' boss after everyone else had gone home seemed like a perfectly natural way to end the day.

Nate was a much more complicated man than I'd originally thought. With his expensive suits and playboy reputation, I'd assumed he was shallow and simple. Of course, I'd known that he was intelligent. People didn't get to be CEO and co-owner of a company like Manhattan Records if they didn't have brains. He'd also been named to numerous lists of the city and the country's wealthiest and hottest men, all of which talked about how brilliant he was.

Honestly, I'd thought that would make him even less likable because nothing screamed decent guy like a rich white male who not only thought he was the smartest person in the room but actually *was* most of the time.

"Which of your artists are your favorites?" I asked, not

responding to his using my first name. I wasn't sure what to say, truthfully.

Things between us had blurred the moment I'd accepted his invitation to be his date for the event. I never should have done that, but then I'd come here to fix that mistake, only to make a worse one. Still, I couldn't bring myself to get up and walk away, not when he was being a nice guy about everything. I didn't want a return of the guy who'd been such a jerk earlier today.

"I don't listen to any of the labels' artists," he said. "I don't want anyone to accuse me of having favorites."

"Why don't you just listen to all of them, then?" I asked. "Equal opportunities?"

He shrugged. "I don't spend a lot of outside time listening to music, so I'd rather listen to something other than what I hear at work all day."

"Do you mind if I ask if you got into the business for the music or for the business?" I asked. "There were a lot of people in my business classes in college who talked about how they didn't have a specific business they wanted to get into. They liked the challenge of creating a company, watching it thrive."

He smiled. "That would be me. Don't get me wrong. I like music, but I picked this industry because I learned fast that I was good at spotting talent and even better at marketing it."

"And the challenge?"

His grin widened, making him look years younger. "That's the best part."

It was on the tip of my tongue to ask him if he felt the

same way about women, but I swallowed the words. I didn't understand it. I'd always been a shy kid. Not insecure but shy, which meant for a lot of my life, people thought I was a snob rather than just keeping to myself.

Except being around Nate – *Mr. Lexington* – made my brain flip around so that I had no problem blurting things out...but I always felt like an idiot after. I supposed if it was something I had any experience with, I'd be a little more confident, but dating wasn't exactly my thing. Let alone talking to someone like him about dating.

"What about you, Ashlee? Do you like a challenge?"

A shiver went down my spine at the heat I heard in the words. Or at least I thought I heard. But that was probably just him flirting because that was what he did. And I wasn't even sure that could rightly be called flirting. Maybe it was more accurately just being charming. From what I understood, being charming was second nature to him. That would make more sense than him flirting with me.

I wasn't one of those women who thought they were plain but only needed a makeover montage to see that they were really beautiful all along. I was pretty and had no issues with my figure, but I also had no illusions about the sort of women Nate dated. I didn't function well in public situations. I wasn't charming, and I'd been told that my attempts at flirting were painful to watch. The sort of women he went out with exuded a sexy confidence that I doubted I could ever match.

"I never shirk away from difficult things or from doing my best," I said finally. "But I don't need a challenge for something to capture my interest."

"Does that mean you're not a competitive person?" he asked.

I considered the question before answering. "I'm not in the sense that I see everything as a win or lose situation, and I don't feel the need to 'beat' other people. That doesn't mean I won't do my best, though."

"Are you saying that because I'm your boss?"

"I don't say things I don't mean," I replied. "I'd rather not say anything at all than say something I don't believe."

He studied me, the intensity of his gaze making me want to squirm. The heat was still there, but it'd been joined by something else. Something I couldn't quite put my finger on.

"A woman of integrity," he said quietly. "There aren't many of your kind left in the world."

He sounded so unlike himself that I didn't know what to make of it. I'd thought I'd seen both sides of him today. The forceful CEO with a temper, and this more relaxed, charming human being. Now, I wondered if either of them was the real Nate. Or was he a combination of those things? A man far more complex than I'd imagined?

An awkward silence fell between us, and I took that as my cue to leave. I'd already lingered too long as it was. I'd come here to say my piece, and I had. How he reacted to that was up to him. It didn't matter that I liked this side of him better than the one I'd encountered earlier today.

"It's getting late," I said as I stood. "I should get going."

He stood as well, taking only two steps to reach my side. "I'll walk you to your car."

"I don't have a car, but thank you," I said. "I don't live far."

"Are you taking the subway by yourself?" He frowned, as if the idea bothered him for some reason.

"Same as I've done every day since I started working here," I said with a smile.

"But you're leaving later than usual."

"I appreciate the concern, but I've been riding the subway by myself since I was a teenager." When he looked like he was going to argue, I added, "I carry pepper spray, and I took self-defense classes in high school."

He still appeared doubtful but didn't say anything as he followed me to the door. Before I stepped out of his office, I turned toward him, feeling like we were on some strange date that needed a firmer ending. I tipped my head back so I could meet his eyes while I spoke, but I couldn't find the words.

He took me by surprise when he bent his head, mouth covering mine even as he settled a hand on my hip. My brain misfired out of shock, and I stood there, letting him kiss me, but that wasn't an excuse, not when heat flowed through my body, eager for more. It took me only seconds to regain my composure and put my hands on his chest, firmly pushing him away, but in those seconds, desire had formed a fist in my stomach, twisting my insides into knots.

"No," I said, wanting to make myself clear. "No."

He took a step back, a smooth mask settling into place. "Good."

I blinked. That hadn't been what I'd expected him to say. He'd respected my wishes, for which I was grateful, but I didn't understand his response.

"Okay?"

He put his hands in his pockets, an expression of nonchalance on his face. As if he hadn't just been kissing me. "I still want you to go with me on Friday."

I tucked a strand of hair behind my ear. "I'm not too proud to admit that I'm confused."

He turned away from me as he began talking. "I had to know that you weren't going to read too much into my invitation."

My head was spinning. "I still don't understand."

"I kissed you to see if you'd think that my inviting you on Friday and then having dinner with you just now meant that I expected more, or if you thought it entitled you to more." His tone was even, business-like. "I needed to make sure that you could keep things professional, no matter what."

"And kissing me was the way to do it?"

"Better that than you assuming there's more to showing up at an event on my arm than looking pretty and keeping me from having to deal with gold diggers all night." He turned back toward me. "I could've asked you, but you could've lied. When you want the truth, catching someone off-guard is a good way to get it."

The concept made sense. Still... "Isn't it risky? Kissing an employee without knowing how she'll react? I could go to HR with a complaint."

"But you won't," he said with the voice of someone who knew what he was talking about.

"How sure are you about that?"

"You didn't go to them when I first asked you to come with me," he pointed out.

"Kissing me is a little different than taking me to a company event."

One side of his mouth tipped up in that half-smile again, but his eyes were guarded. "I'm not the most patient man. I could have waited to see how things played out, but I prefer knowing ahead of time. Kissing you was the best way to figure that out."

If I'd had any sort of attraction or romantic notions toward Nate, I might've been hurt by his matter-of-fact way of looking at things, but I didn't want anything from him that I hadn't earned.

"Now that we're both clear on what we want, there shouldn't be anything else keeping you from accompanying me on Friday."

He was right. Technically.

And if he was looking at this as a business thing, then I could too. I could make a lot of contacts. See how things worked at events like this.

"Okay," I said. "I'll go."

TWELVE

NATE

I HADN'T SPOKEN WITH ASHLEE SINCE SHE LEFT MY office Monday evening. Once she'd agreed to go with me Friday, we'd said goodnight, and she'd gone on her way. I'd called up the security cameras to watch her through the building and wished that I had the ability to follow her all the way to the subway. She claimed to have some self-defense training, and she was a native New Yorker, but if she'd been my woman, she wouldn't have been taking the subway alone at night. I didn't even like it as the employer.

There wasn't really anything I could do to prevent her from getting around the way she wanted to, but I could do something about the rumors at work. People would talk, that wasn't going to change. I could send out a company-wide email using Flora's suspension as an example of what would happen to people caught gossiping about their co-workers – or their bosses – but I knew that would only make matters worse.

What I could do was find out the source of the rumors

and handle it on that end of things. After all, every employee signed a contract that contained certain clauses about acceptable and unacceptable behavior. I hadn't been talking out of my ass when I'd suspended Flora Watts. I had legal grounds to take action against any employee who violated the terms of their contract.

"I understand that there have been some rumors going around about one of your co-workers engaging in less-than-ethical behavior." I leaned back in my chair and leveled my gaze at Myron Leavenworth.

Myron worked in the mailroom and did deliveries, which meant he went to each floor and each employee. If anyone was going to hear rumors and have an idea of where they started, it'd be people in the mailroom.

"I don't gossip." Myron held up his hands, his eyes wide. "Seriously, most people don't even talk to me unless they need something."

"You're not in trouble," I said. "I just need your ears. I want to know what you've heard regarding a young woman in the A&R department."

"Flora?" The tips of his ears went pink.

"What did you hear about her?" I asked. He looked down at his hands. "Myron, I need to know what's going on in my company. What have you heard?"

"I heard that Flora was talking to Ashlee about..." His voice trailed off. When I didn't fill the silence, he continued, "about you, Mr. Lexington. She was talking about you dating and...all that. Then you came in and yelled at them both."

Accurate so far.

"Anything else?" I asked.

"I heard she was suspended for two weeks without pay."

Not-so-accurate. "Who told you that?"

"Um, I think Clara. She and Flora were interns together. She's a receptionist in the lobby."

Shit. If Flora had a friend in the lobby spreading rumors, they could reach much further than if she was isolated in a particular department. But, that also supported my suspicions that the origin of the rumors Ashlee was worried about was the same person who'd been spreading gossip in the first place.

"What else have you heard?"

I watched as he shifted in his seat. Damn, he was twitchy.

"I heard that the other girl, Ashlee, she didn't get in trouble even though she was doing the same thing as Flora."

"That's what you heard? That Ashlee was saying the same things as Flora?"

Myron nodded emphatically, relief on his face. "I'm not saying anything to anyone about what I heard. You have to believe me, Mr. Lexington. Just cuz I heard it doesn't mean I'm saying it to other people."

I held up my hand, silencing him. "I believe you. I just need to know what people are saying. Have you heard anything about why Ashlee wasn't suspended?"

"I-I...Mr. Lexington, I really don't want to say."

I leaned forward. "You don't want to say because the rumors are that either I requested or Ashlee offered sexual favors in exchange for not being suspended." The quick glance he shot at me told me the answer, but I still wanted him to say it so it was clear I wasn't making an assumption.

"You won't get in trouble for telling me the truth. I don't shoot the messenger."

"Yes," he mumbled.

"I'm going to need you to speak up, Myron."

Clearly uncomfortable, the man cleared his throat. "Yes, Mr. Lexington, that's what the rumors are. That Ashlee..." His face flooded with color. "That she did...you know."

"Did you hear this rumor from a lot of different places, or only one or two?"

He thought for a moment before answering, which I appreciated despite how impatient I was.

"I heard it a few places," he said, "but everyone I heard talking about it is from the same group of friends."

Now we were getting somewhere.

"Would these happen to be friends of Flora's?" I asked.

As a kid, I'd had a time where I'd seriously thought about going into law, but I'd definitely learned since that I never could've stayed within all of those laws. Like how, if this had been some sort of trial, I'd have been accused of leading the witness. I'd suspected Flora of being the source of the gossip and everything I was hearing from Myron supported that. I wouldn't need anything else.

"They are," Myron said. "And..." His face took on a pained expression as he twisted his fingers together.

"Go on," I said.

"They've been talking bad about Ashlee on other stuff. About how it took Flora so long to work up to assistant but didn't take Ashlee as long."

A flare of anger sparked in me. No one in my company received undeserved promotions. Not only was it an insult to

Ashlee, but it was an insult to me and the business I'd built. It even gave me pause about taking Ashlee this weekend, but I knew if I did that after inquiring about these rumors, it would look suspicious either way. Best to take care of things this way.

"All right," I said as I stood. I held out a hand to Myron. "Thank you for talking to me."

He shook my hand, his eyes darting everywhere, and the moment I released him, he hurried away without a look back. I crossed to the door and closed it even though I planned to leave in a bit. I needed a few minutes to calm myself down.

I wasn't stupid enough to think that my employees didn't gossip about each other and about me, and while I'd been angry enough to hear what Flora had said about me, her talking about Ashlee had been too much. I'd known women who used sex to get what they wanted. In fact, pretty much every woman I'd ever met was that way. But Ashlee wasn't. Anyone who'd ever had a conversation with her could see that she was a hard worker who'd never take shortcuts, let alone use sex to manipulate.

There were limits as to what I could do, but I planned on doing what I could. I sent off the emails I needed to answer and finished up the last things I needed to do, then let my receptionist know that I'd be leaving. Anything important could be sent to my cell.

I could have waited until Flora came back on Monday to call her into my office, but I didn't want her in my building again. I didn't want her spreading that shit around anymore. I couldn't stop her from talking to her friends outside of this building, but I could control her presence here, and I intended to do it.

I pulled up her file and put her address into my phone. It was time to pay Flora Watts a visit and terminate her employment.

I stared out the window as my driver dealt with the traffic. I hated this time of the year. Sometimes we had sun and warmth, but most of the time, the weather was dreary and wet, hovering at a temperature that could be snow one minute and rain the next. Today was rain, melting away the last bit of snow and slush that had come in last week's storm. It was supposed to freeze overnight, but then temperatures would be going up, though not too much. That would be good for the event this weekend. Too cold and people would stay home. Too warm and people wouldn't want to be indoors.

I didn't need to wonder if Stu or Suzie had seen the weather. They kept three or four weather sites running in the background on their desktops and on their laptops just so they'd never be caught unaware. Granted, weather prediction wasn't always accurate, but it was better than nothing.

"Do you want me to find a place to park, Mr. Lexington?"

I saw the apartment building in front of us and glanced at the clock. He'd made good time. "I shouldn't be long."

"I'll circle the block then," he said as he pulled up to the curb.

I nodded and stepped out into the rain. I pressed the button next to Watts, rolling my eyes at the sugar-sweet voice that came over the intercom as soon as I said my name. I didn't bother with the elevator, jogging up the stairs to reach the second floor. I headed down the hall, wondering what Flora was thinking. I'd simply given my name, not why I was here. Going to someone's house to fire them wasn't exactly normal, but she'd almost sounded happy that it was me.

Maybe she thought I was coming over to offer her the same thing she'd accused me of offering to Ashlee. My gut said if I did tell her I'd end her suspension in exchange for sex, she'd accept. Everything I'd learned about Flora over the last two days told me she was going after Ashlee because she was jealous. I didn't know for certain that her jealousy extended to me, but my gut said Flora was the sort of petty person who'd always think she was entitled to whatever she wanted, and if anyone else had more, she despised them for it.

She opened her door before I even knocked, and judging by what she was wearing and how out of breath she was, she'd changed her clothes and then run for the door. Unless she always lounged around her house in a mini skirt and halter top.

"Mr. Lexington, please come in." She gave me what I supposed she meant to be a seductive smile. "Or should I call you Nate?"

"This won't take long." I ignored her question and tapped the video icon on my cell phone. "First, I need to make you aware that I'm videotaping this conversation." Her gaze dropped to my hand, but she didn't say anything. "And second, after conducting an inquiry into some work behavior that went against company guidelines, I'm here to inform you that your suspension has become a termination."

Her jaw dropped. "What?"

"You're fired, Ms. Watts," I said. "Your things will be shipped to you, and you shouldn't expect a letter of recommendation from me."

"You can't do that!" she sputtered.

I didn't bother to dignify that with a response. I turned and walked back down the stairs while she cursed at me. Even as I tapped the phone's screen to end the video, I didn't care. She was done. Security had an email telling them to keep an eye out for her, and her badge had been deactivated.

One problem taken care of.

Now, I just had my 'date' to look forward to.

THIRTEEN

ASHLEE

I'D THOUGHT THAT MEETING NATE AT MANHATTAN
Records before the event would make this feel like less of a
date. I'd also assumed that it'd make me less nervous because
I'd be able to psych myself up on the way. I was also thinking
that the less time the two of us spent just the two of us, the
better. I'd had lots of thoughts.

I hadn't, however, thought that taking the subway in a
dress and heels would be so problematic. I wasn't wearing
anything expensive, but the floor-length, off-the-shoulder
dress was far from work wardrobe. For my ride home, I'd have
to either call a cab or see if Nate could take me. I wasn't
getting harassed or anything, but I doubted I'd feel like
standing in these heels on the way home. And there was no
way I was going to sit in this dress. I may have found it at a
thrift store, but that didn't mean it wasn't the nicest dress I
owned.

By the time I reached Manhattan Records, I was shiver-
ing, my thin wrap not doing much to keep out the March

wind. Despite that, the moment I stepped into the lobby, Nate frowned, and I was tempted to turn right around and go back to my apartment.

Then he shrugged out of his tuxedo jacket and draped it over my shoulders. "Did you walk here?"

I shook my head, snuggling into the thick material's warmth. "Took the subway. It was a little chillier than I'd imagined."

"I would have sent a car," he said, sounding annoyed. "Or I could've just picked you up at your place."

"I'll take you up on that for the homeward journey," I said. "I've learned my lesson."

Heat flared in his eyes. "Have you now?"

I shivered again, but it had little to do with temperature. He might've said that kissing me was his way of determining whether or not I'd read too much into tonight, but the way he looked at me made me think there was at least some physical attraction there.

Or maybe he simply got off on making his employees bend to his will.

A noise behind us caught my attention, and I looked back to see a security guard looking away in a hurry. Probably hoping the boss wouldn't catch him eavesdropping. I just hoped he wouldn't be sharing any of this with his co-workers. Then again, I'd heard that Nate had been asking questions about people spreading rumors. Yeah, that was a rumor about a rumor, but maybe he really was trying to keep his employees from talking about things that had nothing to do with them.

"My driver just pulled up," Nate said as he tucked his

phone into his jacket pocket, lingering by my side long enough for me to absorb the smell of sandalwood that clung to him even more than it did to the jacket.

"You can have this back," I said quietly. "I'm warm now."

"Keep it for now," he said. "We're going outside."

I didn't point out that the distance from the doors to the car I could see waiting for us was barely more than a yard or two away. Instead, I let him put a hand on my back and lead me to the car where he opened the door for me. When he slid in next to me, he kept space between our bodies, but something still crackled between us.

"I'm not expecting you to touch me." The words flew out of me before I could check myself.

"What's that?" He gave me a look that seemed to say that he wasn't sure if he should be amused or offended.

"There's no dancing at the party, so other than general niceties, you won't need to touch me," I attempted to clarify, but didn't quite get my meaning out. "What you said before about my expectations. I want you to know that I'm not expecting you to touch me like we're a couple or something. Or even like we're on a date."

Why was my mouth still talking? I just kept making things worse.

He angled himself toward me, as if he wanted to see me better for this conversation. "Are you telling me to keep my hands to myself?"

I flushed. "Not those specific words...but yes, that's the general sentiment."

"And if I don't want to?"

It could have sounded like a threat, but it didn't. More

like he was truly curious about what my answer would be if he decided he wanted tonight to be more hands on than hands off.

This was not how I'd imagined any conversation going tonight.

"I, um, I...shit." I clapped a hand over my mouth, mortified that I'd cursed in front of my boss.

He laughed, the sound far more sensual than any laugh had a right to be. "Don't worry, Ashlee. This may be for work, but you'll find I'm a little more lax about the things I expect of employees at events like this than I would be if we were going to a fundraiser or something of that sort." He gave me another of those charming smiles of his. "Though I do ask that you keep the cursing to a minimum." He added a wink.

"Are you going to keep the flirting to a minimum?" I shot back, more than a little shocked by my boldness.

Fortunately, Nate didn't appear to be bothered by it. If anything, he looked impressed by the fact that I'd spoken up. "I make no promises."

I should've turned the conversation serious, made sure he knew that I wasn't joking when I said I wanted him to keep his hands to himself, but there was a small part of me that kept arguing that he might not have been the only one who wanted to touch...

I gave myself a mental shake. No more talking. If I couldn't keep myself from saying stupid stuff, I wouldn't say anything at all. If he asked a question, I'd answer just to be polite, but nothing more than that. He'd have no reason to complain, but neither of us were here to flirt.

Maybe it was only because we were in a car together with

nothing else to do. When we arrived at the event and Nate had to be in CEO mode, he maintain professional distance.

I could've believed that if he hadn't been just as inappropriate in his office after suspending Flora. That reminded me of a question I'd been meaning to ask him, but I wasn't sure if now was the right time to do it. Rumors had been flying at work yesterday and today that Flora's suspension had turned into a termination. That Nate had shown up at Flora's place and fired her because she wouldn't sleep with him. I didn't believe the second part, since, if Nate had really wanted to sleep with Flora, he wouldn't have waited three days to make the demand. I just didn't know if the rest of it was true, and if so, what had prompted the firing.

There was another set of rumors going around, much quieter than the others. Rumors that said Nate had been questioning people about gossip because of what had happened with Flora and me, and that he was taking a hard-line stance on any sort of personal gossip in the office. And that this stance was the real reason for Flora's termination.

These thoughts kept me preoccupied until we pulled up to the venue at one of New York's swankier hotels. I put all of that out of my mind as Nate got out of the car and turned around to offer me a hand. I reminded myself that he was simply being polite and accepted. When he tucked my arm around his to escort me into the building, I told myself the same thing.

I didn't believe it anymore then than I had the first time.

FOURTEEN

NATE

ONCE INSIDE, I LET GO OF ASHLEE LONG ENOUGH TO retrieve my jacket. Some press had been outside, and I had no doubt they'd have a field day with the fact that I'd arrived with a woman wearing what was obviously my jacket, but now that we were inside, she'd be warm enough with her wrap. Besides, she'd had time to warm up in the car. I still couldn't believe she'd taken the subway in that dress. My blood ran cold at the thought of what could have happened to her...and then ran hot at the thought of the men who'd seen her.

If she'd been mine, I'd have taken her up to my office and spanked her ass until it was red and she felt it any time she moved. No one put something of mine in danger, no matter who they were. She wasn't mine, though, which meant my only option was to make certain she got home okay tonight.

"There's going to be a lot of press," I said as I smoothed out the lines of my jacket. "Don't answer anything, even if you think you know the answer. Stu's here so he'll be fielding any A&R questions."

"Am I allowed to say my name, or would that be giving away too much?"

I laughed even though I should have snapped at her to take this seriously. No woman I'd taken to something like this had questioned this much. Ashlee continued to surprise me, and I liked it.

"They're going to try to find out who you are," I said. "As soon as they know you're a Manhattan Records employee, they'll start making assumptions, and there are a few of them who'll print whatever they think, no matter what evidence there is to the contrary."

"Isn't that libel?" she asked.

"It is," I said, impressed that she knew the difference between libel and slander. "I have an attorney on retainer to take care of issues like that. He insists that it's better to be proactive and prevent stories rather than being reactive and trying to minimize the damage."

"That makes sense," she said. "I'll ignore any questions."

I held out my arm again, and she tucked her arm around it, making me wonder if she was truly averse to my touch...or if she just didn't like how she reacted to it. How far could I push her to find out? Walking like this was her touching me through two layers of my clothes, plus it was the gentlemanly thing to do. Were either of those reasons behind her willingness to take my arm? I had no problem continuing to be a gentleman in public, but there were plenty of ways I could maintain that and still test my theory.

If nothing else, it would be a challenge and would keep

me entertained instead of the night dragging on endlessly as it usually did at events like this. In that curve-hugging dress, she would've been quite a distraction on her own, and I found myself glancing down at her as we made our way into the ballroom, appreciating the way she looked.

"We'll make a round before everything kicks off, just to make sure there's nothing that needs my attention. At some point, Stu will check in with me, and when I give him the go-ahead, he'll get things started. The dinner will be last."

"I wondered if you did anything at these events," she said, looking around, her wide eyes sweeping the elegant room.

"You've been thinking about me, then?" I winked at her. She was so easy to flirt with.

"I've been doing my job," she countered. "A job that involved working with Mr. Hancock and Ms. Lamas to plan this event. I probably know as much about it as they do."

She said it in such a matter-of-fact way that I knew it wasn't her being arrogant. She was the A&R assistant, after all, and that meant she'd probably done a lot of research and made most of the calls checking the time and the like. If she hadn't seen my name on much, it made sense that she would wonder what I actually did at these events.

"A great leader knows how to hire great people," I said. "Delegation is key."

She glanced up at me. "Did they teach you those clichés at business school?"

I nodded. "Night class."

My answer surprised a laugh out of her, and her entire face lit up. I'd never seen anything like it. Unfortunately, we were interrupted before I could make her laugh again.

Stockholders, journalists, photographers...person after person approached to make small talk and ask questions, and all the while Ashlee was sweet, charming – and silent – on my arm.

It didn't feel like she was checking out, though, merely being arm candy because I'd told her not to answer questions. The intelligence I'd seen in her eyes and heard in the way she spoke told me that she was probably one of the smartest people in the room. And I considered myself more intelligent than most. I had a feeling she was absorbing everything around her, sorting through it, categorizing it.

I couldn't wait to get her impressions of this entire night. It had been a long time since I'd seen any of this through new eyes, and I had a feeling her eyes would be seeing things I missed. She'd be able to give Stu, Suzie, and me insight into the things she thought worked and those that didn't. Becoming irrelevant was death in this industry, and we needed to stay on our toes. She'd help with that.

"Well, look at you."

A jolt of anger went through me, but years of self-control kept me from showing it. I retained my plastic smile and slowly turned around to face the last person I wanted to see here.

"Roma. You managed to find a way in, after all."

My ex gave me the saucy grin that had preceded so many of our trysts, but it did nothing but turn my stomach now. Her eyes narrowed as they left me and fell on Ashlee, pure venom in that gaze.

"Who's this?" The words were practically a snarl.

"Now, now, Roma, dear." The older man next to her

patted the hand on his arm. "You should be nice to the CEO responsible for tonight's party."

"Good to see you, Bradley," I said mildly.

"Nate."

"Who. Is. She." Roma spoke between gritted teeth.

"Ashlee Webb," Ashlee answered with a smile that didn't look any more real than mine did.

Roma's eyes flicked over Ashlee once and then turned back to me, clearly dismissing her as no competition. Because that's how Roma would see another woman on my arm. Competition for my affection. As if I'd needed a woman at my side to have wanted to break things off with her.

Further confirmation that Roma had never understood how I thought.

"Would you get me something to drink, Bradley?" Roma practically purred.

"You can go with him," I suggested. "I have other people to talk to."

Roma wiggled her fingers at her date – one of New York's bluest bloods who enjoyed rubbing elbows with those in the music industry – but never took her eyes off me. Her voice was low. "Send her on her way, Nate, and the two of us can find a little private space to have some fun. Or maybe a little public space. We can invite some people to watch. I know how you like that."

I felt Ashlee release my arm, and I knew she was walking away, but I didn't look at her. I needed to take care of Roma before anything else. I couldn't let her make a scene, not here, not tonight. I was in charge, and she needed to understand that even though we weren't together, my control still mattered. All she was doing was making it more obvious that I never should have been involved with her in the first place.

"I'm going to say this once," I said firmly. "Stay away from me. Keep your mouth shut. If you make a scene here, your career is over. I will use every contact I have to blackball you from here to L.A. Clear?"

FIFTEEN

ASHLEE

I'D KNOWN TONIGHT WAS GOING TO BE AWKWARD WHEN I saw people who knew me, and I'd known that Nate had a long list of previous lovers, but I hadn't anticipated those two things coming together for one massively embarrassing scene. If Nate wanted to leave with another woman, that was his prerogative. I wasn't his girlfriend, and this wasn't a date.

Still, I didn't want to be present when he made that decision. I'd put up with people like that woman my whole life, and most of the time, I'd been the bigger person. Sometimes, to do that, I'd had to walk away, which was what I'd done a few minutes ago.

Now, I put together a plan of action. I wouldn't be the sort of woman who'd wander around, trying to act as if I wasn't searching for a date who'd disappeared with someone else. Instead, I'd get myself a drink and linger at the bar, looking for Mr. Hancock. Since he was my boss, I could play it off as work-related to anyone who might wonder what I was doing. I'd make some small talk with him, and if I hadn't spotted Nate by the time we were called to dinner, I'd assume he wasn't looking for me and call a cab.

Maybe I could even get home before too late and be able to finish the book I'd been reading. Getting out of these heels would be relief enough, honestly. It was moments like this when I wondered if I was really cut out to be in the A&R department. I was great with the organizational part of things, and I didn't necessarily mind talking to people as I worked out details, but this aspect of the job didn't particularly appeal to me. Small talk. Schmoozing. Pretending to be interested when I wasn't. I could do it, but I didn't like it. The real question was if I disliked it enough to change my career path.

I checked my reflection one more time and ran my pinky finger along my bottom lip, smoothing out my lip gloss. I hadn't come in here to cry or anything like that, but I didn't want anyone to think that's why I'd left in the first place. Any reapplication of makeup would only fuel the rumor mill. It'd be a toss-up if the gossip would be tears or sex – maybe both.

I'd only gone half a dozen steps down the short corridor before stopping abruptly when someone stepped in front of me.

"Hello there, sugar."

I recognized the voice immediately.

"Mr. Hipwood," I said politely. "It's nice to finally meet you."

"Call me Zed, sugar," he said as he leered at me.

I knew Zed Hipwood was in his mid-thirties like Nate, but Zed looked at least ten years older. Dark hair with more product than should have been legal. Blood-shot eyes with pupils almost big enough to completely obliterate the brown irises. A lean body that had a scrawny, unhealthy appearance. The smell of alcohol was almost overwhelming, but my gut said he wasn't simply drunk. No track marks on his arms, but in college, I'd written a paper on the drug epidemic, and I'd learned that a lot of junkies would shoot up between their toes to hide their habit.

"I'm Ashlee Webb from the A&R department." I might've been introducing myself, but I was also making sure that he knew I was here with the record label. I didn't consider myself a cynic, but I also wasn't naïve enough to think that someone who might be a decent enough guy when sober couldn't be something else entirely when drunk and high.

"Are you one of my perks?" He moved closer to me, licking his lips. "Nice to know Stuy-boy knows what side his butter's breaded on."

"I'm not a *perk*, Mr. Hipwood." I kept my tone professional, not giving any indication as to my opinion regarding his requests. "I'm Stu Hancock's personal assistant."

Zed laughed. "And here I thought he was a fag. Must not be if he's banging you."

My hands curled into fists, but I maintained my calm, cool demeanor. "If you'll excuse me..." I took a step to the side, hoping to walk around him, but he moved with me, closing the distance between us even more.

"What do ya say we go find your boss and have him gimme the key to my band's room?" He stared down the front of my dress, not even bothering to try to hide what he was doing. "I get first dibs, but they're all gonna love to get a piece of you."

"I'm not interested." My jaw protested how tightly I was gritting my teeth, but I didn't plan on losing my temper over some drunk asshole's assumptions. Especially a drunk asshole who brought in a lot of money for my employer.

I moved around him and made it two more steps before he grabbed my arm. And then he grabbed my ass.

I quickly twisted out of his grasp and grabbed the hand that was on my ass. Even in a dress, I was fast enough to get his arm behind his back, his wrist on its way to meet his shoulder blades. He bent backward to try to take the pressure off and succeeded only in putting him closer to my height so I could get better leverage.

"Fucking bitch! Get your bitching hands offa me." He struggled, but despite our height difference, his body wasn't in any shape to defend itself. "Dammit! Do you know who I am?! Fucking Zed Hipwood! Unraveling! That's me!"

I'd reacted instinctively to his unwanted touch, but now that I had him off me, I wasn't entirely sure what to do next. The scenarios my self-defense classes had gone through had been about attackers in parking lots, alleys, on the streets, in bars or clubs. Places where the answer was simply getting away as soon as possible. Nothing in those classes had prepared me for what to do when a powerful guest at a fancy party grabbed my ass.

"Let me go! Mother fucking son of a bitch whore..."

"Come now, Zed. You're just stringing a bunch of curses together, and that's not going to get you anywhere." Nate's voice was mild as he entered the alcove. "Can someone tell me what's going on here?"

"Tell the bitch to let me go!"

Shit. I released him and moved back a few steps. I didn't think Nate would let Zed hit me, but I wasn't eager to find out.

"What happened?" Nate asked again. His gaze landed on me and held.

"That little cunt messed up my arm, that's what happened?" Zed cradled his wrist like I'd caused permanent damage.

I could've done just that. I knew how. I'd purposefully held back though. I didn't doubt for a minute that if I'd truly hurt him, I wouldn't get into trouble.

"That's not really the best way to speak to a lady, Zed," Nate said evenly.

If I hadn't seen the hard glint in his eyes or the way the muscles in his jaw clenched, I might've thought he was entertained by this whole thing.

"I came back here to take a piss and this bit...this *girl* was all over me. Wanted me to do her in the bathroom. I turned her down, and she got all fema-Nazi on me."

What the actual fuck?

Was I seriously being blamed *again* for something I hadn't done? Did I have *scapegoat* written on my forehead and no one told me?

Last time, I'd defended my own lack of participation but hadn't blamed anyone else. While I hadn't been suspended, I'd still ended up here and had rumors circulating about me, no matter the measures Nate had been trying to put into place. No way in hell was I going to let Zed Hipwood make things worse. And definitely not about this. I considered myself a level-headed person, not easily angered, but my good nature had been worn down to practically nothing this week.

"That's no—"

"I need to speak with Miss Webb alone." Nate grabbed my hand and practically dragged me past the bathrooms and into a small room that looked like it might be a place where employee interviews were held. "Sit."

I sat, more to take the pressure off my aching feet than wanting to obey him. If he was going to fire me, at least I'd be able to go home. Considering how awful my week had been, I was half-tempted to ask him to let me go just so I didn't have to deal with it anymore. When he shut the door behind him, I knew that was it. I was done.

SIXTEEN

NATE

It had taken every ounce of self-control I had not to explode right there in the hallway.

After I'd finally managed to get Roma to leave me alone, I'd headed in the direction I'd seen Ashlee walking. She needed to know that I hadn't gone off with Roma. When I was with a woman, I didn't leave her to have sex with someone else, not unless the two of us had an arrangement regarding additional partners. Ashlee and I didn't have anything like that because we weren't a couple, but I still wanted her to know that I'd come with her and I'd leave with her.

And then I'd seen Ashlee standing behind Zed, twisting the musician's arm behind his back, a look of fury on her face. Something inside me had snapped.

Now, she was sitting across from me, turquoise eyes flashing, face flushed. She was still angry, but she was trying to reign it in. Such control.

It made me wonder just how far I could push, how long it would take me to break that control and see what was underneath. Or would this be enough to break her?

"Tell me what happened," I demanded. I loomed over her, doing my best to intimidate her into telling the truth. "Don't lie. I'll know if you do."

She looked up at me, emotions playing across her face too fast for me to identify any of them, but I hoped fear was in the mix.

As soon as I thought it, I regretted it, and that disturbed me. I never cared if anyone was afraid of me. I'd never hit anyone who didn't deserve it, but being able to intimidate people was a handy skill. I needed her to tell me the truth, and if she was scared I'd fire her, she'd be honest, which was what I wanted. I just hoped she wouldn't cry. I only knew one way to handle non-sex related tears, and that was to kick the woman out. That wasn't exactly an option here.

Except she didn't cry.

Her voice was flat and matter-of-fact as she spoke, "I came out of the restroom and Zed was there. I greeted him, told him I worked in the A&R department. I could tell he was drunk and probably high, so I ignored his calling me 'sugar.'"

The look on her face would've made me laugh if I wasn't pissed at what she was telling me.

"Zed asked if I was one of the 'perks' he'd told Stu – I mean, Mr. Hancock – he wanted."

Stu and I were going to have a discussion about these 'perks' and what we would or wouldn't be offering in the future. I didn't believe for a minute that Stu had provided women for Zed or the rest of Unraveling, but we were going to make it abundantly clear to all of our artists the sort of things we wouldn't have available for them.

Ashlee continued, "When I told him I wasn't a perk but rather Mr. Hancock's personal assistant, he made a rather crude assumption about my role, and then suggested we get a hotel room key so he and the band could all 'get a piece' of me."

I bit back a growl. The idea of the entire band and Ashlee...no. Just no.

"I turned him down and tried to walk around him." Her mouth flattened into a thin line. "He grabbed my arm, and then he grabbed my...butt."

Hell no. She'd clearly told him that she wasn't interested in him. That was so far over the line...

"I used what I learned in my self-defense classes to get out of his grip and put him into a position of submission."

The word rolled off her tongue and flipped that switch inside me that was definitely *not* work friendly. I wrestled it back into the place I kept it when I needed to be professional.

"Son of a bitch," I said, my voice low as I turned away. I paced, continuing to talk to myself. "This needs to be dealt with. We can't condone this. I knew he was a lecherous bastard, but that's too far. He went too far."

"I'm glad you agree with me."

I turned back toward Ashlee, something about the way she spoke, the earnest quiet of her statement, touched that protective part of me. "You haven't lied to me yet. Zed and I have...history that already made me suspect he was lying."

"But you signed him." She seemed calmer now, more in control of herself. "Unraveling was the first platinum artist Manhattan Records had, if I'm remembering correctly."

I nodded. "Yes, to both. Zed was an asshole back then too."

"I would ask why you signed him, but I already know the answer."

"You do?" My insides froze.

"Rock stars are supposed to make headlines, and Zed being who he is, he makes headlines. Which makes you money."

Right. Money.

"He went too far this time."

I said it directly to her because I needed her to understand that not only did I believe her, but I didn't approve of what Zed did. Sure, I'd kissed her without warning, but as soon as she said *no*, I backed off. Zed hadn't.

"I'm glad you think so," she said. "A lot of men don't."

"I'm going to take care of this." My anger finally bled through my words.

The more I thought about Zed putting his hands on Ashlee, the angrier I got. The control that I had was slipping, and that never happened. What was it about this woman that made me want to not only end Zed's contract but also knock out some teeth in the process?

As a Dom, I'd always been possessive of what was mine until I decided I didn't want it anymore, but Ashlee wasn't mine. Had never been mine. We'd barely interacted. Had a single, brief kiss. But I wanted to protect her.

More than wanted to. I was going to. And I wasn't simply going to protect her. I was going to punish Zed for laying hands on a woman who didn't want him. Just like I would've done for any other woman...but harder because the woman was mine.

Not mine.

I looked at her, and my stomach clenched.

Mine?

"What are you going to do?" Ashlee came over to stand next to me.

"Don't worry about that." I hadn't decided yet, but my instincts told me to walk back out there, find Zed, and punch him in the face.

"You aren't going to do anything stupid, are you?"

She honestly seemed concerned, and I wondered if it was *for* me or *about* me. Did she think I'd make a scene and it'd be her fault? It was impossible to figure out what she was thinking, and that wasn't something I was used to.

"Why would you think that?" I asked.

"Because you seem to have an impulsive streak sometimes," she replied with a smile.

I liked seeing her smile.

"Stay here. I'll be back as soon as I deal with the problem."

I took a step toward the door, and she put her hand on my arm. I stopped, the pressure of her touch more arresting than anything she could've said. Heat flowed through me, diffusing the anger, changing it into something else.

"Please, don't do anything rash," she pleaded.

"You're going to want to step back," I said as my gaze moved from her hand to her eyes. "Because if you keep your hand there, something is going to happen between the two of us."

SEVENTEEN
ASHLEE

I WASN'T SURE WHEN I FIGURED OUT THAT NATE WASN'T going to fire me and that he wasn't even angry at me, but when I did, when I realized that he was furious because of what Zed had done, it changed things. Changed the way I saw Nate Lexington.

He wasn't perfect, and there was still the fact that he was my boss's boss, but I could now see a side of him I hadn't seen before. A part of him that took care of his employees. Except something in my gut said that wasn't all of it, that he wouldn't be getting this worked up for any employee.

I didn't want to know that or think that. I didn't want to complicate things any more than they already were. Except it looked like it was too late to turn back the clock. I'd told him everything that had happened, and now he was talking about 'taking care' of Zed. All sorts of interpretations of that phrase ran through my mind, each one worse than the other.

To think, when he'd first brought me to this room, I'd been worried about getting fired. Now, I was concerned that

Nate was going to do something he couldn't take back. If he got into a fight with the lead singer of his label's biggest artist, he might be okay with it for a little while, but once he cooled off, he'd be furious with himself for losing his temper.

And he might be furious with me for giving him an excuse to fight. Sure, he was on my side now, but he'd been all over the place this past week. Ready to fire me one minute and asking me to come here the next. Kissing me. For all I knew, he'd call me into his office on Monday and demand that I tell him the truth about what happened because Zed was a jerk, but he wouldn't have taken things that far. Or maybe he wouldn't accuse me of being a liar, but would blame me...

No.

I wasn't going to overthink things and come up with all the ways things could go south. I needed to think about the here and now, which meant I had to keep him from doing something stupid like punching the lead singer of Unraveling in front of the press and everyone else.

I went over to stand next to him as I asked what he intended to do, hoping that my presence would maybe calm him, or at the very least distract him.

I put my hand on his arm. "Please, don't do anything rash."

"You're going to want to step back." His voice was quiet, but not at all soft. "Because if you keep your hand there, something is going to happen between the two of us."

That should have made me back off in a hurry, and a part of me recognized that he was trying to scare me into letting him go do whatever it was he wanted to do. He'd tried that posturing earlier when he'd demanded to know what happened. I wasn't any more frightened now than I was then. Even though I didn't know what he might say or how he might act, I did know that I wasn't afraid of him.

Well, not physically.

He wasn't the sort of man who resorted to violence to get what he wanted. If he was, I could think of several different times where he could've used physical force on me. Even the times he'd touched me, I'd been able to feel how much he'd held back.

If I was being honest with myself, that was the part of him I felt drawn to, and the reason my stomach was currently in knots.

I could move back, let him go do whatever while I got a ride home, then text him to let him know where I'd gone. He'd have the weekend to calm down, and then things could go back to normal at work.

But I didn't want to do any of that. I wanted to distract him to keep him from making a mistake he couldn't take back, but more than that, I wanted to know what he'd do next. Wanted to know what that *something* was that he promised would happen between us. I'd never been this curious about another person before, and that should have scared me as much as any almost-threat he made.

I left my hand where it was, my eyes locked with his, and waited to see what he'd do next.

Several seconds ticked by, and neither of us moved or said a word. The room was quiet. The party continued on without us. No one came looking.

Then he moved all at once. His hand catching mine as he

spun me around and pressed my back against the wall. I had a few seconds to register what was happening, seconds to stop him if this wasn't what I wanted. Instead, I tipped my head up, inviting him to kiss me, to see where this would lead us.

Electricity zinged through me the moment our lips touched, scorching its way across my nerves. He devoured my mouth like a starving man, every fiber of his being focused on the way our lips moved together, the stroke of his tongue across mine. His teeth bumped against mine, latched onto my bottom lip, and I moaned.

"Touch you."

The words were a whisper so faint I couldn't tell if they were a request or a demand, but either way, I consented.

"Yes." I kissed his jaw, scraped my teeth across the skin there. "Yes."

His palm was hot as it pushed aside my skirt and traveled up my leg to palm my ass, then moved around until he cupped my sex. I pushed his jacket off and let my hands roam those broad shoulders and muscled torso. I itched to touch him, was tempted to tear his shirt off, but we had a party to get back to, and I doubted he'd appreciate his buttons wrenched off.

The hand not lightly teasing me over my panties caught my chin and held me in place as his mouth found me again. His tongue slid between my lips at the same time a finger moved under the delicate silk I wore.

I gasped as the pad of his index finger grazed my clit, and he swallowed the sound. That one and all the others I made as his fingers skillfully moved over that bundle of nerves, driving me toward the climax I could feel building inside me.

Circles with just the right pressure and then back and forth, a perfect rhythm designed to send me flying as quickly as possible. All I could do was clutch his shoulders and accept pleasure so intense it almost hurt as it coursed through my body. Then I was coming, shuddering as his talented fingers pushed me to orgasm and beyond.

My body stiffened.

Air stopped in my lungs.

Teeth bit down on his lip.

Hands grabbed at his shirt until I was sure it would tear in two.

And still, he rubbed my swollen, throbbing clit, lighter now, coaxing me down from the brilliant white headspace of climax. Holding me up until I could stand on my own. Saying not a single word as he moved my panties back into place. Smoothed down my dress.

And then moving away as we realized what we'd done. The lines we'd crossed. The things we risked if anyone ever found out about this.

But I couldn't bring myself to regret it.

EIGHTEEN

NATE

I DIDN'T KNOW WHAT HAD COME OVER ME. OR RATHER, I did know, but I didn't understand it. I prided myself on my self-control, but it failed me. The moment she hadn't done what I'd told her to do, I'd known that I had a decision to make. I could tell her to go home and then go find Zed like I'd originally planned...or I could do what I'd wanted to do from the first moment I'd talked to her, even when I'd been pissed at her.

So I kissed her. And not a half-assed kiss like before when I wasn't sure if it was a good idea or not. This was an all-consuming kiss that led to me putting my hand up her dress and stroking her to a climax.

Watching her come apart as my fingers worked over her hot, wet skin hadn't been like any of the thousands of other times I'd made women climax. There was something so pure and innocent about it, and while that wasn't usually my thing, when it came to Ashlee, I was starting to think that all my normal rules didn't apply.

I held her while she came down, my thoughts wandering from this experience to what it would be like to have other experiences with her. If she was truly as innocent as she seemed, she might have only done vanilla stuff with other guys.

A spark of jealousy made itself known. I didn't like the thought of her with other men.

I liked the jealousy even less.

What would it be like, I wondered, to be able to teach a sub my likes and dislikes from moment one? To learn the things that turned her on even as I taught them to her. Teach her how pleasure and pain could go together. Dirty that pure vanilla just a little bit. Or a lot, depending how she took to it.

I'd been impulsive just now, though, and I couldn't do that again. I had to be smart about it. Make sure that she didn't think I was coming on to her as her boss. We had to separate sex and work...even though I had just made her come at a work function. That wouldn't happen again. It couldn't. If we were going to do this, we would do it right.

I felt her tense the same time I saw her finish processing the reality of what we'd done, and I took a step back. She needed to get her head around it before I could take things further.

"So..."

I smiled at her. "You aren't going to go all weird on me, are you?"

As I'd hoped, my words made her laugh. A nervous laugh, but still a laugh.

"What about you? Are you going to 'go all weird?'"

"Not at all," I said, bending down to snag my jacket.

Despite already being overly warm, thanks to Ashlee, I put my jacket back on.

"I'm going to need to clean up before I go back out there," she said, her skin still flushed.

I wanted to reach out and touch her skin again. Instead, I offered her my arm. "I'll wait outside the bathroom this time."

"You don't have to do that."

It was on the tip of my tongue to explain everything to her, to make certain she knew that I took my role as Dom seriously, but we weren't there yet. If I started talking Doms and subs and nipple clamps and butt plugs, I'd probably end up getting slapped with a sexual harassment suit before she emptied her desk...or offered to relieve me of my company.

"I'm not letting that bastard near you again," I said. "And I won't let anyone else try it either."

Her expression softened. "Thank you."

The gratitude surprised me. Clearly, she knew how to defend herself, and I'd been prepared to have to argue with her about how I'd rather prevent any issues instead of her having to react after something happened. I hadn't foreseen her thanking me and agreeing to it.

I followed her out of the room and back down the hallway, neither of us saying anything as she entered the bathroom again, and I leaned against the wall next to the door.

The more time I spent with Ashlee, the less I understood her. She wasn't anything like the women I usually spent time with, not the ones in my personal or professional lives. Maybe that was why I was so intrigued with her. I'd been bored with Roma and even bored with the idea of looking for another sub. Someone who wasn't already a sub or at least wasn't knowledgeable when it came to sex would give me a different way of experiencing things.

By the time she came out of the bathroom, I'd decided on my course of action. I held out my arm and waited for her to blow by me. Again, I was surprised by her choice when she took my arm.

"Don't want you getting any ideas about running off to beat the shit out of Unraveling's lead singer," she said as we headed back toward the party.

"That's some pretty unprofessional language there," I teased, my entire being feeling strangely light.

This was...new.

Maybe pursuing things with her wasn't such a good idea after all.

Then I took another look at her and remembered how she'd looked coming apart in my arms. I needed to feel what that was like with my cock buried deep inside her. Soon. Distraction was good some of the time, but if I dragged things out too long, I'd regret it.

"We should check in with Stu," I said, as much for something to say as anything else. "Make sure everything's going as smoothly as possible."

I kept us at the edge of the party as I scanned faces until I found the one I was looking for. As usual, Stu was in the thick of things, smiling and laughing as he moved from one person to the next. If I was the public face of Manhattan Records, Stu was a close second. We had a public relations department who handled announcements, press conferences, that sort of thing. They also handed any press conferences, important announcements, publicity nightmares – considering the sort of shit Zed got up to, they were kept pretty busy. Their faces occasionally made it into media, but Stu was at the parties, and those got a lot more attention than press conferences.

I greeted each person who made eye contact, but didn't let them stop me, moving past with my most charming smile and polite, vague words. When I reached Stu, I waited, however impatiently, for him to finish his conversation with Saya Wong, one of the few agents I genuinely liked, and not in a sexual way. She had three artists with us and handled each one with a professionalism that was lacking in many other agents. She respected not only them and us, but also the business itself.

"Nate," Saya said, extending a hand. She smiled warmly as I shook her hand and then she turned to Ashlee, shaking her hand as well.

"Ashlee Webb." She gave Saya a genuine smile.

Saya glanced at Stu before looking back at Ashlee. "It's nice to meet you. I'm Saya Wong. I represent–"

"Brandy Flick, Golden Words, and The Bright Lights," Ashlee said smoothly. "The Bright Lights is the newest addition to the label."

Saya's smile widened, and her eyes sparkled. "Oh, she's a sharp one, Nate. Where'd you find her?"

"A&R."

Saya and Stu stared at me for a minute before laughing. Ashlee's hand tightened on my arm, and I lightly touched her, an unconscious Dom gesture that I often used on my subs to calm them when they seemed agitated. It seemed to work on her too, and she settled under my touch.

"Miss Webb is my assistant," Stu said.

The fact that he didn't appear to be surprised by her presence here told me either she'd told him or he'd heard rumors. Firing Flora had helped curb people's tongues, but it couldn't make people unhear what had already been going around.

"Before we get distracted by the fascinating rise of Miss Webb's career," I said, "I'd like to know how things are progressing here."

"I'm going to check in on my people," Saya said. "It was nice to meet you, Ashlee." She nodded at Stu and then at me before excusing herself.

"Everything's going well," Stu said, turning his attention to me as Saya walked off. "I have a couple security guys in plainclothes in the crowd, following certain people we know might cause...problems."

My hand clenched into a fist. Apparently, Stu and I needed to talk about those guys because they'd clearly missed following our biggest *problem* earlier. But this wasn't the time for it. For now, I'd offer just a simple instruction.

"Make sure you keep one of those guys on Zed the rest of the night. Don't let him alone with anyone." Stu frowned, his eyes darting from me to Ashlee and back again. I could see him starting to put the pieces together, but I spoke again before he could ask questions. "Ashlee and I are going to head out. My apologies for missing dinner."

I'd fill him in at a later time, but he had to know to keep Zed from groping anyone else at the party. It'd also be a good distraction when Stu inevitably asked why I'd shown up here with Ashlee. I liked that he didn't have a problem telling me what he truly thought, but I had a feeling that would come back to bite me in the ass with this. At least he wasn't as blunt about it as Finley. Stu was, after all, an employee and not my partner.

"Before you go," Stu said, focusing his attention on Ashlee, "I just wanted to tell you what a great job you did, all of your research and work was essential to putting together a great event."

She smiled at him, a genuine, sweet smile. "Thank you. That means a lot. I've learned so much from you."

"You're a quick study," he said. "I can't wait to see what you do with the next one."

I resisted the urge to hurry Ashlee along, to get her somewhere alone where I could tell her what I wanted. I didn't want to make Stu any more suspicious than he already was. I knew my reputation, but I didn't do this with women who worked for me.

But I couldn't walk away unless Ashlee told me to go, and I planned to work to make sure that didn't happen. That was weird for me. Usually, I just had to show interest in a woman to get her into bed. I had a feeling Ashlee wouldn't go easily.

"Thank you," Ashlee said. She glanced up at me, her hand tightening on my arm.

Had she figured out what I was thinking? Did her squeeze mean that she was thinking the same thing? Dammit. I wanted to know what was going on in that head of hers.

"I think you can take things from here," I told Stu. I kept my eyes on Ashlee and told myself that it was because I was trying to imagine what she looked like naked and not because I didn't want to see Stu's disapproval.

He was an employee, not a friend. When it came to my

personal life, I didn't let anyone tell me how to live, not employees or friends. I felt a little twinge as I thought about how isolated that made me, but I pushed that aside. I'd chosen this life, and it was better for everyone that I had. I wouldn't disappoint anyone, and I didn't have to hide who I truly was.

I escorted Ashlee to the exit, pausing just inside the lobby doors to text my driver. While we waited, I finally made my move.

"I want you to come home with me." I covered my surprise that I'd invited her home rather than to a hotel. If I back peddled now, I doubted I'd get another shot. "But I'm not saying that as your boss, but as the man who made you climax with his fingers."

She flushed but didn't pull away from me. In fact, it took her only a couple seconds to give me an answer. "Okay."

Not a ringing endorsement, but I hadn't realized how much I'd been bracing for a refusal until she'd spoken. Based on the expression on her face, she hadn't been expecting her answer either. I wasn't going to waste it.

I made a mental note to discuss Zed with HR and then took Ashlee out to the car. As I slid in next to her, I gave my driver instructions to take us to my place and ignored the look of surprise that he shot me. I was still spinning a bit about it too.

None of this was how things normally went. I wasn't sure yet if that was a good thing or a bad one.

NINETEEN
ASHLEE

When I began today, I'd never expected to end up here, in the back seat of Nate Lexington's car, my insides a mess of aroused knots. I couldn't decide if I was terrified, anxious, turned on, eager...too many different emotions were tangled up inside me for me to identify which one was the foremost.

I'd spent the day trying to pretend that it was just another day at work despite the fact that I was still getting sideways looks from half of my co-workers. My thoughts had been caught up in the possible repercussions of my attending tonight. More gossip. Mr. Hancock and Ms. Lamas looking at me or treating me differently. Nate flirting and me not knowing how to handle it.

Nothing had prepared me for the reality.

From the moment his ex had come up to us, I'd felt things taking a strange turn, and everything from that moment on had made my head spin. Him making me come with his fingers had been the last surprise of the night...or so I'd thought until we were waiting for his car and he asked me to go home with him.

He hadn't spelled out things, but I wasn't an idiot. If I went home with him, we'd be doing a whole lot more than kissing and touching. He'd been careful about making sure I was clear that he wasn't asking me as my boss, and that confirmed for me that if I asked him to stop at any point, he would, but I wouldn't be able to say I hadn't gone into this situation with my eyes wide open.

The only thing that was really giving me pause was that I didn't know how to tell him that I was a virgin. I'd dated a couple guys here and there, but we'd never gone beyond kissing and over-the-clothes petting, which meant that what he'd done tonight was already more than I'd ever done with another person.

I wasn't waiting for marriage, and I didn't have any illusions about love, but I didn't know if Nate would understand that. Being a virgin at twenty-three wasn't exactly abnormal, but most people assumed that if someone made it through college without having sex, there was some deeper reasoning behind it. For me, the timing had never been right, and that had been my choice.

The brush of knuckles down my cheek pulled me out of my head.

"Don't disappear on me, Red." He caught my chin and turned me toward him.

"'Red?'" I echoed as my eyes met his. "You can't do better than that?"

He raised an eyebrow at my challenge, and I had to admit that I'd surprised myself with it, just as I'd shocked the hell out of myself when I'd accepted his invitation to go home with him.

"Sugar?"

I narrowed my eyes. "That's what Zed called me."

His eyes narrowed. "Definitely not *sugar* then."

"Thank you."

"Baby?" The corners of his mouth twitched, and I realized he was teasing me now.

"May I make one request about a nickname?" I asked.

Curiosity sparked in his eyes. "Go ahead."

"Even if you have to call me Red, I don't want you to call me the same thing you've called other women. Especially not that Roma woman."

If he found my request strange, his expression didn't show it. After a moment, he nodded. "All right."

I wasn't sure if that meant he'd just call me 'Red' then, or he was trying to think of something else, but I wasn't going to demand an answer. There were parts of myself I didn't want to share with him. I had to respect his boundaries the same.

He cupped my chin and ran his thumb across my bottom lip. My breathing quickened as I waited to see what he'd do next. He gradually bent his head, as if waiting for me to object. When I didn't, he brushed his lips across mine in a ghost of a kiss. I instinctively leaned forward, wanting more, needing more.

"Not yet." His voice was a low rumble, and when I opened my eyes, I saw that his usual mocha brown had gone to near-black.

"Please," I whispered, wetting my lips. My fingers curled

into the soft fabric of my dress, fists tightening until my knuckles turned white.

He pressed a kiss to my jaw. "Ask me again."

Something sparked inside me. "Please."

His mouth captured mine, and he tried to bury his fingers in my hair, roughly tugging at the pins I'd used to keep my braid coiled around my head. He growled in frustration, his kiss growing rougher as he found himself unable to get at my hair. The pain in my scalp should have had me pushing him away, but instead, it sent a thrill through me, one I didn't quite understand – or maybe I didn't *want* to understand. I grabbed the lapel of his jacket and used it to pull myself closer, my tongue sliding along his as he explored my mouth.

It wasn't until he moved back that I realized the car had come to a stop. Which meant the driver was just sitting in the front seat, waiting, and he had to know what was keeping us. I was far from the first woman Nate had kissed in this car.

That thought was enough to cool me off a bit, though not enough to make me second-guess my decision to come with him.

He got out of the car and held his hand out to me. When I didn't take it immediately, his smile faded, but he didn't look angry. In fact, if I hadn't known better, I would've thought he was...sad.

"Angus can take you home."

His voice was even, but it was the hint of misery in his eyes that prompted me to move. I took his hand, heat rushing through me. "I'm not ready to go home yet."

He smiled again, his eyes lighting up. He helped me from the car and kept my hand tucked tightly to his side. We went up the front steps and past the doorman, who gave us both a nod. When we stepped onto the elevator, he turned his penthouse key, then wrapped his arms around my waist and pulled me against him. I could feel him, half-hard against my back.

"It would be so easy." His voice was low, but loud enough for me to hear. In fact, he was the only thing I could hear. "So easy to take you right here. Lift up the back of your dress and slip off those soft panties I felt before. Maybe just move them aside. Don't need much room for me to slide right inside you. I bet you're all hot and wet for me, aren't you?'

A shiver went down my spine as I nodded just once. He was right. I was both hot *and* wet. My skin was flushed, too tight for my body. It practically hummed, like a thin coating of static electricity that didn't go away. As for wet...making out with guys I'd dated hadn't even come close to making me feel like this. After coming at the party, I'd already needed to change my panties. Now it was worse.

"But I don't want our first time together to be a quickie in the elevator."

First. That sounded promising.

"But maybe later we'll take a ride and have some fun."

I liked the sound of that.

The elevator dinged, and a moment later, the doors opened directly into the penthouse. He slid one hand up to cup my breast over my dress, giving it a gentle squeeze before releasing me.

"Would you like a glass of wine?"

That hadn't been what I'd expected.

"I figured you might want a glass to relax." He caught my

hand and laced his fingers between mine. As my eyes met his, he lifted our hands and kissed my knuckles. "Unless there's another way you'd prefer to relax."

"I'm not really much of a wine drinker." My voice was faint.

"All right." He held my gaze for a moment. "Take your hair down."

I hadn't expected that to be his response to my comment. Or for him to give me what amounted to a command. Because it didn't sound like he was simply telling me what he *wanted* me to do, but rather what I *needed* to do.

I reached up and pulled out the hairpins, setting them down on the first surface I could find, not even bothering to see what I was using. When my braid came down, it reached halfway down my back.

"All the way down."

I pulled out the hair tie and then quickly unbraided it, relieved as the weight eased off my scalp. I ran my fingers through the waves, then dropped my hands, waiting for what came next.

He reached out, trailing a lock between his fingers before releasing it to run his fingers down my arm. Liquid fire blazed a trail down after them, and I waited for him to unzip my dress. He didn't, though. Instead, he took a step back, like he was still trying to figure out what he wanted me to do next.

I tried not to fidget, but there was nothing I could do about the color rushing to my face. I didn't let people walk all over me, which made it difficult for most people to accept that I was actually quite shy. Especially when it came to being the center of attention. I was much better at being behind the scenes than I was having eyes on me.

Particularly when those eyes belonged to someone like Nate.

"Give me your panties."

My face went hot, but I moved to obey. I stepped out of my shoes, knowing I'd never manage to get my underwear off if I tried to do it over my heels, not while I was standing anyway. I reached under my dress, not quite confident enough to take off the dress first. I also got the impression that Nate wanted to dictate what I took off when. Once I got them off, I held them out, and he took them, setting them on the same table where I'd put my hair pins.

"Go sit."

Thanks to the open floor plan, I could see straight from where I was just inside the door all the way to the floor-to-ceiling glass wall. Between it and me were several pieces of furniture, including an expensive-looking couch and matching recliners. I chose the couch, not knowing if he wanted to sit next to me or not.

When he went to his knees in front of me, it took me a moment to realize what he was going to do, which just went to confirm how completely scattered my mind was. I had, after all, been raised by a lesbian who handled the issue of sex and sexuality with a no-nonsense, open approach.

Without another word, Nate pushed my skirt up and pulled my legs over his broad shoulders. I slid down until he was palming both cheeks of my naked ass, and I had a moment to think of how Mom would've yelled at my poor posture before he was lifting my lower half and all of my attention shifted.

"Hold on to the back of the couch."

I reached up and gripped as best I could, every inch of me buzzing with anticipation at what would come next. It became something more as his tongue swiped over my skin. I closed my eyes and let my pulse gallop, my body sing. His mouth moved in now-familiar ways in an unfamiliar place, sending tendrils of hot pleasure snaking through my body until my cells purred with pleasure.

The muscles in my legs began to tremble as the pressure inside me built, and I smacked my hands against the top of the couch, needing to do something with them but not knowing what to do. I was vaguely aware of the noises I was making but couldn't find it in me to be self-conscious. Not with his mouth on such an intimate place.

My back arched as an orgasm slammed into me. I cursed, body attempting to twist but held in place with strong hands as lips and tongue continued drawing out my climax until I couldn't take it anymore.

Nate eased me down onto the couch, my heart hammering against my ribs, little aftershocks of pleasure zinging up and down my nerves. I'd made myself come before, and the orgasm he had given me earlier had been amazing, but this...wow.

He ran his hands up and down my thighs until I finally managed to open my eyes and look up at him. The smug expression on his face didn't annoy me as much as I would've thought. The man had serious skills. Not that I really had anything to judge by, but I felt fairly confident in my opinion since he'd managed to give me two orgasms and we hadn't even gotten to sex yet. Then again, maybe he did that because he wasn't any good at actual sex, though I doubted that was the case. No matter how much I tried to avoid gossip, certain things were hard to ignore.

"I'm trying to decide the best way to fuck you." His conversational tone struck me as strange considering his lips and chin were wet, and one of his fingers was moving up and down my slit, but I wasn't about to complain. "I could put you on your knees and take you from behind right here."

I felt like there was something I needed to say before we got that far, but my brain wasn't exactly working at the highest levels.

"Or I could sit down and watch you ride me." His gaze dropped to my breasts. "I'd love to watch those tits bounce."

I gasped as he slid his index finger inside me, my hand shooting out to grab his forearm. My eyes went wide as his gaze snapped back to mine.

Shit. Now, I remembered.

"Ashlee," his voice was even and his expression unreadable, "is there something you want to tell me?"

"Um, yeah." I looked down to where his hand was still under my dress. "Maybe without your finger inside me would be better."

To my surprise, he actually flushed as he pulled back to sit on the low table in front of the couch. "Speak."

I pushed myself up until I was sitting rather than slouching and tugged my skirt down to my knees. The material was still bunched, but at least I no longer felt entirely naked. Despite that, I couldn't quite bring myself to look anywhere but at my clasped hands on my lap.

Direct seemed like the best approach under the circumstances. If he still wanted me, we could move on, but if he was going to send me away, I didn't want to drag that out.

"I'm a virgin."

A beat of silence before his response. "I see."

I risked a quick glance, but I still couldn't tell what he was thinking. "It's not a big deal."

He raised an eyebrow.

I hurried to explain what I meant. "It wasn't something I felt like I needed to just 'get over with' because people thought it was weird that I hadn't had sex yet, but I'm not waiting for some perfect moment or perfect person or anything like that." I was vaguely aware that I was rambling, but I wasn't sure how to stop myself since Nate didn't seem like he was going to. "I won't read more into this than there is."

He held up his hand as I finally said something he wanted to comment on. "What is it you think is between us?"

I twisted my fingers, all of my previous pleasure vanishing as anxiety took over. "A good time. Enjoying something physical."

He leaned forward and put his hand over both of mine. "Look at me." I raised my head and let my eyes meet his. "Do you know what I am?"

I frowned. "That sounds like the sort of question where any answer is going to get me in trouble."

One corner of his mouth ticked as if what I'd said amused him. "You've heard plenty of rumors about my...proclivities, and you're not an unintelligent woman. I'm certain you can put it together."

My brain scrambled to put together pieces but kept coming up empty...until I remembered something Flora had said about how Nate could tell her what to do. "Are you saying you're a," I searched for the correct word, "Dominant?"

Nate leaned back, a pleased smile on his face. "I am. That's a broad term that covers a wide variety of preferences, but it should tell you at least two important aspects of my personality." His smile remained, but something about it darkened as his voice lowered. "I'm in control, and I don't like secrets."

I shivered, goosebumps breaking out across my skin, but I wasn't afraid. Not of Nate or of what he would want to do. Maybe I should have been, or maybe I should have hated it. But I didn't. I wanted to know more. I wanted to know *him*.

"You kept a secret from me," he continued. His hand slid off mine and onto my knee. "A big secret." His fingers moved under the hem of my dress. "And I want to punish you for it."

A nervous thrill went through me. "Punish?" The word came out in a squeak.

"I want to fuck you tonight," he said plainly, "and I want to do it my way. If that's not what you want, I'll call for Angus, and he'll take you home. No hard feelings, no repercussions. If you want to stay, we'll move forward, beginning with your punishment. It's your choice to make."

TWENTY
NATE

Nothing tonight had gone the way I'd envisioned it, and while I normally hated things to not follow my plans, it had definitely been...interesting. Considering I'd ended things with Roma because I was bored, I wasn't going to complain. Especially not after I'd made Ashlee come twice.

Except I thoroughly expected this to be the end of it. The moment I'd slid my finger inside her, I'd suspected, but it had been the way she'd grabbed my arm and the expression on her face that had confirmed my suspicions. Her telling me that she was a virgin had been more about finding out if she'd be willing to admit it to me than it had been about the actual information.

Between her explanation about why she hadn't yet had sex and the fact that she hadn't freaked out when I'd mentioned punishment, I thought there was a distinct possibility that she might stay.

But I didn't want to hope that was the case, because if I did and she left, I'd feel like an idiot. I had to make her think that it didn't matter what she decided, that I'd be fine. It wouldn't devastate me when I called Angus, but I would be disappointed. I'd never had sex with a virgin, and it wasn't something I would've thought I wanted, but if it meant getting to feel and see Ashlee come apart underneath me, getting to teach her all the ways I could bring her pleasure...

All the ways?

This wasn't a relationship. It wasn't even an arrangement. This was one night of sex. On Monday morning, we'd return to being employer and employee. Nothing more.

But I still wanted tonight.

It had to be her choice, though.

"Beagle."

I blinked. Where had *that* come from?

Those sensual lips curved up in a saucy sort of smile that sent blood rushing straight to my dick.

"It's my favorite dog," she explained.

Sort of.

"It can be my safe word."

I froze. I had to have misheard her.

"How do you know what a safe word is?" I asked the question carefully, not wanting to insult her, but needing to ask a question that could've gone so many different directions. If she thought I was questioning her virginity after I'd made her confess it, or if she thought I was implying she was *too* innocent, things could end badly.

Fortunately, she looked pleased with my question. "I read."

"You read?" As soon as I asked the question, I realized what she meant. "You've read romance books about BDSM."

"I have." She put her hand over mine, her fingers soft as they stroked the back of my hand. "And I may have done a little research to see how accurate those books were."

The thought of her sitting at a computer, looking through BDSM sites annoyed me. I wanted to be the one to teach her about everything. If this meant she stayed, there'd be no more computer knowledge. I'd be her teacher. Her *only* teacher.

"Are you saying you want to stay?" I asked. I didn't want any misunderstandings. The situation we were in was a delicate one. I needed her consent to be clear before we went any further.

Her eyes met mine, and turquoise irises blazed. With the slightest pressure on my hand, she slid both of our hands between her legs. "I'm saying I would like to know what my punishment is."

It took only a few seconds for her statement to process, and then I was on my feet and pulling her up as well. "You remember what to say any time you want things to stop?"

"Beagle," she answered promptly. "Now, are you going to de-virginize me or what?"

She looked as shocked as I was by the comment, but I wasn't going to shy away from it. "First, I'm going to spank you."

Her jaw dropped, and color flooded her face, but she didn't protest when I led her down the hallway and through the second door on the right. Guest bedroom. I rarely came in here, but I wasn't taking her into my bedroom. That would be a step too far.

Even though we were the only two in the place, I closed the door behind us. She needed to feel absolutely safe for this to work. Since I wasn't counting on this being a regular thing, and she wasn't a normal sub, I'd take it easy on her...but I still planned on learning what it felt like to turn her ass a nice shade of pink with the palm of my hand.

I released her hand and moved over to the bed, sitting on the edge. "Dress off."

She reached behind her and unzipped the dress, letting it fall to the floor, leaving her in only a sheer black bra that did more to enhance those amazing breasts of hers than if she would've been naked. Her waist was soft, and her hips curved in ways that was nothing like the previous women I'd been with. The trimmed curls I'd felt on my fingers and mouth were the same brilliant red as the thick locks cascading over her shoulders.

She was gorgeous.

I'd known she was pretty, of course, but how had I not seen that Ashlee Webb, personal assistant to my A&R department, was fucking *gorgeous*. How the hell would I ever be able to look at her at work and not picture *this*?

I held out my hand and gave her an expectant look. Her expression turned shy as she took my hand, but she let me pull her to me. She was short enough that our eyes were level as I explained to her what would happen next.

"I'm going to put you over my knee and spank you." I put my hand on her hip and smiled when I saw her sway. "Normally, for a lie, I'd say twenty, but since it's your first offense, we'll go with ten. Five on each cheek."

"I've never done this before," she blurted out. "That really didn't need to be said, did it?"

I raised her hand to my lips and kissed her knuckles, a

Dominant need to soothe her nerves. "One word and I'll stop, but give it a chance. I'll make it good for you."

She nodded. "I trust you."

I allowed myself a moment to wonder what I'd done to deserve that sort of trust from someone like her, and then I pulled her down onto my lap, arranging her over my thighs with her delightful ass right in prime spanking position. My cock was already pushing against my zipper, and I had a feeling that by the time I was finally ready to be inside her, it was going to take all of my self-control not to come right away.

I ran my hand over one ass cheek and then the other, earning a breathy moan. I made the first smack a light one, easing her in as I did the same thing to the other cheek. When she didn't try to get away or protest, the second time my hand came down was harder. She gasped at the third, and her skin started turning pink.

Four.

Five.

She squirmed, but judging by the way she was pressing her thighs together, I was taking it as a positive reaction.

For the final two blows, I put a little extra force into them, and she gasped both times, her head falling down as her hands gripped the comforter, but unless I was completely off base, those had been sounds of pleasure more than pain. Once I was done, I ran my hand over the flushed skin, appreciating the shudder that went through her body. Then I dipped my hand between her legs, and she made a squeaking sound that made me smile in amusement as much as it did in arousal.

"In a minute, you're going to move to the bed. Stay on your stomach. I'll join you, and we'll get to that de-virginizing."

I waited until she nodded and then helped her over to the bed. I stood, removing my clothes while keeping my eyes on her. She'd folded her arms under her head to allow her to keep her face down, her hair hiding her expression. Her breathing was slow and steady, which I hoped meant she wasn't regretting her decision.

She'd said she wasn't looking at this as some big thing, but I knew she'd always remember her first time, and everyone who came after would be measured by this bar. At least I hoped she'd remember it. My own first time was a blur. Fourteen, I'd been half-drunk during my first high school party when Hallie − a sixteen-year-old cheerleader − had pulled me into a room. It'd been over in minutes, and neither one of us had taken off our clothes. I was pretty sure she'd been a brunette, but I couldn't swear to it.

That wasn't going to happen with Ashlee. I planned to make it so that every other man would fall short in comparison. Maybe that was selfish of me, but I couldn't bring myself to give her less than an incredible first experience.

Reaching into the bedside table, I retrieved a condom. I might not have brought a woman to my home in the past, but I believed in being prepared, which meant I had condoms stashed all over the house. It also made it easier to grab a couple when I was heading out.

I rolled the condom on, for once grateful that it would dull sensation. It'd help me last long enough to make this good for her too. I was so hard it hurt, and I could already feel my control slipping, neither of which I'd experienced any time recently. This was going to be a challenge, and in all honesty, that alone turned me on more than Roma had in weeks.

Ashlee's breathing caught when the bed dipped under my weight, and I put my hands on her calves. Her entire body jerked, and I stilled, waiting to hear her safe word, but it didn't come. I ran my hands up her legs, parting them as I settled between her knees. My palms continued to skim over her soft skin until I reached her hips.

"Up." I helped her arrange herself until she was exactly how and where I wanted her: on her hands and knees, that fiery curtain of hair cascading down her back and over her shoulders.

I let my hands roam, gliding across her back, down to her stomach, between her legs, along every crease and dip. She still wore her bra, but it was easy to undo those hooks and let the filmy undergarment hang from her shoulders. I was tempted to turn her over so I could pay attention to her breasts, but I didn't want to do this face-to-face. Some women thought looking into a lover's eyes meant something more, and I couldn't risk that with her.

I cupped her breasts, teased her nipples until they were hard, and she was panting, soft sounds spilling from her lips. When I tugged on them, her entire body twitched, ass pushing back against me, and I wondered what she would do if I sucked on them. They seemed sensitive enough I'd have to ease her into using clamps, but I could only imagine the way she'd writhe with them on.

"I'm going to fuck you now," I warned her, pinching her

nipples hard enough to make her yelp. "I can't promise to be gentle. I'm not gentle."

"It's okay. I don't want...I mean, I want...fuck." The last word came out in a frustrated growl.

"What do you want?"

She shook her head. "I don't know."

"I think you do," I countered. "Tell me, *le soleil.*"

The endearment slipped out before I even knew I was going to use it, but I didn't take the time to consider what it meant because she was answering me, and my responsibility as a Dom was to take care of my sub first and foremost. For tonight, she was *mine.*

"I don't want gentle. I want it to hurt a little. I want to feel it tomorrow."

I closed my eyes and cursed. Who the hell was this woman? I opened my eyes and used one hand to guide my cock as the other held onto her hip to keep her from moving away. If she said the word, I'd let her go, but if she didn't, I was going to give her what she said she wanted.

Once the tip of my cock was resting on her entrance, I asked, "Ready?"

She nodded, and I could see her muscles tightening.

"Ashlee, relax." I squeezed her hip. "Trust me, *le soleil.* I'll make it good for you."

She inhaled slowly and then let the air back out the same way. I felt most of the tension leave her and took that as my cue. One smooth thrust, and I was buried deep inside her. She cried out, muscles tensing again, and I ran my hand up and down her spine, all the while trying to ignore the way her pussy had clamped down on my dick.

"Breathe, *le soleil*, breathe," I murmured the words over and over until she relaxed. Only then did I move inside her.

A couple shallow, easy strokes to start, as much for me as for her, and then I gave her what she wanted. I pulled back until I was almost completely out and then drove right back in. She cursed, but rocked back against me, and I knew I could do it again.

I reached for her hair, wrapping some of it around my hand to use as leverage. Any doubts I might've had about taking her this way vanished as I fucked her. Less than a dozen strokes, and she was moving with me, driving me deeper and harder until the sound of flesh slapping against flesh became louder than our harsh breathing, an accompaniment to the curses that flowed freely from us both.

The pressure building at the base of my cock told me I was getting close, and I reached under her to get her there first. Three rough circles over her swollen clit, and she came, her screams muffled as she buried her face in the comforter. My hips moved in short jerks twice, three times, and then I was coming too.

It wasn't until I'd come down and was lying next to her that my brain reminded me of what I'd called her.

Le soleil. The sun.

It was what my grandfather had called my grandmother.

I was so fucked.

TWENTY-ONE

ASHLEE

I didn't dream.

When I got home last night, I took a quick shower and collapsed into bed, exhausted. Seconds later, I was asleep, and I didn't remember anything until my alarm woke me up. No dreams. Nothing.

For a minute after I woke up, I didn't remember anything either, but then I rolled onto my back, and the still sensitive skin on my ass stung like a sunburn. With that pain came the memory of how my ass had gotten that way. Then I realized that other parts of my body were aching. My muscles felt like I'd been doing a hardcore workout for an hour or so, and anytime I moved my legs, my pussy protested.

I regretted nothing.

But as the memories of everything Nate and I had done came flooding through my brain, reality set in, and with it came embarrassment.

I'd slept with my boss. Technically my bosses' boss, but that didn't make it better. And I hadn't just had sex with him.

He'd been my first. And it hadn't been some basic vanilla sex either. He'd used his fingers to make me come at a work event, and then he'd gone down on me in his living room. He'd spanked me and then taken me on all fours until I'd come hard enough to see stars.

Not exactly how I'd pictured losing my virginity. Though, in all honesty, I hadn't really done much thinking about it in general. By the time I'd been old enough to have sex on my mind, there had been enough other things going on in my life that being a virgin hadn't even been close to important.

But still, if someone had asked me how I thought it would happen, this wouldn't have been it.

Another alarm went off on my phone, and I frowned as I reached for it. I cursed when I saw the reminder. *Brunch with Mom.*

At least I could be thankful that, despite everything we'd done together, Nate hadn't given me a hickey. I would've had a hell of a time explaining that to my mom. I planned on telling her, but I didn't want it to be the first thing we talked about. There had to be some way to ease into the conversation.

———

"I'VE NEVER SEEN that outfit before. It's lovely." Mom gave me a hug before pulling back and tucking some hair behind my ear.

"Thank you." As I did every time I saw her, I looked her

over from head to toe, taking in every new wrinkle, anything that could indicate that something was wrong.

Even though she was only fifty, her hair was pure white, styled in short, tasteful curls. I'd gotten my red hair from her, but when it'd come back after chemo, it had been solid white. I actually looked a lot like her, even without the same hair color. Same face shape, same build. We'd been through a lot together, and she wasn't just my mother. She was my best friend.

Which meant she knew me far too well.

Her smile faded. "What's wrong?"

I shook my head but couldn't meet her eyes. "Nothing, Mom." I motioned behind her. "Our table's ready."

We followed the hostess to the corner table where we always sat when it was too cold to be outside. With the sun shining, Mom might've tried arguing that she was fine and we could sit outside, but she was giving me a look that said she'd conceded our seating rather than debating it with me because she had other things on her mind.

Things that had to do with the wince I had to hide when I sat down.

"Would you both like your usual drinks?" The waitress that came over had been serving us almost every week for the past three years, and she always had a smile for us.

"Yes, please," Mom said with a polite smile. "How are you doing, Tiffany?"

"I'm great, Ms. Webb. How did your appointment go on Friday?"

For a moment, panic flared up. Mom had been in remission for five years, but the word *appointment* still conjured up images of hospital waiting rooms and doctors with masked expressions.

"You tell me." Mom put her hands on display, showing off her nails. "They wanted to do these great big claw-like things, but I told them I couldn't scare small children."

Mom glanced at me when she said it, and I glared at her. Her desire for grandchildren was an ongoing joke between the two of us. Some days it was funnier than others.

Tiffany's eyes lit up. "Are you–?"

"No," I cut her off, holding up a hand. "I'm not."

As Tiffany headed off to get our drinks, I pointed at Mom. "I thought we talked about this."

Mom put her hands together and rested her chin on them. "We did, but since you're not giving me grandchildren, you could at least give me humor."

I rolled my eyes. "You do realize that I'm still two years younger than you were when you had me, right? And most people now consider mid-twenties to be on the young side for having kids."

Her eyes narrowed. "That's not your usual comeback."

Shit.

"What?" I tried for an expression of innocence.

"Usually, when I harass you about grandchildren, you first say that you need a man. And then I say that there are ways around that. Then you tell me that you don't want to have a baby before you have–"

"I know what I say," I interrupted.

Tiffany appeared just then, and I breathed a sigh of relief. She set down our drinks and then took food orders. All of it was a nice distraction from a topic that I still wasn't sure how to bring up without it being completely awkward.

"How was the party?"

I blinked, confused. "What?"

"The party you told me you were helping plan."

I flushed. "There were a few hiccups, but it went well."

I'd already gone online to see what the media had to say, and there didn't appear to be anything negative. A few were just blurbs that seemed almost bored with the whole affair, but more praised the diversity of Manhattan Records' artists and complimented how eco-friendly the entire party was.

Fortunately, none of them mentioned Nate or me. I'd hadn't realized it at the time, but looking back, I could see how he'd steered us out of the path of most of the reporters. I wasn't so sure about *why* he'd done it, but I was glad he had. The last thing I needed was for pictures of Nate and me to be on the internet.

"I know that look." Mom put her hand over mine. "What's going on, Ash?"

I sighed. "I didn't just plan the party this time. I went. With a...guy. And then, I went home with him."

Her eyebrows shot up, and the surprise in her blue-green eyes was clear, but she simply squeezed my hand and waited for me to continue.

"We had sex."

A few seconds of silence followed my announcement, and then Mom spoke, "Do you want to talk about it? It's okay if you don't."

"I do," I said. "It's just...complicated."

She smiled, a slightly sad smile. "When it comes to matters of the heart, it's rarely simple."

I opened my mouth to tell her there was no heart involved but found that I couldn't do it. I didn't plan on telling her all the details, but I didn't want to flat-out lie. Therein was the problem. I didn't know if I'd be lying or not if I brought feelings into it.

Better to stick to the non-feeling facts.

"Well, it's more about who the guy is than about my heart. You see, he's kinda my boss..."

TWENTY-TWO

NATE

THERE WAS SOMETHING TO BE SAID FOR MINDLESS physical repetition.

One of the main reasons I'd wanted this particular penthouse was because it had come mostly furnished, complete with an in-home gym. I'd always been a muscular guy with a good metabolism, but I wasn't a teenager playing football or a twenty-something burning off calories left and right anymore. I was thirty-five and had a sedentary job. I was vain enough that I didn't want to completely let myself go, but not vain enough to let exercise become an obsession.

It was one of the few areas in my life where I consciously practiced moderation.

I really needed to start doing that with sex too. I'd had one-night stands in my life, but I'd gone into those with my mind already made up that it would be a physical release and nothing more. I'd had no prior contact with the woman or any contact with her after, at least if I could help it, I didn't.

Ashlee was different. I was her boss. Granted, she didn't

report directly to me, but it wasn't like I'd never see her again. And if I couldn't stop thinking about her when she wasn't around, how much harder would it be then? Could I ignore her when I saw her in a simple business suit and remembered what she looked like without anything on at all?

"Fuck!" I hit the sandbag one last time and pulled off my gloves. Usually, if lifting didn't clear my head, beating the shit out of something did. I'd channeled my frustration into pounding the heavy bag, but I hadn't gotten the single-minded clarity that I needed.

I'd tried counting. I'd tried going through specific sequences. I'd tried half a dozen other ways to focus on working out rather than the memories of last night, but nothing had worked. I'd get a minute or two into it, and then something about Ashlee would pop in my head and make it impossible to concentrate.

The sounds she made when she came, first on my fingers, then on my tongue, and finally, on my cock. Each had been slightly different, and I wondered if she always had a new noise or if they were dependent on how she got off. Or maybe the strength of the orgasm had something to do with–

The bag hit my side with enough force to make me stumble, and if I'd been standing any closer, I probably would've ended up with a wicked bruise. This was exactly the problem. I let myself get distracted, and things got messy. I didn't like it when that happened.

I looked at the 3-in-1 step machine I'd purchased a few months ago to replace my older model. It had all sorts of interactions and options when it came to running or walking. It could simulate various kinds of terrain, making the workout as easy or difficult as it would be on a real road or path. It even had video functions that could give me a similar visual to what I would see outside.

I didn't feel like any sort of virtual reality today, though. My life had taken on enough of a surreal quality lately. I needed something real. Something solid that I could touch.

Ashlee was real. More real than anyone I'd met in a very long time. Strange, now that I thought about it, that someone so very *present* could make me feel like I was in a dream. I'd never cared to be an introspective person before, but I found myself wondering what all of that said about me.

Outside.

I needed to go outside. It was a gray and overcast day, chilly and misting rain. All things that made me want to avoid leaving my building, but unpleasant stimuli might be exactly what I needed to free my thoughts. A run in this weather should do the trick nicely.

I wiped my face off with a towel and tossed it into the laundry room before heading into my room for more March-appropriate clothes. I'd cooled down enough by the time I'd changed that I considered taking the stairs, but I wasn't crazy. My penthouse was on the top floor. I waited until I was in the lobby before quickly stretching out and bouncing a few times on my toes to warm my muscles. I heard women talking behind me and then heard low laughs that confirmed they were watching me.

I ignored them. The only thing stupider than fucking a woman at work was fucking one where I lived. No, thank you. I didn't need some ex pounding on my door at two in the morning because she was drunk and horny. Or drunk and pissed. Or just pissed.

I headed for the doors, starting with a jog as soon as I stepped outside. It was mid-morning, but because of the weather, the sidewalks weren't as full as they could have been. I picked up speed as I went, easily making my way around people as they hurried to wherever they were going. I almost envied them, having a specific purpose, somewhere they needed to be. I was running to run, not to get somewhere, but having to concentrate on not knocking someone down at least gave me something for my brain to focus on.

I paused at a crosswalk, jogging in place so I didn't get cold. Before the light changed, someone grabbed my arm. Startled, I jerked back. I recognized the laugh even as I saw the woman in front of me. Nearly six feet tall and still slender even though it had been a decade since I'd seen her last. Her brown hair was longer, and she didn't seem to care about hiding the hardness in her bright green eyes.

"Calah?"

"I'm surprised you remember my name, Nate." She twirled her umbrella and gave me a coy look. "Perhaps I left a bigger impression than I realized."

It was on the tip of my tongue to tell her that she hadn't, but that would've been a lie. I hadn't forgotten a single moment of the time she'd been around, but it wasn't a part of my life I liked to think about much. Nothing about her impression had been positive.

"Would you like to get some coffee?" She touched me again, but this time, she kept her hand on my arm. "I don't have long before I'm supposed to meet my boyfriend, but I'm sure he won't mind me catching up with an old friend."

I raised an eyebrow at her word choice. We hadn't been friends. Ever.

"Don't let me keep you." I used my most dismissive tone and turned to continue on my way...except the light was against me again. Dammit. I considered going a different direction, but Calah had seen me waiting for this light, and if I changed direction, she would assume – correctly – that it was because of her. I refused to give her that satisfaction.

"Don't be that way." She pouted. "You can tell me how Joshua's doing."

I tensed but still ignored her.

"Fine," she snapped. "I don't really have the time anyway. My boyfriend and I are going to go back to my place and fuck. He's a wonderful lover. Best I've ever had."

The light turned, and I jogged off without a word. I knew what she was doing. She'd done it before. Calah Evenstar had a one-track mind, and that one-track was usually on things she couldn't have. She thought she was entitled to everything she wanted, and to hell with anyone in her way.

As I went around the block to head back home, I pushed thoughts of Calah from my mind. It wasn't hard.

Ashlee, on the other hand...

TWENTY-THREE

ASHLEE

I'D HAD TWO MOTHERS UNTIL I WAS THIRTEEN. My biological mom, Roberta Webb, and her girlfriend, Mona Wadsworth. They'd been together three years by then, and they'd agreed they wanted a child. For physical reasons, Mona hadn't been able to carry me or even use her eggs, so Mom was the only one tied to me by blood. Since Mona had never formally adopted me, when she finally left, she had no legal or biological claim to me. Something I'd always been glad for.

Mona leaving us had made Mom and me closer. Then, four years later, Mom was diagnosed with breast cancer. Since Mom's family had disowned her when she'd told them she was a lesbian, all we'd had was each other. And we'd always been enough.

After I told her about Nate, she hadn't chided me about anything except the work thing, but I couldn't blame her for that. When I'd left his place, he'd assured me that this aspect of our personal lives would never cross over into business, but Mom had still told me to be wary.

I reminded myself of that as I washed up my dinner dishes and put them away. I needed to stop obsessing over what had happened. I had to be able to show up at work on Monday morning and act like it was completely normal for me to have been out with Nate on Friday night. My work had to be impeccable until it became clear to everyone that I'd earned my place at Manhattan Records with quality work. Not sex.

With Flora having been fired, I'd be the only one doing everything for A&R. Which meant if I went in on Monday looking like I had a debauched weekend, the gossip mill would eat me alive. But, if I came in with a list of artists I'd researched on my days off, specifically because I knew I had to pick up the slack, it would be a huge step in the right direction.

I grabbed a water from my fridge and settled on my couch with my laptop. As I pulled up various sites and tapped out notes, I found myself getting into the rhythm of the work, remembering that even though I hadn't chosen this profession because of a long desire to be a part of the music industry, there were parts I'd learned to love.

A knock on my door drew me out of my work headspace, and I glanced at the time, surprised to see that I'd been doing this for more than an hour. I set down my laptop and went to the door. A quick peek through the peephole gave me another surprise.

Nate.

What the hell was he doing here?

I opened the door and stepped back, motioning for him to come inside. Whatever conversation he wanted to have, I wanted it to be away from my neighbors. My business with Nate was *my* business, and I didn't want it spread around, no matter what he was here to say.

He looked different than usual, wearing a pair of jeans and a t-shirt rather than the suit I was accustomed to seeing him wear. His hair looked damp, as if he'd showered not too long ago.

"Is everything okay?" I asked, suddenly aware that I was wearing a pair of two-year-old leggings, as well as a ratty t-shirt that hung off one shoulder and did nothing to hide the fact that I wasn't wearing a bra.

"No." Nate's gaze raked over my body, moving from head to toe, and then back up again. "Everything's not okay."

His voice was rough, but the heat in his eyes made me think that he wasn't talking about work. I crossed my arms and tried not to read too much into things. He wasn't my boyfriend. I needed to wait until he spelled things out a little more clearly.

"I can't get you out of my head." He ran his hand over his hair, not seeming to notice or care that his normally impeccable hair was a mess. "Why can't I get you out of my head?"

He looked at me expectantly.

"Seriously?" I laughed and shook my head. "Are you really expecting me to have an answer for that?"

One side of his mouth tipped up. "Honestly, I was hoping." He sighed. "This isn't...dammit."

This was the point where I could tell him that I couldn't help him because I wanted things to go back to how they'd been before he'd even met me. Maybe he'd be a bit embarrassed, but he'd have all day tomorrow to get over it, and even when we were both at work, we didn't have to see each other.

Except...

"You've been on my mind too," I admitted quietly. "But I don't know what that means any more than you do."

I waited for him to say something. Anything. Though what, I didn't know. All I did know was that I needed him to be the one to initiate what we did next. Honestly, I wanted to sleep with him again, but I wasn't going to be *that* woman. I'd promised him that I wouldn't be weird because he'd been my first, and I intended to keep that promise.

He closed the distance between us, and it suddenly became hard to breathe. How had I forgotten how much bigger he was than me? Adrenaline dumped into my system, but I wasn't afraid. Maybe a little nervous, but mostly excited, eager.

Would it feel different when he kissed me this time because my body now associated Nate's kisses with more intimate things?

"Do you remember your safe word?" he asked.

I nodded, but when he didn't say anything for several seconds, I spoke, "Beagle."

He reached out and hauled me against his body hard, his other hand moving to cup the back of my head as he bent his head and covered my mouth with his. I wrapped my arms around his neck, pushing myself up on my toes as high as I could go. I made a soft sound as his tongue slid across the seam of my lips, and his fingers dug into my scalp. I parted my lips, and his tongue plundered my mouth, exploring even as the hand at the small of my back dropped to my ass.

He picked me up, and I wrapped my legs around his waist, not wanting to take my mouth from his, not even for a moment. I didn't know if I'd get this opportunity again, and I wasn't going to waste it. I knew all too well how quickly life could change.

I wasn't aware we'd moved from in front of my door into my bedroom until he was setting me on my bed and breaking our kiss. My head spun, but I didn't take my eyes off him as he took a step back. He'd left his shoes out in the other room, and now as I watched, he tugged his shirt forward over his head with one of those one-handed movements that some men managed to make look graceful.

Damn.

I'd originally thought I had no regrets from last night, but now I realized I'd had at least one. Having him behind me for the act itself and then me leaving so quickly had meant I hadn't gotten to see much of his body.

And what a body it was.

He stood in front of me, thumbs hooked in the waistband of his jeans, his broad, muscular chest gloriously bare. I licked my lips, wondering what it would be like to taste every inch of that skin, to mark it with my teeth.

"Enjoying the view?"

I let my gaze linger on that golden trail of curls a moment longer before raising my eyes to meet his. "I am."

"Look your fill then," he said, his smile nothing but wicked. "Because once I've tired of you, we'll be done."

The words were harsh, but I hadn't expected declarations

of intent and love. The challenge in his eyes made me wonder if he'd said them because he wanted to know if I'd push him away or cry. He'd misjudged me if he thought either of those things were possibilities. I'd faced much tougher things than Nate Lexington.

"And if I tire of you first?"

I almost laughed at the surprise on his face, but I had a feeling that'd earn me another spanking, and my ass wasn't quite recovered enough for that. Part of me doubted my pussy had recovered enough for another pounding, but I wasn't going to turn him away. Who knew when I'd find another man who looked like him and could do what he could in the bedroom?

"You might get tired *from* me, but never *of* me." He shoved his pants down, revealing that he'd worn nothing underneath. Then he straightened, and I only had eyes for one thing.

I let out a low whistle. "How the hell did *that* fit inside me?"

He laughed as he fisted his cock with languid strokes. Impossibly, it seemed to grow even more. "It was a tight fit."

My pussy throbbed at the memory.

"Sit up," he ordered. "Have you ever sucked a cock before?"

I shook my head. Butterflies took off in my stomach, and I swallowed hard. I slid to the edge of the bed and waited for him to tell me what to do. While nerve-wracking in its own right, I couldn't help but think how much more freaked out I'd be if I was getting ready to give my first blowjob to someone who wouldn't have thought to ask and just expected me to know what to do. Sure, I understood it in theory, and I'd had a few entertainment choices that'd given me ideas, but it was actually kind of nice to have someone tell me what to do.

He caught my chin and tipped my face back so he could see my expression.

"Watch your teeth. Breathe through your nose." His eyes danced with humor. "And remember that a blowjob never looks like it does in porn. It gets messy. If it's done right anyway."

My laugh eased some of my tension, but it didn't stay away long, returning the moment he put his hand on the back of my head and nudged me forward. It was all the prompting I needed. I wet my lips, then flicked out my tongue to lick the tip of his cock, then circled the soft flesh, smiling when Nate moaned in approval.

"More."

All right. Time to move past using my tongue and start using the rest of my mouth. I wrapped my lips around the head and slowly moved down, taking an inch and then another. Letting the silky skin slide across my tongue. The taste and weight of him made heat coil in my stomach. When I pulled back, I sucked on the hard flesh. When Nate cursed, I knew I was on the right track.

He was far too long, and I was far too inexperienced for me to take all of him, but I intended to do the best I could. I didn't know if all he wanted was this, but if that was the case, I intended to continue to make it difficult for him to forget me.

His hand pushed at my head, and I took the hint and

went down again. This time, I went as far as I could, not stopping until I felt myself start to gag. Now knowing my limit, I reached up to wrap my hand around the base of his cock as best as I could. It took me a minute to get a rhythm that worked, but once I did, I applied myself with my usual work ethic and a hell of a lot more enthusiasm. I'd heard enough women complain about giving head, particularly when men didn't return the favor, and maybe one day I'd be annoyed enough at men to feel the same, but right now, I was thoroughly enjoying myself.

I put a hand on his thigh, the hair rough against my palm, muscles bunching as his fingers dug into my hair. I'd put it up in a messy bun, and he appeared to be enjoying the way he could grip it and pull on it. And I couldn't begin to describe the way it made me feel. The bright pain that somehow managed to move my mind into a strange, surreal place. New and different where all of my troubles and confusion were distant and unimportant – for the moment at least.

When he used my hair to pull me off him, his cock was slick and glistening, curving up toward his stomach, thick and full. I gasped, trying to catch my breath as my mind spun. What had I done wrong? I'd thought he was enjoying himself.

"Clothes off." His voice was hoarse, but no less commanding.

Oh.

The shirt went first, my nipples already hard and begging for attention. I slid back on the bed, pushing off my pants and underwear as I went. By the time I reached my pillows, I was naked, and Nate's eyes were nearly black.

"Do you have any scarves?" he asked.

"It's not cold."

The moment I said it, I knew it wasn't even close to the right reason he was asking for a scarf. I flushed, completely embarrassed, and felt the urge to cover myself.

He reached down and took one of my nipples between his thumb and forefinger, rolling it and tugging on it until he had all of my attention.

"What can I use to tie you up?"

"Oh – ahhh..." I grabbed his arm as he pinched me. "Socks!"

He released me and leaned back. "Socks?"

"Second drawer down, left side," I pointed. "I have these long socks I wear when it's cold. The heat isn't great here."

"Long socks?" He went to the dresser and opened the drawer I'd indicated. He held up a pair of black socks with red reindeer, then picked up another pair and gave me a questioning look. "What are those?"

"Golden snitches." I gave him my best serious expression. "Don't tell me you aren't a Potter fan."

He tilted his head, like I'd said something he wasn't sure was funny or not. "Perhaps we'll come back to that sometime in the future."

Future?

"Since you don't have the right type of bed for me to restrain you the way I want, I'll have to get creative."

How the hell was he thinking about tying me up when his cock looked ready to break something? My own body was begging for him to do something...anything.

"On your back, off the pillows." Once I did that, he continued, "Arms over your head."

He quickly tied my wrists together, tight enough to keep me from moving them but not so tight as they would leave marks. I had the feeling that if this was a regular thing, he wouldn't care about that. Honestly, I wasn't so sure I would care. A part of me actually liked the idea of being marked by him.

He looped the other sock through the one binding my hands and pulled them up high enough that he could tie them to my headboard. After he finished binding my hands, he stood for a moment, looking from me to the snitch socks still in his hand.

"Dammit," he muttered. "This is what happens when I try to improvise."

I couldn't help but smile at that. He really was a control freak.

"You find this funny?"

I immediately flattened my lips into a line and shook my head. "Nope."

A dangerous gleam came into his eyes, and he pulled one sock free.

"Now that we're doing this again, I think we need to address an important part of this dynamic."

He sounded more like he was in a boardroom, discussing business strategy than he did like he was standing in a bedroom, stark naked, and sporting a magnificent erection.

"What should you call me? Master? Sir?"

"I could call you Mr. Lexington," I suggested cheekily. "Like I do at work."

For a moment, I thought he'd turn me over and paddle my ass again...and a not-so-small part of me wished he would, even though I knew it'd hurt like hell.

He knelt on the bed and leaned over me, his face mere inches from my own. "I think I like that idea. That way, every time you speak to me at work, I'll be reminded of all the sweet ways you can scream my name."

Shit.

That's what I got for not thinking things through like I usually did. I'd just totally screwed myself because I'd never be able to use his name without thinking that exact same thing.

"Now, let's have you answer my question with the proper respect." He trailed his fingers over my breasts, then my stomach, and down between my legs, the feather-light touch making me want to squirm. "Ashlee, are you ignoring me?"

"I don't remember the question," I said, fighting to stay still. "That tickles."

"Do you find this funny?"

I didn't remember what *this* was referring to, but it wasn't really the point anymore. There was only one correct answer.

"No, Mr. Lexington."

He closed the distance to brush his lips across mine in an all to brief kiss. He didn't completely straighten when he pulled back, however. Instead, he took another sock and tied it around my head, completely covering my eyes and leaving me in the dark, both literally and figuratively. So many limitations I put on my interactions and relationships didn't seem to apply to him.

It was just sex, I reminded myself. It wasn't like I was

trusting him with my heart. Just my body, and I knew enough about him to tell myself that wasn't too crazy.

I gasped as he took my nipple into his mouth, tongue swirling around it. When he took the tip between his teeth, I tried to reach for him, not remembering that I was restrained until my hands jerked to a stop before they'd gone an inch. He chuckled, the vibration moving down my nerves, joined by a different sort of pleasure as he worried at the skin with his teeth.

I couldn't stop the sound of protest I made when he released my nipple, but it cut off the moment he latched on to the other one. This one he sucked on, each hard pull of his mouth making a direct line to my pussy. I arched my back, needing more, but his response was to put a hand on my stomach and push me back down to the bed. A thrill went through me at the strength I felt there. He'd never force me, but knowing that he could easily overpower me was a turn-on I hadn't been expecting.

"Fuck!" I jerked against my restraints as he shoved one thick finger inside me. I had the fleeting thought that my socks were going to be stretched out of shape by the time we were done, but it flew out of my head the moment he added a second finger.

"You're nice and wet for me, *le soleil*," he said as he worked his fingers in and out. "Tight too. I need to loosen you up so you don't squeeze my dick off."

There was that phrase again. *Le soleil*. I'd meant to look it up earlier today, but I'd forgotten. I didn't want to bring it to his attention though because I liked it, and I had a feeling if I asked him about it, he might stop using it.

"Do you like my fingers inside you?"

He twisted said fingers, his knuckles brushing against my g-spot. At least, I assumed that's what it was because, one touch, and it felt like electricity shot through my body.

"Yes, Mr. Lexington."

He made a growling sound, and I was suddenly disappointed I couldn't see his face. I wanted to know what he looked like right then. It wasn't a bad or disapproving sound, but I wanted to know if it was only approval, or if there was something more.

His fingers curled inside me, and I cried out as he found that spot again. Back and forth the tips of his fingers moved, the friction just hard enough to push me closer to the edge with each pass. Then his thumb brushed over my clit, and I came hard enough to see stars even with the blindfold on. I was still coming as he pulled away his hand, and I'd barely begun to come down when I felt something much larger push against my entrance.

He gripped my hips, tilting them up as he slid inside. One thrust, stretching me all around him without any respite, and I came again. Or maybe it was the same climax, just growing stronger with the new burst of sensation that my brain couldn't categorize as either pain or pleasure because it was too much of both. He didn't pause or ask me if I was okay, but proceeded to hold me as he drove into me with punishing strokes.

My back and neck muscles protested the angle, but the rest of me screamed at them to shut up because I never wanted this to stop. I tugged at the restraints, wanting to feel him, wanting to rip off this blindfold so I could see that he was with me, really with me, and not thinking about another woman...

Pain, bright and sudden, made me cry out, and it took me a moment to even register that he'd twisted my nipple. Hard.

"Stop thinking," he snapped. "I can see it on your face."

"Yes, Mr. Lexington." The answer came out automatically, but I found that I meant it. "No more thinking."

"Now, let's see how many times I can make you come."

He shoved himself even deeper inside me, and I screamed.

TWENTY-FOUR

NATE

I COULDN'T QUIT STARING AT THAT STUPID SOCK. I hadn't realized that I'd accidentally stolen the snitch sock I'd used to blindfold her until I'd already gotten home and headed for the shower. When I'd taken off my pants, I'd seen there was something in the pocket. That something happened to be one knee-high dark green sock with a ball from a fictional game on it.

I picked it up as I moved to my library. The room wasn't massive, but I'd filled it, floor to ceiling, with bookcases. I had some leather-bound classics and first editions that I didn't read, but most of the books here were ones I loved. I knew I didn't come across as a reader, and I did little to dispel that notion. I had a reputation that allowed me to get done the things I needed to get done. The fact that my reader copies of a certain British series about a wizard were dog-eared and worn would do more harm to my reputation than good.

The only two chairs in the room were plush and comfortable, bought specifically for this room, for me to sit in when I wanted to read. I'd never liked reading in bed. While my bedroom was personal space, this place was my sanctuary.

I selected another one of my favorites and took a seat. T.S. Eliot's *The Wasteland*. I'd had to read it in college, and I'd been surprised at how much I'd liked the poetry. I'd gotten into the habit of reading it every year, even though I had most of it memorized.

Except I couldn't lose myself in it as I had so many times before.

It was that damn sock. I told myself not to carry it around like some kid with a stuffed animal, but every time I put it down, I found myself picking it back up, remembering what I'd used its twin for last night.

What had I been thinking? Going to Ashlee's place and having sex with her hadn't been part of my plan for yesterday. Tying her up with those ridiculous socks of hers. Taking her so hard that my own muscles were feeling it today.

When I'd left her yesterday, I'd tried telling myself that the oval bruises on her hips couldn't be from the first time we'd been together, but I'd known them for what they were. I'd held her too tight, too close. And then I'd done it again. Been too rough and taken things too far.

Except...she hadn't asked me to stop, either specifically or with her safe word. I'd been with plenty of women over the years, and I liked to think that I knew when they enjoyed themselves. Unless I was losing my touch, Ashlee had liked what we'd done, rough as it was.

And I couldn't quit wishing for more.

I'd read the same page three times before I set the book aside. It was a little after noon right now, which meant it was far too early for me to go back to Ashlee's or to ask her to come to me. *Tell* her to come to me. Not ask. Never *ask*.

My phone rang, and I reached for it, needing a distraction – any distraction, even if it was a telemarketer. But it wasn't one. It was my mother.

Shit.

Today was their anniversary, and I'd forgotten. Well, sort of. I'd arranged for a gift to be sent yesterday. A nice gift with a sentimental card that my mom would appreciate.

"Hey, Mom." My hand curled into a fist around Ashlee's sock as if it was some talisman. "Happy anniversary."

"Thank you, Nate. And your gift was lovely. I know that took some doing to get those tickets."

I shrugged, then remembered that Mom couldn't see me. "It's your fortieth anniversary..." Fuck. I gave a weak laugh. "Sorry, thirty-ninth. Didn't mean to make you a year older. Or me a year older."

I tried to pass it off as a joke, but we both knew it wasn't that funny. I'd honestly forgotten how long they'd been married. I was now glad that I hadn't gotten a card with any of those specifics on it.

"Your dad says thank you too," she said. "He's at the store right now, or he'd tell you himself."

"Of course." And I didn't doubt Dad had specifically planned to be there when Mom made the call. Herman Lexington's hardware store was his life, and my older brother David was his legacy. Joshua was the baby, and I was the disappointment.

"Are you coming to the party today?"

I was tempted to tell her that I didn't know there was a

party, but that would mean she'd get upset with David and David's wife, Julia, who most likely had been doing the planning. I couldn't do that to Julia or to my mom. David and my dad could go to hell for all I cared.

"Sorry, Mom, I've got work to do."

A few moments of silence between us made me close my eyes and hope she believed the lie.

"I understand. Being a CEO takes a lot of time and attention."

Another silence and I waited.

"Have you talked to Joshua recently?"

There it was. Mom's true purpose for calling. The question she always asked in some form or another. Usually, she wasn't this blunt about it, but it still always happened.

"I haven't."

I didn't need her to tell me what she was thinking right now because we'd been here before. Mom wanted all of us together and getting along, but that hadn't been our family in a long time. Maybe since I was a kid. Even then, I wondered. At what age had David become Dad's favorite? When had Joshua and I reached the point where we wouldn't talk things through, wouldn't trust each other?

"Did I remember the restaurant correctly?" I asked, more to fill the space rather than actually wondering. I knew I'd gotten it right.

"You did." Her voice was warm, but I could picture the expression on her face. I'd seen it plenty growing up. She loved me...but she was disappointed in me.

Nothing new.

"Well, let me know how the shows are," I said, faking a smile even though she couldn't see me.

I didn't bother telling her to pass along my love or tell anyone that I missed them. They all knew the truth of me, of who I was. My family all knew that it would be nothing for me to leave my place in Manhattan and go to the Bronx to see all of them. All but Joshua, of course. He was in L.A., and while I doubted he was coming home for the party, I didn't want to risk seeing him. Better for everyone if I stayed home.

Mom and I exchanged a couple more words of small talk, and then she ended the call. I stared at the screen for a minute, waiting for her to call back, half-hoping she'd want to convince me to come to the party, tell me that it had been too long since she'd seen me.

I let myself hope those things for five minutes. No more than that. If I let myself hope longer than those five minutes, I might actually think that something might change.

I reached for my book but stopped when my phone rang again. This time, it wasn't my mother's number and name on the screen. It was my brother's.

"Afternoon, David."

"You couldn't even bother to come up with an original excuse?"

I sighed and rubbed my forehead. "Come on, we both know you don't want me there today. I might as well make everyone happy and stay away."

"Come on," he mimicked my tone, "we both know you aren't staying away because you want to make anyone happy. This is all about you, same as it always is."

"You're right," I said, not wanting to draw this out. "It's

about me. Now that you've dragged out that confession, can we go back to radio silence? I'm actually busy."

"I can't believe you're making our parents' anniversary about you," David snapped. "Or, I guess I can because you've always been selfish."

"Nobody wants me there, David. Fuck off."

I stood up as I ended the call. I couldn't sit around here and read, holding onto a fucking *sock*. I needed to blow off some steam, and there was only one place I could do that.

I was going out.

TWENTY-FIVE
ASHLEE

The weather had taken a crazy turn today, the temperature dropping from dawn on until it would have been snowing had the precipitation been right. It'd still be cold in the morning, which would suck, but right now, I was enjoying being snuggled under a fluffy blanket, sipping hot cocoa and watching a movie marathon about my favorite wizarding world.

By the time the most recent movie ended, it was eleven o'clock, and I was ready for bed. Not only did I want to be up early enough for work that I could beat everybody to the office, but my Friday and Saturday nights had both been more physical than I was used to, and it wasn't like I never exercised at all.

I winced as I stood, further proving my point. I felt like I'd done some sort of crazy exercise challenge or something. I was more grateful than ever that the new marks Nate had left on my body would be easily covered by my normal work clothes. Nothing like a turtleneck a couple days after being spotted on the boss's arm to make people immediately think of hickeys.

It truly was sad how much the corporate world was like high school.

I was exhausted enough that I fell asleep not long after I turned out my light. A night of deep, dreamless sleep was exactly what I needed to fortify myself for tomorrow.

A thump on my door jerked me out of sleep, bleary and disoriented. My heart pounded in my chest, and I reached for my phone. Half past midnight. I'd been asleep for a little over an hour. I didn't get out of bed, hoping that the thump had been on a neighbor's door rather than mine. Only a few seconds passed before two faster thumps came, one after the other.

Knocks.

Someone was knocking on my door.

"Ashlee! Open!"

Fuck me. It was Nate. What the hell was he doing here? And at this hour? Was he determined to keep me from sleeping at all this weekend?

I threw off my covers, fully awake, and even more fully annoyed. He was going to have to explain to Mr. Hancock and Ms. Lamas why I was falling asleep at my desk.

I didn't even consider the possibility of not opening the door. I could have made excuses later when he asked why I hadn't come when he'd called. Plenty of people could sleep through anything. Mona had always been like that. I doubted that excuse would work though if Perry or Gary thought I was in trouble, or Mrs. Posner got annoyed, and one of them called the cops. As much as he'd reassured me that sex and work were two entirely separate things, I couldn't help feeling like that'd be the end of my career, at least at Manhattan Records, and I didn't want to jeopardize that.

Continuing to justify my choice, I made my way to the door and opened it, glaring up at him as I grabbed his sleeve.

"Get in here before you wake up the whole damn building!" I hissed.

I closed the door behind him, preparing myself as I faced him. He wasn't going to be happy that I'd...

"You're pretty when you're pissed." He gave me a wide grin that confirmed everything my nose was telling me.

"And you smell like expensive alcohol and cheap perfume." I kept my tone mild despite the anger and hurt roiling in my belly.

I wasn't naïve enough to think that he and I had anything special. We weren't dating, but we had just spent the last two nights fucking. I would've thought that at least earned me the right not to know that he'd hopped into a new bed the next day. I'd thought he respected me, as an employee and fellow human being if nothing else.

"I'm not drunk," he insisted. "I went to the club to fuck someone, but all I could do is drink."

"Yeah, you're not drunk at all." I assumed he was too out of it to catch sarcasm, but I probably would've said it the same way no matter what.

"There were all sorts of women there," he continued, either oblivious to how rude he was being or not caring.

I wasn't sure which option was worse.

"One sub crawled over to me on her hands and knees. Offered to suck me off while her Domme watched. Not a stitch on her and I couldn't get it up. Great tits and ass, but I got nothing."

I gritted my teeth. "I think you should go home. Give me your phone, and I'll have Angus come up and get you."

He shook his head. "Nope. Angus didn't drive. I took a cab."

"A cab?" I raised an eyebrow. "Is it waiting downstairs?"

"Nope." He grinned at me. "Didn't want him to wait while I got laid."

He took a step toward me, and I put up a hand, stopping him from coming any closer. "You're not getting laid. At least not by me. You should've found a woman at the club."

"I didn't want any of those women." He sounded like a petulant child.

I refused to take that to mean that he wanted me. I was fine with the two of us having sex when we were both on the same page. Him showing up in the middle of the night for a drunk booty call because he couldn't get it up for some naked woman at a sex club...no thank you. That wasn't the same page at all. We weren't even in the same fucking book.

"Let me call Angus to come get you," I said, forcing my voice into something soft and coaxing, even though all I wanted to do was shove him into the hall and tell him that I didn't give a damn where he went next.

Nate patted his pockets, frowned, and gave me the saddest puppy-dog eyes I'd ever seen. "I lost my phone."

"Do you know Angus's number?"

"Number one speed dial."

"That's not going to help."

He shrugged. "Can't find my phone."

"I'm sure it'll turn up." I sighed. "I guess that means you'll have to stay here tonight because I'm not putting you into a cab drunk."

"Yes!" He came toward me again, and this time I had to put my hands on his chest and shove him back.

"No," I said firmly. "Let me make this perfectly clear. We are not having sex. Period. You're going to sleep on my couch right there, and I'm going to sleep in my bedroom. Alone. With the door closed and locked, so you don't wander in."

He pouted – wealthy CEO Nate Lexington who could pick up women without even trying – was actually *pouting* because I wouldn't have sex with him. He was lucky I wasn't the sort of woman who'd stoop to blackmail because this would have been great.

"Couch." I pointed. "There are pillows and a blanket there already. That's all you get. And if you throw up on anything, you better clean it up yourself, because if I have to, you and I are going to have a serious problem."

It really was too bad, I thought as I walked back to my bedroom, that he wouldn't remember most of this in the morning. I'd never have the guts to say all of that to his face if he'd been sober.

Who was I kidding? If he'd been sober, we'd already be fucking.

TWENTY-SIX

NATE

Why did my head feel like I'd stuck it into a fucking drum?

And why did my mouth taste like someone had taken a shit in it?

And what the *hell* smelled so bad?

Gradually, the truth came to me as I remembered what had happened the night before. Pieces of it, anyway.

I'd needed a distraction, so I'd gone to Club Privé, the elite BDSM club where I was a member. It was exclusive and discreet, two things that a man in my position needed. There'd been plenty of women there. Not all of them were subs, but enough that I'd had my pick; I generally had my pick wherever I went. I could have taken any woman into a room and spent hours doing all sorts of things to her. Club Privé offered everything anyone could ever need to have a good time. No improvising necessary.

But I hadn't wanted any of the women. Not the ones who

played at being coy, and certainly not the ones who threw themselves at me.

Since I hadn't wanted the women, I'd taken advantage of their excellent liquor selection. That's where things got even more hazy.

I was hungover. I now had an explanation for how I felt and the smell. What I didn't have was answers for new questions.

Like why my knees were practically in my chest, and things were way too loud. I could hear cars and people, though those were faint. I could also hear someone moving around, and I couldn't for the life of me figure out who it could be.

Then I opened my eyes. This wasn't my place. It was too colorful, for one. After a moment, I realized that I knew this place. I'd been here before.

Fuck it all.

I was at Ashlee's apartment. On her couch, apparently, because this wasn't her bedroom. Judging by the way I smelled and the fact that I was still wearing the same clothes as I'd put on last night, she hadn't had any reason to take me to bed.

Heat rushed to my face as I realized how I must have appeared. Drunk enough that I could barely remember anything about the interaction. Reeking of booze, sweat, and various types of perfume, most of them cheap. Had I made a pass at her? I must have because there was no other reason for me to have come here than to get what I hadn't taken at the club.

I pushed myself up, muscles complaining at the way I'd

slept, contorted onto a couch that would've been uncomfortable for anyone over five and a half feet, let alone someone over six feet tall. My head spun, and my stomach churned, but I managed to keep myself from throwing up. The last thing I needed was to humiliate myself even more.

"Good morning." Ashlee smiled at me as she came over from the kitchen. She held out a mug of coffee.

"What time is it?" I snapped as I sipped at the steaming dark liquid. It wasn't even close to the expensive kind I had at home, but it was decent enough.

"About six-thirty," she said. "Plenty of time to get cleaned up and get to work."

"We're not going into work together." I stood up, swayed, and then caught myself. I took another gulp of coffee. "I don't know what sort of shit I said last night, but drunken sex talk doesn't count when sober."

She raised an eyebrow. "We did a little talking last night, but we didn't have sex at all, so there was no drunken sex talk."

She was missing the point. "We're still not going into work together. We're not a fucking couple."

Her face went blank, wiped clean of all emotion, of everything. "I'm aware of that."

"Are you?" I glared down at her as I put the coffee mug on the closest flat surface. "You talk about going in to work together, make me coffee like we were some sort of–"

"I'm getting in the shower," she interrupted. "And then I'll be getting dressed. I suggest you see yourself out."

"You can't talk to me like that." I took a step toward her. "I'm your boss, not some fuck budd–"

"You're in my home." She made the statement simply, plainly. "*You* came to *me*. Don't let the door hit you in your ass on the way out. Or do. It's all the same to me."

I opened my mouth to yell at her, to tell her to come back so I could keep telling her how we weren't anything, but she closed her bathroom door with enough force that I knew if I opened that bathroom door, I'd regret it, probably more than I regretted being here at all.

I needed a shower.

On my way to the door, I reached into my pocket for my phone and found nothing. Shit. I turned around and ran my hands over the couch cushions, dug under them, looked under the couch...what the *fuck*? Where was my phone?

I heard the shower turn on and wondered if she'd been waiting to hear the front door close, but then realized she needed to make it sound like she was following through...

My head was spinning too fast, too far. I was way too hungover to be dealing with any of this shit.

I had enough money. I'd buy a new fucking phone.

TWENTY-SEVEN

ASHLEE

I'D FINALLY HAD ENOUGH OF HIS MOUTH, AND THE FACT that I didn't think anything dirty about his mouth was evidence of just how fed up I was. Taking personality into consideration was one thing. Being verbally attacked when all I'd done was give him a safe place to sleep off a hangover after he'd gone to some sex club...? I ground my teeth together just thinking about it.

I'd dealt with assholes like him before. People who felt like they could treat me like shit because there was something about themselves they didn't like, so they made it about me, tried to make me feel bad about who I was. Fortunately for me, I'd learned how to deal with that sort of bullshit.

By proving that I was above it all. That I was a stronger person than they were.

I told myself all of that when I was in the shower. It was easier to give myself a pep talk when the only other sound was the white noise of falling water. I just hoped he'd be gone when I got out. I had a hell of a time saying no to him, and I refused to become one of those women who let assholes walk all over them because they didn't want to 'lose' him.

I'd lived just fine without him, and I'd do it again. I'd only spent a single weekend with him, after all.

I breathed a sigh of relief when I came out of the bathroom, and my apartment was my own again. I emptied his cup and washed it quickly. I hated taking the extra time, but I didn't want to leave behind any reminders of the stupid things I'd done the last couple days.

I'd have enough of those when I got to work.

THANKS to my late-night visitor and the overly awkward morning after, I was late for work. Not actually late, thanks to my intention to be here early, but arriving on time, which was later than I'd wanted.

I passed Clara and knew today was going to be as bad as I'd feared. She hadn't been at the event on Friday, but someone who had been there had let the cat out of the bag, so to speak. I supposed I was grateful that the only thing anyone had any evidence about was us attending a work event together. Some of them might guess at the rest, but as long as Nate and I kept our mouths shut, no one could claim anything but rumor.

"Damn cold out, isn't it?" An intern from the PR department got onto the elevator with me. He leered at me. "Must've been nice to have someone drive you in this morning."

I plastered on my best fake smile and pretended to not understand what he was saying. "I wouldn't know. I took the subway. Wasn't too bad that way."

"He made you take the subway after spending a weekend with him? That's harsh. Or maybe sex with you wasn't good enough for a private car ride. What do you think?"

I liked to think of myself as fairly laid-back, but there was only so far I could be pushed. He'd just reached my limit.

I turned toward him and gave him the most patronizing once over I could muster. "I think you must be under the impression that it's acceptable to speak to people the way you just spoke to me, but let me educate you on something. It's not. Particularly in a work environment. I'm going to assume that you're an immature boy who doesn't know any better because if you were anything else, I'd be stopping at HR and filing an official complaint."

The elevator dinged, and I stepped off, ignoring him as he followed me off. I walked at my normal pace, waiting to see if he'd say anything else, but he didn't. Still, I felt his eyes on me along with everyone else's as I made my way to my own department. I might've been able to tone things down a bit, but it had felt good to defy expectation and speak up.

And it'd felt damn good to not stand there in silence when someone was being blatantly disrespectful. I wondered if I'd feel the same at the end of the day. Judging by the whispers I could hear behind me, I had a feeling my little outburst was going to be as much a part of the rumor mill as everything else. It would most likely end up twisted and hardly even close to what I'd actually said, but at least I wouldn't need to deflect the truth. I had, after all, had sex with Nate, even if it hadn't been planned or part of an agreement to keep my job.

How many people would believe that, though?

What a mess.

TWENTY-EIGHT

NATE

I DRAINED MY SECOND BOTTLE OF WATER ALONG WITH another few aspirin. My head hadn't stopped pounding since I'd woken up, and I wanted to blame it on the fact that I'd slept on the most uncomfortable couch in history, but I couldn't do that. I'd been hungover enough times to know that, by now, I should've been fine. I'd gone home and went through my usual post-hangover routine of food, water, sports drinks, and aspirin, but nothing had helped. Sure, it'd taken the edge off, but that was it.

I didn't want to be here, and that just pissed me off even more. Work was my refuge. I always wanted to be here. This took my mind off things, let me focus my attention somewhere other than the shit going on in my life. I'd been hungover at work before. Hell, I was pretty sure I'd founded the company when I was hungover.

Except, right now, the pain in my head was sort of taking over everything else. I hadn't been able to think straight, concentrate on anything. All I could think about was how much I wished I was in a dark room, passed out until my headache went away, and I could function again.

At least, that was what I'd been trying to convince myself of all morning. That the fact that I felt restless and uncomfortable in my own skin was because I'd gotten shit-faced at Club Privé last night. That it wasn't about where I'd ended up *after* the club.

While a lot of last night was hazy, including what I'd said when I'd gotten to Ashlee's place last night, my conversation with her a couple hours ago was crystal clear. No matter how much I wished it wasn't.

Why the hell was I in knots over a woman I'd only fucked twice? It'd been easy to walk away from every other woman I'd ever had. This one got under my skin like no one else, and it didn't make any sense.

"Mr. Lexington?"

The name made my head snap up...which then made my head spin. "Come in."

I should've known it wasn't her. Aside from the fact that she wouldn't have come to see me after the way I'd treated her, that wasn't her voice. Still, I was disappointed when my office door opened, and a short brunette with glasses came in.

"Mr. Lexington, I'm Kandace from the art department." Her eyes darted from me to the iPad in her hand. "Um, I was, uh, supposed to bring you this?"

She said it like a question, and while that would normally have annoyed me, I was even more on edge than normal. When she didn't immediately continue, I snapped, "Then bring it to me."

"Right. Sorry." She scurried over to my desk and held out the iPad. "Here."

I practically snatched it from her hand. What did the art department need me to look at so desperately that they'd send some intern or whatever she was?

"What is it?"

"Um, I'm not sure. They, uh, said you'd know."

"That's unhelpful."

She winced, and I probably should've felt bad for being an asshole, but it wasn't like this was a new thing for me.

I ignored her and hoped whoever had sent this had provided some direction or heads were going to roll. A little voice in the back of my head told me that I couldn't go fire my entire art department, but I told it to fuck off. If I wanted to fire them all, then I would. Manhattan Records was mine. I could do what I wanted. Wasn't that the whole point?

Fortunately for them, I knew exactly what it was they were asking, and it was a simple enough question to answer. So simple that I wondered why they hadn't just emailed me, but I didn't bother asking Kandace. She wouldn't know, not if she'd been sent up here without an explanation in the first place. I made the appropriate notes and handed the iPad back to her.

"Tell them the next time they send a person when an email could do, they'll be the one running errands."

Her eyes went wide, and she nodded. I made a dismissive gesture, and she hurried away without another word. I couldn't decide if she was naturally timid or if my reputation was getting worse. Maybe she'd heard about me firing Flora and calling others into my office to talk. If she wasn't a gossip, then she didn't have any reason to worry.

I might snap at the messenger, but I wouldn't kill the messenger. Probably.

I went back to my computer and read the same email I'd been reading for the past hour. It wasn't a particularly important email, but it was still one I needed to reply to personally. The problem was that I couldn't reply to what I couldn't seem to remember. I did finally figure out that I could do things one paragraph at a time, and that was the way I managed to respond to a few emails before someone else knocked on my door.

Before I could say anything, the door opened, and my partner came in. It was a fairly normal occurrence, Finley coming to see me on Monday mornings, but I'd forgotten about that. What did it say about Ashlee that she could make me forget something that had been happening nearly every Monday for the past decade?

"You look pleasant." Finley's words dripped with sarcasm. "Tough night?"

I glared at him. "You're a bastard."

He grinned. "Yes, actually."

I closed my eyes. "Shit. Sorry, Finley. I forgot."

"Then you also forgot that I don't particularly care that my parents weren't married." He was always so good-natured.

It annoyed the shit out of me.

"What's got you looking like you woke up on the wrong side of the bed?" He leaned against my desk. "Or did you just wake up in the wrong person's bed?"

"I can't decide if you're asking because you know me or because you've heard something."

He wiggled his hand back and forth. "A little of both?"

"Dammit," I muttered. "Guess I shouldn't have taken her on Friday."

"Please tell me that you're using the word 'taken' in a platonic sense."

I glanced up at him but couldn't meet his eyes. I couldn't bear to see his disappointment. "I might have intended it to be that way, but..."

"But you had sex with her anyway." Some of that good-naturedness faded away. "An employee."

"Yes," I said with a sigh. "She's an employee, and yes, we had sex. Before you say anything, though, it was completely consensual."

"I think HR might disagree on that point," Finley said. "You can't date an employee."

"I'm not *dating* an employee," I said.

"Then you're just sleeping with her, and that's even worse."

"How is that worse?" I asked, even though I already knew the answer.

"It's worse because if you were actually dating, it'd be a lot harder for the employee to convince HR that you're leveraging her job for sex."

I decided that I disliked serious Finley more than smiling Finley. "I'm not blackmailing her into sex."

"I didn't say you were," he said. "But is that what she'll say?"

Ashlee's face immediately appeared in my head. The

expression she'd worn the first time I'd seen her. How she'd looked underneath me. The blank mask I'd gotten this morning when I'd yelled at her.

"She won't go to HR."

Finley walked around the desk and put his hand on my shoulder. "Look, I know that one of the reasons this business between us works is because neither one of us tells the other how to live their life, but you know you can't keep seeing her. Dating or sex. Doesn't matter. It has to be done."

I gritted my teeth. "It's not an issue."

Finley squeezed my shoulder. "I'm not going to let it be an issue. Give me her name. I'll make sure she has the same understanding that you do."

TWENTY-NINE

ASHLEE

I could say one great thing for being the only assistant in A&R: I was being honest every time I told someone that I didn't have time to talk to them. I spent so much time moving from one task immediately into the next that I barely took five minutes to eat, and I even did that while I was working. My brain was so busy that I didn't have time to dwell on anything that other people might be saying.

It was nice.

At least Mr. Hancock and Ms. Lamas hadn't mentioned my presence on Friday. I was sure Ms. Lamas knew I'd attended with Nate – I couldn't use 'Mr. Lexington' now any easier than I did his first name – but she hadn't said a word about it. I appreciated how they were both handling things, but it couldn't have been easy for either of them, having our department be the subject of gossip like this.

"Miss Webb?"

My head jerked up, my heart in my throat. I knew that voice. Finley Kordell, the less-visible CEO of Manhattan

Records. I'd seen him around, heard him too, but I'd never been this close to him before. Never spoken to him directly.

"Mr. Kordell." I flushed at the squeak in my voice. He was going to think I was an idiot.

"You're Ashlee Webb, correct?" His expression was serious, but not angry.

I could barely breathe. He rarely talked to anyone here. Half the time, he wasn't even in the building. He was the label's silent, seldom-seen partner. Most people didn't even know he existed.

I wasn't most people.

"Yes," I said, pressing my sweating palms against the tops of my thighs. "I'm Ashlee Webb."

"Finley Kordell." He held out his hand, and I shook it. "I understand you've been working for us for a while."

I nodded. "Yes, sir. Started as an intern, then moved up to runner. Promoted to assistant three months ago."

I was rambling.

"Mr. Hancock speaks highly of you," he said. "And despite his cheery personality, he doesn't actually do that very often."

I wanted to ask him what he was doing here, why he'd decided to come talk to me after all this time, but I was too afraid that I wouldn't like his answer, so I didn't ask the question. Maybe it was cowardly of me, but I only had so much courage and getting through today had taken a lot of it.

"I understand that you were Mr. Lexington's...date on Friday." His pleasant expression looked strained over his word choice.

Was that it? Was he concerned about me dating a known

player like Nate? Had he thought cautioning me would be a better tact to take than warning Nate away? Or had he already spoken to Nate?

My already flushed face grew hotter at the thought of those two men discussing...no, I couldn't even go there. Not unless I absolutely had to, and I really hoped it wouldn't come to that.

"Yes." I kept my answer simple and hoped he wouldn't ask me to expound on exactly how much time Nate and I had spent together, or what we'd been doing that whole time.

"I'm not privy to all of Mr. Lexington's personal matters," Mr. Kordell continued, "but when it involves this company, those are times I intervene on his behalf."

Company involvement. *His* behalf.

I was such an idiot.

He was here about Nate, but not for me. He was here for *Nate.*

His sudden appearance and interest made sense now. I should have seen it from the first.

"Whatever occurred between you and Mr. Lexington is over." Mr. Kordell's voice was firm but gentle. Professional and non-judgmental. "There will be no more events together, nor will there be anything else between you save work-related conversations that should take place via email unless it's absolutely necessary to have said conversations in person."

I held up a hand, not wanting to endure another minute of this torture.

"Whatever you may have heard, there is nothing between Mr. Lexington and me. This weekend was a one-time incident that will not be repeated."

He gave me a searching look, and I hoped he could see that I wasn't the girl he thought I was. I hadn't slept with my boss for any sort of gain. I never wanted anything from Nate. Not before and most certainly not now. In fact, I was starting to wish I'd never heard his name.

"I'm glad to hear that, Miss Webb," Mr. Kordell said. "If you have any concerns or questions that Mr. Hancock or Ms. Lamas are unable to answer, please come see me. I know I'm not always out and visible in the company, but my door is always open."

"Thank you." I barely managed to get the words out and return his smile before he walked away.

Could my life be turned upside-down anymore?

Maybe this was a sign that it was time for me to start making plans for what came next. I had a degree I could use in numerous fields, and once I left here, I wouldn't need to worry about bumping into Nate. Our paths wouldn't cross without Manhattan Records.

I took a deep breath. I had something I needed to do before I left, but I'd put it off long enough.

THIRTY
NATE

THE MOMENT FINLEY LEFT, I WAS TEMPTED TO GO AFTER him and tell him to ignore the whole thing. I could tell him that I'd deal with it and then figure out what it was I actually wanted to do. The thing about Finley and me, though, was that he knew me better than anyone else. He'd seen me at my lowest point and knew all of my strengths and weaknesses. While I hadn't shared every single dirty detail of my life, I'd told him plenty, which meant he knew that, even if I said I'd handle things, I probably wouldn't do it the best way for the company.

I tried going back to my email, but it was even harder to concentrate than before. I kept wondering if Finley had talked to Ashlee yet and what he'd said to her. He was the diplomat. I could fake it when I needed to, but brute force was usually my method of handling things. I dealt in threats and promises. He knew the art of compromising without giving away too much. I didn't like to compromise.

All of these were reasons why it was better for him to talk to Ashlee, but it didn't mean I had to like any of it.

I made it two hours before calling her desk.

"Ashlee, it's Nate."

Silence for a beat. Two.

"Mr. Kordell spoke to me." Her voice was flat. "I'm clear on what you want."

I doubted that.

"I want to talk to you."

"Go ahead."

I sat up straighter, annoyed at the lack of emotion in her voice. I didn't want this bland version of her, not after I'd seen how passionate she could be.

"Not on the phone. Come to my office."

Another two beats of silence. "Mr. Kordell was clear that I keep my distance from you, and I agree that's the best course of action."

"And if I don't agree?"

"I suggest you speak to Mr. Kordell. Is that all, Mr. Lexington?"

"For now." I hung up before she could.

Dammit. This wasn't going to be as easy as I'd anticipated. She'd managed to reduce my name to something without even a hint of the sensuality that she'd put into it this weekend.

It didn't seem possible that our first date had been just three nights ago. We hadn't had nearly enough time for me to get bored with her. I wasn't ready for things to be completely done.

Sure, I'd behaved...poorly this morning, but she had to

understand where I was coming from. Whatever she wanted from me, she had to ask for it so we could be on the same page. Acting like she'd done me a favor when she could've just sent me away wasn't the way the world worked.

The business part of me knew that Finley was right, knew that Ashlee and I had to keep our distance from each other, but my libido said it didn't want any distance that meant I couldn't see her naked.

I waited thirty minutes before leaving my office for the A&R department. I generally liked reaching out to Stu and Suzie after any large event, but I typically summoned them to my office or took them out to lunch. Today, I felt like going to see them.

It had nothing to do with Ashlee.

And it didn't annoy me that she got up and left just as I reached her desk. Nope. Not at all.

I didn't pause at her desk or even glance in that direction, just in case she was watching to see if I was going to look for her. I wasn't. I was working.

When I got back to my office, I had an email from Finley waiting. I scowled as I opened it. If he was going to scold me for going to A&R, he and I were going to need to re-evaluate who was in charge of what. Fortunately, that wasn't the case. Unfortunately, however, his email still pissed me off, though not at him.

I spoke with Miss Webb, and she informed me that whatever happened between the two of you this past weekend wouldn't happen again. I don't believe she'll cause any problems here. She seems like a decent girl.

She was more than a decent girl, but that didn't stop me

from being irked at her for telling Finley that she and I were done, as if it were some unilateral decision that I had no say in. I'd never force a woman to have sex, but it wasn't right for her to make the decision to end things without at least talking to me about it.

My hypocrisy came back to bite me in the ass less than a minute later when I realized that in every single relationship, arrangement, and understanding I'd ever had, I'd done just that. I'd decided that things had been over, and I'd informed the woman. I'd never sat down and talked to any of them about it.

Shit. Had this been what it'd been like for all of them?

I imagined that it'd probably been worse for a lot of them because I wasn't as invested in this thing with Ashlee as, say, Roma had been in me. Not that I was disillusioned enough to think that Roma was in love with me. Maybe two or three of the women I'd been with had fooled themselves into thinking that they were in love, but most of them had been just as opportunistic as I was. We'd all gotten something out of our various arrangements.

That had to be the problem.

Ashlee hadn't said what she wanted, so now she was keeping me at arm's length until she saw what I had to offer. Two nights of great sex was fine when fucking was the only goal. That's what I wanted more of. Ashlee didn't strike me as the sort of person who was only after sex, though. If that was all she wanted, she wouldn't have stayed a virgin so long, no matter what excuses she gave. She could find another man to fuck her, just not one who could measure up to me.

My chest tightened at the thought of her in some other

man's bed. I wasn't going to accept that. Not until I was done with her. Not unless she spelled it out to my face. I'd been an ass earlier, and I'd make that up to her. After that, if she didn't want us to hook up anymore, then we'd both walk away.

Now that I had a plan in place, it was easier for me to focus on real work. Easier, but not as much as it should have been. I still kept glancing at the clock on my computer screen, waiting for it to get down to the last half hour before everyone went home for the day. I refused to give Ashlee any room to wiggle out of us talking. Thirty minutes would give her enough time to finish whatever she might be doing for Stu and Suzie but not enough for her to ask for something new so she could avoid me. And if she somehow managed to get away, I'd visit her apartment again. Sober this time.

One way or another, she and I were going to have a talk.

THIRTY-ONE
ASHLEE

As soon as I picked up my phone, I regretted it. I'd guessed that it'd be Nate, but I hadn't realized how perfect his timing would be.

I was only a few minutes from finishing the last thing on my list from Mr. Hancock, and he'd told me I could leave when it was done. He hadn't mentioned anything about Friday night, but I knew he'd heard at least some of the gossip because he'd given me things to do that allowed me to be away from people. I was pretty sure that was why he was going to let me cut out early, so I wouldn't be caught up with everyone else as they left.

Except I wasn't going to leave early because, as soon as I was done with tightening up these last two memos, I had to go see Nate. Which meant by the time I was leaving with everyone else, they'd all see me come out of his office, or they'd be told about it by someone who had seen me.

Had Mr. Kordell even talked to Nate at all? How was I

supposed to stay away from him if he kept after me? Didn't he realize that if I went into his office alone today that it would only serve to make the rumors worse? It wouldn't matter if I came out right away or not until everyone else was gone. Either one would be a story.

I could refuse to go, of course, but it was entirely possible that he had something work-related for me to do and I was the only one reading more into things. He wasn't exactly known for being sentimental about his relationships, let alone a fling like the one we'd had. If I presented myself professionally, then I could show him that what had happened between us meant as little to me as it did to him.

The main problem with me maintaining proper work behavior had less to do with the two nights we'd spent together and more to do with the fact that he'd brought Finley into our personal lives. Maybe me being angry about that was a good thing. I could go to his office, listen to whatever assignment he gave me, and then I could tell him that I didn't appreciate what he'd done. If he had something he wanted to say to me, he could either say it to my face or not at all. No more sending someone else on his behalf. No more talking about our private business with anyone, especially not Mr. Kordell.

All of this flashed through my mind in half a minute and then I was telling Nate that I'd be there as soon as I finished this last project. He sounded pleased as he ended the call, but that could have been my imagination.

By the time I was ready, I had fifteen minutes before I was technically off the clock, and as I headed toward Nate's office, I wondered if I should have told someone where I was going and why. Then again, it wasn't like I had an email to show anyone that I'd been summoned.

If I asked Mr. Hancock or Ms. Lamas to go with me, or if I told Mr. Kordell that Nate had insisted on seeing me, it would've been simple for Nate to deny it. My word against his, and it was tough to decide which of us would have come out ahead.

Two nights of great sex wasn't worth all of this.

"Miss Webb, take a seat."

Even though I'd wanted him to be professional, his bland tone made me bristle. If he'd brought me here for some twisted cat-and-mouse game where he could flaunt how much power he had over me, he and I were going to have a serious issue. For the moment, however, I would hold my tongue.

I sat in the seat directly across from him.

"Ms. Lamas passed along some of your suggestions for possible artists for the label to sign." He shuffled a few papers in front of him, and I wondered if he'd printed them off for this exact moment, thinking that this made him seem more important, more in charge. "I have to say, the notes you took were seriously lacking."

I swallowed a protest. If he explained and I was in the wrong, it'd be better for me not to speak at all. If he was wrong, I should keep my mouth shut and wait until I had proof before I told him.

"For each artist you found, you included what social media platforms they were already on, as well as how many followers they already had, but you don't have notes about each site. What the artist had available. Picture, video, audio. How often they post. What sorts of interactions they have."

Ms. Lamas had specifically said that she wanted a brief mention of their online presence, not details. In my opinion, that made her the only one who could judge whether or not I'd provided enough information. I filed that bit away as Nate moved on to the next item on his list. I'd wait until he was completely finished so I'd have a more complete idea regarding his opinion of this particular assignment.

"You didn't include possible name changes for the ones whose names won't work."

Name changes? Was he kidding me? Still, I held my tongue.

"If you're going to work in A&R, you need to know that a name is just as important as talent. With the name comes a brand, an image, and that's what we sell. A person or group with a stupid name isn't going to sell shit, no matter how good their music is."

I wondered what he considered a stupid name, because there were a few band names I could think of off the top of my head that wouldn't have been my first choice. Then again, I didn't have a record label with numerous best-selling artists. He might have a point about the names.

What he *didn't* have a point about was how it was my responsibility to do those things when I hadn't been given those instructions. This sounded more like he needed to tell Mr. Hancock and Ms. Lamas that he wanted their assistants to do more when they were told to search for potential artists.

"Do you understand what I mean when I say that we cultivate an image?"

And that was enough.

"Yes, I understand what it means to cultivate an image," I snapped. "I may be fairly new to the business, but I did actually pay attention in college."

His eyebrows shot up. "Is that so?"

"Look, I got your message, okay? You didn't need to follow up. It's not like I was planning on stalking you or anything. This morning pretty much did it for me." I could barely believe the words coming out of my mouth. First the guy on the elevator and now my boss. What had gotten into me today?

I already knew that answer, though. It was Nate who was the issue. Instead of him making me more likely to hold back, it seemed like being around him just pushed all the buttons that made me want to push back.

"I wouldn't think you were the type to let a little bickering keep you from the best sex you'll ever have."

"Since I don't have anyone to compare you to, I'll have to take your word on how good you are." I tightened my grip on the arms of my chair. "But I would think that sex would be like anything else...if you have to say it, maybe you're not as good as you think you are."

The corners of his mouth tightened. "I guarantee that when the next guy you're with won't be able to find your clit, let alone your g-spot, you'll think twice about that."

"I'll keep that in mind." I stood up. "If you're done criticizing my work for things I hadn't been told to do, I'd like to go home."

M. S. PARKER

He stood up, and I had to admit that it was a lot more impressive when he did it. Probably something to do with the fact that he was more than a foot taller than me.

"I'm done talking about your work, but I'm not done with you."

That should have been menacing. It shouldn't have been hot.

"And what is it you plan on doing with me?" I crossed my arms and tried not to look like my panties were getting wet. Treacherous body.

He came around the desk and stood in front of me, well within arm's reach, but he kept his hands to himself. For now, he kept only to words, and those slipped over my skin like warm water.

"I'm going to teach you some respect." His low voice rumbled over me even as his gaze caressed my body. "And you're going to enjoy every minute of it." He paused, and then amended, "Well, most of it. Sometimes new things are... disconcerting before they're pleasurable."

His vocabulary kept surprising me.

"First, I'm going to blindfold you so you'll have no choice but to wait to find out what I'm going to do to you."

A shiver went down my spine.

"Then I'm going to have you turn around in that chair, put your knees on the seat, bend over the back, pull down those snug pants and panties..."

I swallowed hard.

"Once I have you how I want you, I'll open the door to my office. People should be gone, but if they're not, all they'll need to do is come down this hall to see me fuck you."

My pulse raced. I couldn't decide if he was joking or not. Not about any of it. And I didn't know how I felt about any of it. I did, however, have a feeling that if I didn't walk out that door right now, I was going to find out, one way or another.

THIRTY-TWO

NATE

.

I NEVER MINDED WOMEN WITH PASSION, BUT DEFIANCE had always been too complicated for the straightforward arrangements I wanted. Dominating strong women was appealing, and Ashlee was one of the strongest I'd met. I didn't know why I kept pushing her, testing her limits.

She was right about everything. About our conversation that morning. About the fact that I was complaining about parts of her work that she most likely hadn't been told to do. I'd done it on purpose, intentionally provoking her until she finally snapped. When she had, it'd been more of a rush than any sort of planned seduction from any woman I'd ever been with. And every woman I'd been with had planned their seductions from the shade of their lipstick to whatever lingerie they had or hadn't been wearing.

Ashlee wasn't like that. She'd flirted with me, but it hadn't been seduction. There was a difference between the two, and I was surprised at how much I liked that difference.

About as surprised as I was at how much I liked Ashlee and couldn't get her out of my head.

Maybe this would finally do it. Maybe if I pushed her right up to her limit and got to see her enjoy that, maybe I would finally get her out of my head.

Because that was what I wanted. Her out of my head and just doing her job so I could do mine. I wanted to be able to concentrate instead of thinking about all the ways I could tie her up, the things I could do to her, the things I could have her do to me.

First, we'd start with what I wanted here and now.

I loosened my tie, raising my eyes to meet hers. I didn't tell her to leave. I didn't tell her if she stayed, I was going to do everything I'd just told her I wanted to do. She'd been with me twice now. She knew me well enough when it came to sex that she knew how to stop me, and she knew that if she didn't say the word, we were going to fuck again.

Color flooded her cheeks, and her pupils dilated. The sharp intake of breath when I pulled the tie off told me that this desire wasn't one-sided. She might not like me, but she definitely wanted me.

I could work with that.

I moved with a slow deliberateness that she watched but didn't try to stop. Neither one of us spoke, and I wondered if she felt the same sort of reluctance as I did, a feeling that if either of us said a word, this spell would be broken and this opportunity would disappear.

My fingertips brushed her skin as I wrapped my tie around her head, covering her eyes as thoroughly as any blindfold. This wasn't my first time using a tie in sex games. It was always a convenient prop, though I'd rarely had to use it in an improvised situation. The fact that I hadn't planned any of these encounters wasn't lost on me.

I took her hand and turned her toward the chair, using my hands to guide her up onto the seat. Even over her clothes, the feel of her curves made my already-interested cock thicken. Once she was settled, I ran my hand down her spine and over that amazing ass of hers. I'd been her first in a lot of ways, and the thought of being the first to take her ass made my mind immediately pipe up that there was yet another fantasy I wanted to fulfill with her. Maybe tonight wouldn't be the end after all.

I walked backward toward the door, wanting to watch her thoughts cross her face when she realized I actually planned to open my office door. She would have no way of knowing that just how far I left it open would depend on whether or not other employees were still in the building. If Roma – or any of the other women I'd been with – had been the one on the chair, I might've considered leaving the door wide open, no matter who was out there. Well, probably not here, since this was my place of business, but it would've been because of that, not out of any need to keep her safe from prying eyes.

Yet another way Ashlee was different from the others. The idea of anyone seeing her, seeing us, bothered me. I wanted to believe it was just because she worked for me, and I wanted to keep sex separate from our professional lives, but I knew it was more than that. I was the only person who'd gotten to see this side of Ashlee, and I wanted to keep it that way.

M. S. PARKER

I pushed aside the little voice that suggested it might be more than that.

I turned the doorknob, and the faint click was enough to make her tense. She still didn't say her safe word, so I opened the door partway, glancing out long enough to ascertain that we were alone. At least as far as I could see. Since I had no way to know with absolute certainty, I left the door open only an inch. Enough to still be a little risky, but not enough that anyone would be able to see into my office without pushing the door open more.

And if we were quiet, no one would bother us.

I returned to where Ashlee was waiting and slid my hand across her torso, squeezing one of her breasts before going to my desk to retrieve a condom. When I reached around to undo her pants, she stiffened, and I stroked my fingers over her stomach until she relaxed.

Well, more or less.

"Do you remember what to say if you want to stop?"

"Beagle." Her voice was soft but without hesitation.

"Come as often as you can," I said as I hooked my fingers in her waistband and eased her pants over her hips. "But unless you want to attract attention, I suggest you do so quietly. And if you don't come by the time I do, you don't get to at all."

She nodded, and I got the impression she was literally biting her lips in anticipation. Her hair was pinned up, giving me the sight of enough skin to know that she was blushing. Once her pants and underwear were down to her knees, I slid my hand between her thighs, then up until I felt her skin, hot and slick.

"Damn," I muttered. "It didn't take much to get you wet, did it?"

This time, she shook her head, but she still didn't say anything. I'd had responsive lovers before, but the fact that someone this innocent and inexperienced could be turned on so easily made me proud in a way I'd never been before.

If she'd been anyone else, I would've just slammed into her, tested her silence with a little bit of pain. This was going to be quick, and I wasn't going to be gentle, but she'd had fairly intense sex two nights in a row, and she wasn't used to this sort of thing. A little bit of prep was warranted.

I swiped a finger between her lips, teasing her entrance for a few seconds before moving up to her clit. Her head fell forward as I made brisk circles around the sensitive nub, more moisture leaking onto my finger. When I heard the second shuddering breath, I moved my hand back, sliding a finger inside her. Two strokes and then I added another. I twisted my fingers as I thrust them into her, but as soon as she pushed back against my hand, I took it away.

She made an annoyed sound that brought a smile to my lips and made me wish I could take my time, draw things out until I had her screaming and begging. Maybe that was another thing to add to my growing list, even though I should've been thinking about how to get her out of my thoughts.

I made short work of my pants and the condom, then brushed my cock between her legs so she'd know what was coming. I eased inside her, steady and relentless until I bottomed out, and she shook around me. As much for me as for her, I took a few seconds without moving, my usual self-control slipping at the feel of her fitting around me like she'd been made for me.

"You can play with your clit, if you want."

One hand immediately dropped, and I took that as my cue to move. I drove into her at a fast pace, wanting to see how quickly she could get herself off with me inside her. Half a dozen strokes later, I heard a low curse, and she tightened around me. I thrust past her spasming muscles, drawing out her orgasm until my own exploded out of me.

She was still coming when I pulled out, squeezing off the condom with one hand and patting her ass with the other. Once I washed up in my private bathroom, I'd give her the chance to do the same. At least we wouldn't need to have some awkward morning-after conversation or talk about our feelings. A great fucking was always better than talking.

THIRTY-THREE

ASHLEE

I'D NEVER FELT LIKE A BIGGER IDIOT THAN I DID WHEN I walked out of Nate's office, the space between my legs aching even while my stomach twisted. I was grateful that everyone had already gone home because I didn't think I would be able to handle the humiliation of seeing the people who'd gossiped about Nate and me and knowing they'd been right all along.

I might not have slept with him to get or keep my job, but I had done it at work, despite the fact that he'd been picking apart a project I'd worked on for days. He hadn't surprised me. He'd wanted me, no matter how many times he'd behaved as if he didn't, and even though he'd said awful things to me, I'd wanted him too.

Shame colored my cheeks. How could I want someone who treated me the way he did? What did that say about me, that I'd let a man talk to me the way he did, and then I'd let him fuck me?

No, I hadn't *let* him. I'd *encouraged* him. I'd had a way to stop him. A single word and he would've backed off because, as much as he was an asshole, he wasn't a rapist. One word. That's all it would've taken, and I would have already been on my way home, unembarrassed and looking forward to ordering some food and reading a good book.

Instead, I was approaching the elevators and praying that no one I knew would be on it. I couldn't handle pretending that my entire world wasn't spinning backward. The doors slid open, and I stepped onto the elevator, breathing a sigh of relief. A sigh that didn't last very long because, before the doors shut, I heard someone call out for me to hold it.

My hand was between the doors before the owner of the voice registered, and my entire body went immediately cold and then hot when the absolute worst person possible joined me in the elevator.

"Mr. Kordell." I barely managed to get his name out.

"Hello, there, Miss Webb." He smiled at me as he leaned against the wall.

"Good afternoon." I hoped my smile didn't look like the grimace it felt like.

"Leaving work a bit late?"

"Yes."

Shit. What was I supposed to say to him? How could I tell him why I was leaving after everyone else had? Was I a good enough liar to convince him that I hadn't been doing something with Nate I really shouldn't have been? I couldn't tell the truth, obviously. Even if he hadn't specifically told me to stay away from Nate earlier that day, I couldn't have told him what I was doing.

"Just finishing up a few things." I laced my fingers

together so he couldn't see them tremble. "I have double the workload until a replacement assistant is hired."

That, at least, was true.

"Heading home for the night, then?"

Any other CEO would've ignored an employee that he didn't really know unless he was discussing something important. Not Mr. Kordell, though. He wanted to make small talk during our short trip down to the lobby.

"Yes. And you?" It was a lame question, I knew, but a polite one, and one I could ask honestly.

I didn't like lying in general, and I certainly didn't like lying to him. I hated it, in fact. But I couldn't show that either. So much I couldn't say or do. How did I keep getting myself in this situation?

"The same," he said. "Maybe a little wine with dinner while I binge watch a show I've been waiting for."

"I'm in the middle of a good book." I offered that bit of information without much forethought.

"I've been looking for a good book. I spend far too much time watching TV." Mr. Kordell straightened as the elevator dinged the arrival into the lobby. "What's the title?"

Even more color flooded my face, and I was certain I was never going to have a conversation with this man that didn't involve my total humiliation.

"*Desi's Dream Harem,*" I mumbled.

Dammit.

THIRTY-FOUR

NATE

I HATED NEW YORK TRAFFIC.

After Ashlee had left my office – not bothering to look back a single time – I'd waited behind, giving her enough time to leave the building before I went to my car. We'd had our fun, but the thought of the awkward silence that an elevator ride would bring made me all too glad that she didn't expect that sort of thing.

I'd almost been whistling when I reached my car, and based on the strange look Angus gave me, I'd thought for a moment that I'd done it out loud. Maybe he'd just been surprised to see me...happy. I supposed that's what I was feeling. Happiness.

It had been so long since I'd felt anything besides... honestly, I didn't know what I'd felt all these years. I couldn't call it contentedness because I didn't know what that was either. I could remember happiness from when I was a kid, but I didn't think I'd ever been content.

Even if I couldn't name it, I still knew that I felt better

now than I ever had with any other woman. Except I wasn't with the woman right now. I was just thinking about her. Thinking about what we'd done, how it had felt to take her right there in my office. I wouldn't be able to look at that chair without thinking about how hard her pussy had gripped my cock when she'd come.

It was going to make working difficult.

And this traffic was making everything else difficult at the moment.

"Are you all right, sir?"

I looked up to see Angus giving me an eye via the rearview mirror. "I'm fine."

He fell silent, and I stared out the window. It was a fairly gray late afternoon, chilly and dreary, but at least it wasn't raining. I wasn't a fan of the rain.

Then an image of Ashlee popped into my head. Her standing outside in the rain. Clothes molding to fit those amazing curves of hers. The hard points of her nipples poking through her shirt because, of course, she wasn't wearing a bra. I imagined kissing that Ashlee, mingling the taste of the water with the taste of her.

Fuck.

It hadn't worked. Time with her hadn't lessened my desire for her, it'd just made me want her more.

The problem I had now was that I didn't know if Ashlee wanted the same thing. Had this been all she'd needed to get *me* out of *her* system?

I still had those thoughts running through my head when I arrived home. I thanked Angus and headed inside. I'd almost convinced myself that I could figure out a way around all of it, but then I stepped off the elevator only to find that I wasn't alone. For one brief moment, I thought it was Ashlee, coming to tell me that there were things she wanted me to do to her and that she wouldn't be satisfied with any other man–

Fuck.

When had I turned into this guy?

"Nate, baby!"

Dammit. Not Ashlee. Not even close to Ashlee.

"How the fuck did you get in here, Roma?"

My ex grinned up at me and held up a key.

I sighed and repeated the question with a slight change. "How the fuck did you get a key, Roma?"

"I might have borrowed a spare so I could surprise you sometime. Surprise!"

She bounced up and over until she was only a few inches away from me. I didn't back away even though I didn't want her to touch me. If I gave her the slightest inch, I'd lose the power I had over her, and I had no intention of that happening. The smell of alcohol poured off of her in waves, and I wasn't sure if I wanted to gag or curse. She could be a nasty drunk if things didn't go her way, which meant I needed to get her out, the faster, the better. When I got worked up, it turned Roma on. The best way to get her out of my house was to act like I didn't care. Fortunately, I didn't care about her, so it was easier to keep my head.

I held out my hand. "Key. Now."

She stuck out her bottom lip in a mock pout. "Don't wanna."

"Roma." I made her name a warning.

"Don't be that way," she put her hand on my chest. "You can punish me for being bad. You like doing that."

"I told you that we were done." I wrapped my hand around her wrist and moved her hand off my chest. "I meant it."

"But I don't wanna be done." Her eyes narrowed, and I knew she was transitioning from flirty drunk to mean drunk.

"That wasn't the arrangement," I reminded her. It was essentially pointless to argue with her when she was like this, but I needed to say the words, if for no other reason than to remind myself that this wasn't about me treating Roma like shit, but about following the terms we'd both agreed to when we started things.

"Fuck your arrangement," she snapped.

"It wasn't *mine*," I said through gritted teeth. "It was *ours*. As in something that both of us made. One point of which was that either of us could end things whenever we wanted. I wanted us to be over, so we're over."

"You're a real bastard, you know that?" Roma poked my chest with one long, manicured nail, something she never would have done when she was my sub.

I'd always suspected that Roma hadn't been a true submissive, but she'd been willing to play the part both in and out of the bedroom. At first, at least. Ashlee wasn't playing a part at all. Even when she was quiet, she had a strength that told me she had certain limits that would never be breakable, and when it came to sex, she either flatly rejected it or immediately submitted. I'd always thought I preferred women who were submissives all the time, but Ashlee was making me reconsider.

"I'm tired, Roma," I said as I pushed thoughts of Ashlee from my mind before they could give me a hard-on. The last thing I needed was Roma thinking it was for her.

"Then let's go to bed," she practically purred.

Her zero-to-sixty shit was another reason I hated it when she got drunk.

"You should go to bed," I said. "Alone. In your own apartment."

She closed the last bit of distance between us and reached down to grab my cock through my pants, frowning when she realized I was soft.

"Fighting always gets you hard."

I took her wrist more firmly this time and pushed her hand away from my crotch. "Not with you. Not anymore."

She stumbled backward, confusion on her face.

"Stay there," I said. "I'll call you a cab."

"Don't want a cab." She sat down.

"You need a cab," I countered. "You can't drive home, and I don't–"

She wasn't listening. She was passed out.

"Motherfucking–" I bit back the rest of the curses. I needed to decide what to do now. I could call Angus, but he usually had a standing dinner date with his daughter on Wednesday evenings. I'd always respected that, taking other forms of transportation on the odd Wednesday's I wanted to go out. I didn't intend to interrupt his dinner because my ex had done something stupid.

I could still call a cab, but now I remembered that I didn't have a key to her place, which meant I'd either have to dig through her purse or pockets to find hers or I'd have to break in. Neither of which were good options since she could end up feeling vindictive enough to accuse me of something.

Which meant the best option I had was to let her stay here.

I really didn't want to do that, but it was the choice I could live with.

After I got her settled into a guest room, I went to the kitchen to find something for dinner. I was halfway through my reheated stew when my phone rang. Finley's name on the screen was the only reason I answered it, and as soon as I had, I wished I hadn't.

"What the hell are you thinking, Nate?"

I wasn't sure which surprised me more: the intensity in his voice or the fact that he hadn't made his usual polite small talk before getting to the reason for the call.

"If you tell me what you're pissed about, I'll tell you what I'm thinking."

"Ashlee Webb. I thought we agreed that you needed to leave that girl alone."

I put down my fork, my food forgotten. "Are you spying on me?"

"I don't need to spy on you, Nate. You're rarely as discreet as you think you are, especially when it comes to someone who knows you as well as I do."

I didn't bother pointing out that he was the only person who knew me well, the only one I didn't hold at arm's length. It didn't mean he was my father, though. He couldn't tell me what to do.

"Spit it out, Finley," I snapped.

"I saw her leaving your office this afternoon, and I took the elevator to the lobby with her."

"And?"

"And I've seen enough of your women to know what they look like after you've...had your way with them."

I barked a laugh. "*Had my way with them?* What is this, some gothic romance novel? There's nothing wrong with consensual sex, Finley. And honestly, I'm surprised you're being so prudish about it."

"Prudish? There's nothing prudish about this." The frustration level in his voice was as high as I'd ever heard it. "She's your *employee*, Nate, and she could ruin everything we've worked for if she decides she was coerced into sex with you."

"She won't do that."

"And how do you know that?" he asked.

"She hasn't yet."

He sighed. "You've got to walk away from her. She clearly isn't going to heed my warnings. Maybe she's gathering as many complaints as she can before going public or trying to blackmail you. Or maybe she's some innocent kid you're taking advantage of, and if that's the case, there's a special kind of place in hell for people like you. Stop messing with her before you do something you can't take back."

I stared at my phone as the call ended.

What in the actual fuck was that?

THIRTY-FIVE

ASHLEE

I WASN'T GOING TO HAVE SEX WITH NATE. AGAIN.

I repeated that every time my mind started drifting toward my boss and everything that came with it. Which meant it was in my head nearly non-stop until Mr. Hancock gave me a set of figures to look over. I'd never been bad at math, but double-checking the list of expenses for the event with the various receipts took all of my concentration. I was grateful for it.

The work took me all the way up to lunch, and I tried to make the distraction last through my meal, but as soon as I closed the file and sent it off to Mr. Hancock, there the thoughts were, just waiting for an opening. Halfway through my lunch, I came up with something new to distract me.

Something that made my gut churn with anxiety and my palms sweat. Something, though, that needed to be done. Something that, technically, I wanted to do, even if the execution of it wouldn't be pleasant.

I needed to speak with Mr. Kordell. I didn't know how

much he knew about what had happened between Nate and me, but he needed to know that it was completely over. And that I'd tried to stay away from Nate. Maybe Mr. Kordell could talk some sense into his partner, get Nate to quit pursuing me.

Then again, I hadn't gotten a single call or email from him all day today. Maybe he'd finally given up. I tried to pretend that was what I wanted, but the pulse low in my body told me a different truth.

I went back to my desk and did a quick check for any important emails or messages to see if Mr. Hancock had anything else for me to do. Since there was nothing immediate that A&R needed, I had the time now to find out if Mr. Kordell was here. I had a feeling that if I waited, I'd lose my nerve, be too embarrassed to say the things I needed to say.

I wrote a note so that if anyone came looking for me, they'd know I'd be back in a bit. I doubted anyone would read it, but it was there just in case. I didn't want anyone thinking I'd gone to see *someone* for a non-work-related purpose. I hadn't heard new rumors, but it wouldn't take much to get them going again. Maybe worse this time.

I hurried down the hall before I could change my mind about talking to Mr. Kordell. I was furious with myself for letting things go this far. I'd been here for years, built up a good reputation, was working toward presenting myself in the best possible light. Okay, I'd been procrastinating for other reasons, but all of the hard work I'd done would be for nothing if I couldn't get Mr. Kordell to believe that I hadn't slept my way to my current position.

I didn't know for certain that he was in his office, but it

wouldn't take much to check. Just walk down the hallway and turn to the door on the left rather than the right. Of course, I also had to ignore the fact that I'd turned to the right less than twenty-four hours ago and now wished that I hadn't.

Well, my brain and heart wished that I hadn't. Other parts of my anatomy were still thanking me for it.

I was only a foot or so away from the door when Nate's door opened. I froze, mind scrambling for any excuse I could have for being here, any excuse that didn't involve having come for Nate. I opened my mouth to say something, but any words I might have uttered died in my mouth when I saw who came out of Nate's office.

Roma.

Maybe Nate's ex wasn't so ex after all.

Though, judging by the pure fury in that woman's eyes, I wasn't the only person he pissed off. Then, her eyes met mine, and they narrowed. She'd recognized me. Shit.

"Piece of advice from someone who's been where you are," she practically snarled, "get everything in writing, so you have proof of what you're fucking him to get. He's not great at keeping promises he makes when he's trying to get into your pants."

My jaw dropped, and she laughed, one of those mean laughs that certain girls always seemed to have, the ones that let people know that they aren't in on the joke – they *are* the joke.

"Oh, sweetie, are you really that naïve? Sex is just another transaction to him. It's how he does things. How he *always* does things. Be smarter than I was and get it in writing."

229

As she stormed off, I ducked into the closest room, suddenly desperate to see absolutely no one. I'd thought I knew Nate in at least a basic sense, but I clearly didn't. How could he be like all of those other men that had been in the news recently, extorting sex from women who just wanted to further their careers?

How could I feel what I did for a man like that?

THIRTY-SIX

NATE

Before Roma had come into my office to complain about how I'd been rude when I'd had Angus waiting in my place to take her home this morning. Apparently, I should have made her breakfast and seen her home myself, after making up for my rejection last night by having sex with her. Or she'd said something like that. I'd been thinking more about how I was going to get her out of my office and how I was glad I'd already had my locks changed at home.

I hung up my phone and hoped to hell the security guys were clear on how important it was to make sure Roma never got any farther than the lobby downstairs, not without a specific order from me. One of the perks of owning the building, I could say who was or wasn't allowed inside. Granted, only a few people knew that I owned the building, but the people who mattered did.

Now that I was done with today's interruption, I got back to what I'd been doing before Roma had shown up.

Reading Ashlee's job application.

I went from there to finding her on social media. She had a couple accounts, fewer than most people her age, and she definitely frequented them less. Almost all of her posts were words rather than pictures, which made me wonder if she just didn't take many pictures or if there was some deeper reason.

Most of the information was made up of things I'd already learned, some from Ashlee herself, some from her job application, but I did catch a few other things. Like the fact that she was a John Perry's fan, and her favorite book was *A Hitchhiker's Guide to the Galaxy*. Interesting, but I wasn't sure any of that gave me any insight into the conundrum that was Ashlee Webb.

"Are you busy?"

There was something strange in Finley's voice, and in the way he looked at me.

"Not really." I closed all the tabs I'd opened to do my...research.

When Finley took a seat in the chair across from me, I realized what was wrong. He was disappointed in me, and it hurt me as much as it surprised me.

Did he know what Ashlee and I had done in the chair right next to him?

"How's the planning for the Golden Words release party next month?"

Okay, not what I'd expected.

"I haven't heard anything about it, so I assume that means everything is going well." I leaned back and laced my fingers together, hoping I looked more casual than I felt.

"Are you planning to take Miss Webb as your date?"

I'd had so many people be disappointed in me over the years that Finley's should have been expected. It'd been a long time coming.

Instead of reassuring him that I had no intention of doing the thing he'd warned me against – even though I'd already done it – I did what I always did when someone thought the worst of me.

I proved them right.

"I am."

He sighed and rubbed his forehead as if I was giving him a headache. "Does she know this?"

My fingers tightened, but I didn't let my tension leak into my voice. This was *my* life, not his.

"She will. I've got plenty of time between now and then to ask her."

"Are you going to ask her, or are you going to 'ask' her?"

I could hear the air quotes, and the knife in my gut twisted a little more. How could he think I'd use my position to force someone into going to...fuck. That's what I'd done to Ashlee the first time we'd gone out.

"I'll make sure she knows that she can refuse my request without fear of repercussions." My tone was flat. I didn't want him to know how much this conversation was hurting me...no, *bothering* me. No one hurt me. I didn't let them. Maybe this was just a sign that I'd let Finley too close, and I needed to put some distance between us. This was as good a time as any.

"Ashlee and I are both adults, Finley, and Manhattan Records doesn't have a policy against co-workers dating."

Not that Ashlee and I were *dating*, but that'd be way too much information to share.

"You're not her co-worker," he pointed out. "You're her boss."

"Trust me, she doesn't have any problem making her thoughts known. If she doesn't want to go with me to the party, she'll say so."

Finley stood, something almost sad passing over his face. "I just don't want things here imploding when you end things with her. I've seen too many of your former relationships go toxic. Just a couple hours ago, Roma—"

"Ashlee isn't Roma," I cut him off. "She's different."

"I have no doubt she is," Finley said. "But *you're* not."

I glared at his back as he left. He was wrong. And now I wanted to prove it.

THIRTY-SEVEN

ASHLEE

I MANAGED TO AVOID SEEING ANYONE FOR THE REST OF the day and slipped out of work without speaking more than two words. I still wanted to talk to Mr. Kordell and make certain that he understood I wasn't the woman he thought I was, the woman almost everyone here thought I was, but I'd have another opportunity tomorrow.

Except when I got to work, I had several emails I needed to respond to right away. Those took an hour, and by the time I finished, I wasn't alone at my desk anymore. Nate stood in front of me, expression unreadable. I tensed, waiting to see if I was going to be yelled at or just talked to about something work-related. I was leaning toward the latter. We were out in the open here, after all.

"What are you doing tonight?"

Dammit. That didn't sound like anything to do with work.

"Normal Friday stuff," I replied, keeping my tone crisp

and light. "Probably much different than what you have planned."

"Not at all," he said. "You're coming with me tonight."

I raised an eyebrow. There was that bossy tone of his. "I am?"

"We're going to a club. You'll like it."

When it came to sex, I was okay with him telling me what to do and what I'd like. He seemed to know how to play my body better than myself.

That didn't mean he could dictate what I did with my body when we weren't fucking or working. And since I didn't plan on us having sex again any time soon, he now only got to order me around at work.

Going to a club with him wasn't work.

"No, thank you," I said politely.

His lips pressed together into a thin line, but I didn't say anything else as I waited for him to respond to my answer.

"Haven't I made you come?" He stepped closer, dropping his voice so that only the two of us could hear. "I can make you come again tonight. This club, it's private, discreet. Its members can indulge in all sorts of...desires. Things we haven't done yet. Things I could teach to you, do to you."

My breath caught, and I was certain he heard it, but I kept staring at my computer screen, wishing he couldn't see the heat in my cheeks, wishing he didn't know that the color was only half from embarrassment, the other half desire.

"We won't need to worry about anyone knowing who we are. Many members and guests wear masks to protect their identities. Not that anyone would dare breathe a word about who we are. If anyone betrays the trust of the owners of Club

Privé, their membership is revoked, and depending on the severity of the crime, they could be blackballed from most other clubs."

"It doesn't matter," I said before he could go any further. If I didn't speak now, he might actually end up convincing me to go with him, and I didn't want that. Or, rather, I knew I *shouldn't* want it. "I'm not going with you."

He looked both surprised and annoyed, though he should have expected a refusal from me after the way he'd been behaving. Then again, I hadn't said no when he'd told me to get on the chair so he could fuck me.

"Why not?"

I gave him my most recent reason. "I spoke to your ex-girlfriend, Roma." When he stiffened, my suspicions about the truth of Roma's statement grew. "She told me to get in writing whatever you promised me because you'd go back on your word."

"She's jealous and angry because I dumped her."

That was a plausible reason, but I still needed to know if it was the truth. "She also said that you'd promised her things in exchange for sex."

He shrugged. "You know how the world works. Men want sex. Women want things. People always *want*. I don't see the problem with exchanging one thing for another. As long as it's all consensual."

"What she said is true then?" I told myself I shouldn't be disappointed, but a part of me was.

"You're not that naïve. Women look at me and see something they want. You can't tell me that there isn't something you can think of that I could give you."

I stared at him and took a slow breath to calm myself before speaking. I didn't want to assume anything. "Are you asking me if I had sex with you so you'd give me something in return?"

"It's natural to want to get something when you give something. What is it you want, Ashlee? Tell me, and I'll try to get it for you." He reached out, the touch of his fingertips ghosting down my arm. "Name it."

I jerked my arm back. "I don't want anything I haven't earned, and I don't mean by 'servicing' you."

Maybe my word choice offended him. Maybe it was guilt over the fact that he'd suggested I'd whored myself out to get something in return. Maybe he was just annoyed that I'd refused him.

Whatever the reason, he turned around and walked away without another word.

THIRTY-EIGHT

NATE

Hours later and I was still fuming. I'd invited her to come to Club Privé, and that's not something I did with everyone. Ashlee had no clue what it meant for me to want to take her there. It wasn't really about the place, but the fact that I'd tried to bring her more into my world, and she'd rejected it.

She'd rejected *me*.

After I'd had some dinner – most of which was made up of two glasses of my favorite scotch – I knew I wasn't going to stay home and brood. I needed to release some tension, and that meant getting laid.

I didn't owe Ashlee anything. We weren't in a relationship. We weren't even in an arrangement. We'd fucked, and I wanted to keep doing that, but she didn't seem to get how this worked. I told her what she was supposed to do, and then we were supposed to do it. Maybe she'd get a little snippy, and I'd have to spank her or punish her in other delicious ways.

But to have her flat-out refuse to join me, to act like I'd done something wrong? No. Too much drama involved in that.

My phone dinged with a message from Angus saying he was here. I pushed thoughts of Ashlee out of my head and made my way to the elevator. Just because she didn't want to go out to a club with me didn't mean I had to stay home. She had no expectation of monogamy. For all I knew, she was out with someone else right now.

"Dammit," I muttered under my breath.

Why couldn't she stay out of my head?

"Where to, Mr. Lexington?" Angus asked as soon as he got back into the driver's seat.

I'd told him he could call me Nate, but he always refused, saying it wasn't appropriate when he was working.

"Club Privé."

Tonight wasn't a special event at the club, but it was a Friday night with decent weather, which meant the place would be packed. I knew most of the regulars and had been with a handful of them. They were just fun. New ones could be that too. I wasn't going to be picky tonight. All I wanted was someone who could make me forget.

A MAN in an expensive suit walked by, a woman in a latex bodysuit following close behind. Her head was bowed, hands bound in front of her. Only her mouth, eyes, and part of her nose were visible, but the bodysuit conformed to every dip and curve, showing off the bars through each of her nipples and the hoops through her labia.

In the corner across from me sat one of the city's best defense attorneys getting his cock sucked by his wife. They'd been one of the club's regulars since it had re-opened with its new design and owners.

I'd been fascinated with this place since I first learned of it a couple years ago, and I often wished I could've been a part of the story of how it had come to be. I also wondered how different it would've been for me if I'd had a place like this back when I'd first been exploring the BDSM world. It had taken me a while to accept that just because I liked kink didn't mean I was some sort of pervert.

I emptied my glass, and before I could raise my hand to wave over the pretty waitress who'd served me my last one, she was there. When she smiled at me, her teeth flashed bright white against her rich brown skin. She was dressed in one of the club's more risqué uniforms, one that showed off plenty of that gorgeous flesh and signaled to patrons that she liked to play. No one here was paid to have sex, but any employees who wanted to schedule 'playtime' within their schedules were allowed.

The gleam in her ebony eyes told me she'd be up for whatever I might suggest, and the possibility appealed to me...but not enough to make me take her up on her offer. I already knew that if I went with her, I'd be picturing Ashlee, and I wasn't bastard enough to think of another woman during sex.

Three people walked by, their identical masks doing more than simply hiding their identity. Matching masks were one of the ways people made their exclusivity known without having to say a word. No one would approach a couple or group with a proposition if they had masks that said they were already with someone. Only a member of the couple or group could do the approaching as they would know their particular selection guidelines.

I'd been a part of a few groups and threesomes when I was in my early twenties, but it hadn't taken me long to realize that I preferred to be the one calling the shots in those situations. Joining an already existing couple or group didn't appeal to me. I wanted to be the primary focus, whether it was me and multiple women or if it was my submissive having sex with other men.

What would Ashlee think of sharing me with another woman? I sipped my drink and let my thoughts continue along that path. Would she refuse, and if so, what would her excuse be? Would she say that she wasn't interested in women sexually or would she say she didn't want me to be with another woman, even if she was there?

The possessiveness of that last one should have made me uncomfortable, but it didn't. Mostly because I understood it. I didn't want to share her with another man. Actually, I realized, I didn't want to share her with another woman either. Considering, talking, or even spinning a fantasy about those sorts of things didn't bring with it the same gut-churning sensation that came when I thought about another person touching her. I wasn't even sure I could have another person touch me when she was watching. I could imagine the hurt on her face, and it was enough to make me stop thinking about the subject altogether.

I tossed back the rest of what was in my glass. Between the drinks I'd had at home and the ones I'd consumed here, I was starting to get buzzed. Not drunk like I'd been the last time I'd been here. The staff at Club Privé were really good at keeping their patrons from getting too plastered, but I was good at hiding how much alcohol affected me, which was how I'd ended up at Ashlee's, drunk enough to say a whole lot of shit that I shouldn't have said. Shit that I didn't even completely remember.

I wasn't going to do that tonight.

Except the more I drank and watched everyone else, the more I wanted to see Ashlee.

A pretty blonde with a leather corset and collar doing a scene with a statuesque brunette wasn't enough to capture my attention for more than a few seconds. When a waitress in a barely-there mini skirt and a sheer bra walked past with a smile, I gave a polite nod but had no interest in asking her to play.

I kept seeing that long, henna red hair as it brushed against my thighs. Turquoise eyes darkened with lust, pupils wide. Porcelain skin flushed. Curves the perfect fit for my hands.

Dammit.

I set down my glass and stood. As much as I liked this place, this wasn't where I wanted to be.

I'd had Angus wait for me, even though I hadn't known when I'd be ready to go, and now I was glad that I had. In the time it took me to reach the front door, Angus had arrived. If he was surprised by the destination I gave him, he didn't show it. Merely nodded and started driving.

When I found myself standing in front of the same apartment door as I had less than a week ago, I had a moment of doubt. What if I'd read her wrong? What if she didn't want me the way I wanted her? What if, despite what she'd said to me in my office, she did want something from me and was only waiting for an opportunity like this to demand it?

I had to know.

I knocked, then realized I had no idea what time it was. If she was already asleep, I was going to feel like a complete idiot. I knocked a second time, telling myself that if she didn't answer this time, I'd leave and never talk—

The door opened.

"Nate?"

I didn't remember what she'd been wearing the other day, and the times I'd imagined seeing Ashlee in her pajamas, it'd been all silk and lace, the sort of lingerie every woman I'd ever been with would wear. She'd had fancy bras and panties on every time we'd fucked, so I'd assumed that would carry over to what she slept in. Not that I really knew what most women wore to sleep. Waking up next to one wasn't a common occurrence.

"What are you doing here?"

She had on a pair of hot pink boy shorts that just barely covered everything important and a simple gray t-shirt that said *Grr Power* in glaring pink. Her hair was in a ponytail, and her feet were bare.

"Nate?"

Her hand on my arm made me realize that she'd been talking to me the whole time I'd been staring at her pajamas. Maybe I was a little more drunk than I realized.

"Sorry, what were you saying?"

She crossed her arms, and the shift of her breasts made me wonder if she was wearing a bra underneath, distracting me yet again. Then she reached out and took my hand, pulling me into her apartment.

"It's past midnight, Nate. You can't keep standing in my hallway, knocking on my door and staring at me."

I grinned at her. "You invited me in."

She sighed. "You're drunk again."

I shook my head. "Not drunk. Just buzzed enough to act on what I want, no matter how stupid I know it is."

Ashlee walked around behind me and closed the door. "What you're saying is, you wanted to come see me, but couldn't do it until you were...buzzed?"

"Yes," I said, proud that there was something I could answer. "Exactly."

"Should I call for a cab, or do you want to sleep on my couch again?" Her voice was tight, and everything about her posture forbade me to come any closer.

Lucky for both of us that I wasn't much in the mood for behaving myself. Not unless she said her safe word.

"I don't want to sleep," I said, taking a step closer to her. "And I don't want a cab or a car."

Her head tipped back, reminding me once again of our height difference. "Nate, we've been down this road more than once. This isn't a good idea."

I put my hand on her waist, and she didn't pull away. "Maybe it's not, but that doesn't change what I want, and I know it's what you want too."

"Is it?" Her voice was soft.

"Tell me it's not." I brushed the back of my hand down her cheek, and when she leaned into my touch, everything in my world narrowed down to her and me. "Tell me that you don't want me to strip those clothes off you and fuck you so hard that you'll forget your name."

A shiver ran through her. "Nate, we can't–"

"Do you want me?"

She hesitated, then nodded. "I do."

That was all I needed to know. I pulled her tight against me, my arms wrapping around her as I lifted her off her feet. My mouth crashed into hers, and all the reasons this was a bad idea vanished. My senses flooded with her. Her taste, her scent. The sounds she made when my tongue swept between her lips.

Securing her with one arm, I reached up with the other, wrapping her hair around my fist. When I tugged on it, she gasped, head falling back until I could move my lips to her throat, kissing my way down the smooth column.

"Yes, please," she moaned, fingers digging into my shoulders.

"Are you going to be a good girl?" I asked. "Or am I going to have to spank you?"

She squirmed against me, and my cock pressed painfully against my zipper.

"Does that mean you want me to spank you?" I grabbed her ass, squeezing it. She made a squeaking sound, and I laughed. "All right then."

I carried her into her bedroom and dumped her onto the bed. She laughed and squealed as she bounced, the joyful sound making me wonder if I'd ever had a lover make sounds like that.

"Clothes off," I ordered. "Do you have any belts?"

Her eyes went wide. "Um, yes, one, I think. It'd be on the top shelf in my closet with the things I don't wear very often."

"I'm going to get some...supplies. When I come back, I want you naked, on your stomach, and your ass in the air."

THIRTY-NINE

ASHLEE

I TOSSED MY CLOTHES TOWARD THE HAMPER I KEPT NEAR the foot of my bed and rolled over onto my stomach. I had only the faintest idea of what was in store for me, but I was more than ready for it. I pressed my thighs together as I moved up onto my knees, the space between my legs throbbing.

"There you are, *le soleil*. Such a good girl."

I kept forgetting to look that phrase up. I had an idea of what it might mean, but I didn't want to think too much about what could be something as meaningless as any other overused endearment.

"This is going to hurt more than my hand did, but you'll enjoy it just as much."

I appreciated the honesty, but the way my stomach twisted at his words made me wonder if there was such a thing as *too* honest when it came to stuff like this. Then again, that might've been the point, I realized. The anticipation could be a part of it. Like when he'd blindfolded me. He'd told me what he was going to do to me, but I hadn't been able to see him. Every touch had been a surprise.

"Do you remember what you're supposed to say if you want to end things?"

I wasn't certain if I imagined the double meaning of his question, but either way, the answer was the same. "Beagle."

I didn't plan on saying it, but I appreciated the reminder that I had a way out if things got to be too much. I trusted him with sex; that hadn't changed. At times over the past week, I'd wondered if he knew my body better than I did.

"Close your eyes," he ordered. "You need to get out of your head, or this will just be pain. Focus past the pain to your other senses, the other sensations you feel."

I closed my eyes and nodded, clenching my fists in an attempt to relax the rest of my body. The sound of cheap leather cutting through the air registered a moment before it cracked against my ass, and I cried out as bright pain burst across my skin. He'd hit horizontal rather than vertical like I'd expected, and it scrambled my brain for a moment. For some reason, that made it easier for my mind to break the sensations into categories and prepare for what came next.

Neither of us counted out loud, and I stopped keeping track after three. My hands kept flexing, wanting to grab on to something, and the muscles in my legs shook as my ass burned. I wouldn't be able to come like this, but I couldn't deny the moan that came out as many times as a cry. Over and over that belt came down, a rhythmic cadence to each stroke until I started pushing my body back, almost eager for more. Then, he stopped as abruptly as he'd started.

"Rest for a moment," he said. He pressed his lips to the small of my back and gently lowered me to the bed, keeping me on my side to avoid friction on any extra-tender parts.

I opened my eyes but concentrated on breathing rather than looking around. We were far from done, and I wanted to stay in this headspace where things were warm and safe, even when there was confusion and pain. When I was like this, I didn't have to worry about anything. I had no pressure on my shoulders, no decisions to make, no obligations or expectations. Logically, I knew that I placed most of those on my own shoulders but getting rid of them wasn't as easy as most people would think. Having someone else take control of at least this aspect of my life was more appealing than I would've imagined.

"Roll onto your stomach and spread your legs."

I did as he said, anticipation stoking the embers inside me to full flames.

"I always keep a few condoms in my wallet," he said. "But lube isn't something I generally have on hand. You'll need to start keeping supplies here."

My mind spun on what that last statement could mean. Was that his way of saying that he wanted this thing between us to continue? It didn't sound like general advice, something to fill the silence, more like something specific he wanted me to—

Lube.

He chuckled. "Your entire body just tensed up." He put his hand on the small of my back. "Relax. I'm not going to fuck your ass tonight. Just play a bit."

I wasn't sure I liked the sound of that any better than anal sex, but I hadn't thought I'd enjoy being spanked either. I'd trust his judgment on what he thought I could handle and what I'd like. Still, my decision didn't keep me from gasping when a finger went down my crack, stopping only to apply a cool gel I couldn't quite identify.

"Vaseline works, but I prefer lube for anything more than a minor bit of playing."

How the hell did he sound like he was carrying on a completely normal conversation while doing what he was doing?

Any other questions I might've had disappeared when he touched my clit. A light touch, it felt more like he was trying to shift my attention, and I let him. He started with circles, using just enough friction to keep me in the headspace I'd gone to when he'd spanked me. Ripples of pleasure moved outward along my nerves, reminding me of how good he could make me feel.

Something unyielding rubbed over that ring of muscle, but before I could tense, he moved his finger from my clit to my pussy, sliding inside with ease. In and out, his finger moved until all of my focus was on that, and then he added a second finger. Twisting his fingers inside me, he made rapid circles over my clit with his thumb, and just as the sensations were going to be too much, he pressed whatever he had in his other hand against my anus. For a brief moment, nothing happened, and then my muscles gave way, and it slid inside.

I let out a moan, turning my head so that my face was to the mattress. Fingers and other things moved in tandem, sending a strange, pleasurable burn to mix with the more familiar electric sort of pleasure that came from his fingers.

The strokes came faster, less in rhythm, twists sending knuckles rubbing against my walls, thumb movements becoming more aggressive until I was writhing on the bed, not knowing if I wanted him to stop or if I needed more.

"Come for me, *le soliel*. I want to see you come like this, my fingers in your cunt and something in your ass."

I shuddered, the combination of his words and talented fingers bringing me to the peak. How did he always know what I needed? Now wasn't the time to try to figure it out. Thinking became impossible as I tipped over the edge, my blanket muffling the shout that would have woken far too many people

He pulled his fingers out but left the object still inside me. He ran his hand up my spine and pushed my hair back from my face.

"One day soon, I'm going to take your ass," he promised. "And eventually, I'll show you how good double penetration can feel. But not tonight."

I nodded to show that I understood, though a question floated into my head. Did he mean to share me? That wasn't something I wanted. But he'd said that would be in the future. Not something to bring up or worry about tonight.

He removed whatever it was he'd put in my ass and then moved off the bed for a moment. I heard him throwing something away, then turning on the sink – I assumed to wash his hands. He was back in seconds, already opening a condom wrapper.

"I owe you one of those hair chopstick things."

I frowned, not understanding. But when he spread my legs farther apart and settled between them, it clicked, and heat flooded my face. *That* was what he'd had in my ass. I didn't have the chance to dwell on it much because the heavy weight of his cock against the overly sensitive skin of my butt cheek made me flinch. He leaned down, pressing a kiss to the base of my spine before kissing his way up to a spot between my shoulder-blades.

As I relaxed, the tip of his cock notched against my entrance. He held himself above me as he snapped his hips forward, burying him inside me without any of the gentleness that he'd shown with his kisses. I cried out, back arching instinctively. His hand landed in the last place he'd kissed and held me down. If he hadn't paused, as if waiting for me to say something, I might've forgotten that I was the one who had the final say in what happened between us. That hesitation spoke volumes about the man above me, reinforcing the trust I had in him.

Neither one of us said a word for several long seconds, and then he grabbed my ponytail, yanking my head back. Bent at an awkward angle, I should have been turned off, but I wasn't. If anything, it added another element to the multitude of sensations coursing through me, a different sort of pain. My nipples chafed against my blanket as he drove into me with deep, fast strokes, sending me rocketing toward a second orgasm that promised to be even more powerful than the last.

His thumb ran down my crease, stopping at my still slick anus. Thicker than the chopstick, he had to apply more pressure, but when it popped inside, it was the last thing I needed to come. My mouth opened, but no sound came out, even though I heard the scream in my head. It was too much, too intense, but I never wanted it to stop.

At some point, I'd realize how dangerous this was, how easy it would be to lose myself in him, and in this.

But not tonight. Not now.

FORTY
NATE

I KEPT WAITING TO GET BORED. WE'D ONLY FUCKED A
few times, but that didn't matter. It was how things went with
me. If a first encounter was good and both of us agreed that
we wanted more, we discussed terms and went from there.
We could push our limits, delve into whatever depravities
appealed to us. Sometimes, we ventured into new territory
for one or both of us, but I'd never been with someone who
was new to *all* of it.

Not jumping straight to something extreme because it
might freak her out was new for me, but it shouldn't have
been a positive thing. It should have annoyed me, but instead,
it spoke to a part of my Dominant nature that hadn't really
been awake before. The part that made me truly want to take
care of my sub.

I'd done that in a way for other women, making sure they
had the time and care they needed to come out of their
subspace, but it was different with Ashlee. I trusted her to
speak up if she wanted to stop, but I also knew that she didn't

have the experience that I did, and she needed me to look out for her in ways that no one else ever had.

I was used to looking after myself. I was the stereotypical 'invisible' middle child with a 'perfect' older brother and the 'baby' younger brother. I loved my parents, but we weren't close. I did things my way, and when something went wrong, I took care of it myself. I'd never even thought about taking on someone else as a responsibility, but my subconscious, it seemed, had already accepted Ashlee.

She stirred next to me, and my arm tightened around her automatically. When we'd finished, she'd closed her eyes and fallen asleep. I doubted she'd be out for long, but I'd pushed her body in a way it wasn't used to, and it needed some time to recuperate. Honestly, I'd needed a couple minutes to recover myself. I'd come so hard I'd seen spots. Now, though, it was time to get cleaned up and go home.

I eased away from Ashlee and climbed out of bed, careful not to wake her. I went across the small hall to her bathroom and cleaned myself up, not bothering with a shower. I'd take one of those when I went home. At the moment, a washcloth and a sink would do the trick.

I didn't want to leave while she was sleeping, even though that had never bothered me before. I wasn't going to stay the night, but I'd give her a little more time to sleep. I was tempted to climb back in bed, wrap my arms around Ashlee, and enjoy having a few peaceful minutes. We never seemed to have peace. We were always either at odds or fucking, and there wasn't much in between.

Maybe that was why it felt weird to think about...cuddling.

I made my way into the kitchen, opening and closing the few cabinets as I went. I told myself I wasn't snooping; I was merely satisfying my curiosity. I supposed if Ashlee caught me, she'd make a distinction. Or maybe not. She surprised me more often than not.

A stack of papers sat on her desk, and I glanced at them as I reached for a picture frame that sat behind them. In it, a young Ashlee stood with a short, curvy woman with the same winning smile. I took it in for only a few seconds because it took that long for my brain to process what I'd seen sticking out from underneath the top paper.

I set the picture back down and pulled the newspaper clipping out so I could see the whole thing. I was mildly impressed that she actually read physical newspapers, but then I finished processing.

Four or five years ago, Finley and I had thrown a charity fundraiser where artists on our label played a concert where all the proceeds had gone to fund an LGBTQ safe house for anyone who'd been kicked out of their homes or was in danger because of who they were. It had been a rare event that both of us had attended, and the reporter who'd done the story had taken a picture of both of us. In the article itself, several things had been circled, and notes were jotted in the margins. Things like "co-founders," "internship," and "degrees needed for promotion."

What the fuck? Why did she have this? She hadn't been working for us when we did that fundraiser. I remembered her starting date from when I'd looked at her file.

"Looking for something?" Ashlee asked from behind me, even as I was researching for the folder marked *MR Research*, wondering what other types of research she'd been doing on me.

I turned around, clipping in hand. She stood a few feet away, her t-shirt and shorts back on. If I hadn't been holding incriminating evidence of...something, I might've been distracted by how completely fuckable she looked.

"Found something." I cut the distance between us in half. "You want to tell me what this is about?"

The muscles around her mouth tightened. "It's an article about some of the charity work Manhattan Records has done."

"An article from a paper that was printed before you came to work for us."

She crossed her arms. "I'm not sure what the problem is."

"I think you do," I said, my heart beating in my temples. "There are notes written in the margins."

"Spit it out." Her voice was hard, and I knew that whatever I said next would determine where things went from here.

I didn't care.

"You're stalking me. You found this article, saw that I was rich and decided this was how you were going to get money from me." The words tumbled out of me. "You've had this planned all along. Get hired at the label, meet me, fuck me–"

"Out." She walked past me to the door and opened it. "Get out."

"Gladly."

I didn't bother going back into the bedroom to get my shirt. My phone was in my pants, and that was all I needed. I texted Angus from the lobby and waited near the door.

She should have just told me what she wanted. I wouldn't have been hurt or surprised. Everyone wanted something. At least every other woman in my life had been honest about what they'd wanted from me. She didn't need to lie about it. And not just one lie either. She'd been lying from moment one.

I thanked Angus when I got into the car but didn't say anything else, my thoughts still on the way people had always used me.

In high school and college, girls had wanted to be with the good-looking, popular guy. In college, I'd had those things and a bright future. Then, just a few months after graduation, the record label that I'd started suddenly took a downturn. It'd been while I was out trying to drum up financial support to get me through the unexpected crisis when I met Isti Mollen.

In her mid-forties, Isti had lots of money and certain... tastes. It'd been an open secret – and still was – that Isti found young men who needed money and offered them 'financial assistance' in exchange for sex and companionship. I'd been no different.

I'd been working as a bartender at a high-end restaurant not far from where Manhattan Records stood today, trying to talk up patrons who looked like they might have money to spend. She came in for a business dinner and stopped at the bar afterward. By the time my shift was done, she'd promised me an investment of a couple thousand dollars if I spent the night with her.

Age had never really mattered to me, and I'd figured if I'd already planned on finding someone to fuck later, I might as well get paid for it. So I'd done it. And then she'd offered to make it a regular thing. She'd keep my record label going if I became her boy-toy.

My only other option at the time had been to go back home and admit I'd failed. Needless to say, I'd taken her up on her offer. I'd moved in with her, had my own room where I'd slept after she'd finished with me each night. The one thing I hadn't counted on was that Isti had been into the BDSM, heavy on the S. She was a sadist, and enough of one for me to learn that I wasn't a masochist. It hadn't been too bad at first, but she'd gotten worse the longer we'd been together, and when things had inevitably reached a certain point, I'd gone elsewhere to meet my own needs.

I'd been an idiot. Fucked Isti's maid at the house. She'd caught us, fired the maid and kicked me out. I'd been twenty-three and out on my ass. I'd refused to go to my parents' place, not wanting to have to explain anything to them, so I'd been on the street.

I thanked Angus when he opened my door and told him I wouldn't need him this weekend. I didn't plan on doing anything but drinking and not leaving my penthouse. This second blow up with Ashlee had hit me harder than anything else had in a long time. I didn't think I'd felt this bad since Isti had kicked me out.

As I took the elevator up to my floor, I let myself remember how that part of my story had played out.

I'd been out on the street for nearly three months, working at different clubs and bars as extra security, paid in cash, when this guy had found me. Finley Kordell. He'd been the only person I'd ever known who'd wanted to help me without asking for something in return. Sure, he'd become my partner when we'd started Manhattan Records, but it'd been an equal fifty-fifty split, and there'd been no 'extras' that I'd owed him. Our history was why he was the only person I truly trusted.

What had happened today had been the reminder I'd needed to not let anyone else close.

FORTY-ONE

ASHLEE

I'D SPENT ALL WEEKEND TRYING TO WRAP MY HEAD around what'd happened Friday night. It wasn't that I didn't *understand* but rather that I still couldn't believe that it'd happened. Sure, when I'd invited Nate inside, a part of me had known he'd initiate sex and that was my own fault. No matter how angry I'd been at him or how many times I'd told myself that I was through, that deep physical attraction hadn't gone away.

It had left the moment I'd told him to leave.

Objectively, he hadn't become less good-looking, but the thought of him produced more negative emotions than it did positive. One of those negative emotions was directed more at me than at him, though.

Guilt.

Not for having sex with him, but rather guilt over not having been truthful regarding my research into Manhattan Records prior to applying for the internship. I hadn't been stalking Nate, no matter what he thought, but I had known more about the company than I'd let on. Omitting that information years ago might not have been the most honest thing to do, but it hardly had any bearing on my relationship with Nate. Or my non-relationship. Or however we would have labeled it if things hadn't completely blown apart. The private parts of my personal life didn't need full disclosure just because he thought they did.

These were the sorts of things I'd had circling my mind almost non-stop since I'd kicked him out. Little voices telling me how I'd done the right thing and equally loud voices saying that he'd been right to be suspicious of me. That was the biggest problem. I could understand why he'd gotten upset. I told myself that if he'd simply asked questions, then he could've taken the higher moral ground, but he'd lost his temper and started accusing me of things.

I wasn't going to put up with that, no matter what my own wrongs had been.

The last time I'd gotten this angry at him for being an asshole, he'd pursued me at work. If he tried the same thing this time, I needed to have a plan in place. Unfortunately, by the time I finally managed to fall asleep, I still hadn't decided the best way to handle the situation.

I arrived early enough to avoid the main morning rush and went straight to my desk, the day's plan firmly in place. Once I checked through my email, I'd have an idea of any pressing matters I needed to discuss with Mr. Hancock when he got in. Once I finished talking to him, I'd go to Ms. Lamas to see what she needed done. Unless she called me in first.

I was becoming quite adept at juggling the two schedules.

Since they hadn't yet found another assistant to take Flora's place, I was still doing twice the work. I appreciated the distraction as well as the excuse to avoid people, but it didn't make the work any less involved.

If I decided I needed to leave Manhattan Records, I wanted to be sure I could get good recommendations from both Mr. Hancock and Ms. Lamas, and doing quality work was the best way to do that. I wondered if I should give them a heads up that I was considering going somewhere else so they could up the hunt for an assistant. I wouldn't feel right, leaving them in the lurch.

I couldn't believe I was seriously thinking about quitting.

Before I'd gotten involved with Nate, I'd never considered leaving. I didn't have some overwhelming desire for a career in the record business, but I didn't have something else I wanted to do either. Why would I throw away the years I'd put into something that could be a career because I'd made a stupid decision? Okay, I'd made the decision more than once, but it'd really been the same decision...right?

It wasn't going to be an issue, I reminded myself. Because I was done with Nate. Forever. No more going to his penthouse or his office or opening the door when he showed up drunk. No more sex.

Ever.

I'd done just fine without it, and no matter how good it was, it wasn't worth all the shit that came with it.

I could focus all my energy on work. That'd be good. Build a great portfolio to help me find a job when I left here. There was a goal I could get behind.

"Miss Webb."

I looked up to see Mr. Hancock standing in front of my desk. The somber expression on his face made my stomach flip. Something was wrong.

"Yes, Mr. Hancock?" I rubbed my palms dry on my pants and tried not to look like my heart was in my throat.

"Mr. Lexington would like to see you in his office."

Dammit. I didn't want to go. Every time I went, I ended up doing something I regretted. But he'd called Mr. Hancock instead of calling me directly. That had to mean something, right? That he wanted things to be professional.

Still, I couldn't help but try to put it off. "Right now?"

"Yes." Mr. Hancock started to walk away, but then he turned back. "Is everything all right, Miss Webb?"

I smiled and nodded, hoping my expression didn't look as fake as it felt. "Everything's fine."

The lift of his eyebrows told me he didn't believe me, but he didn't call me out on it. As he walked away, I stood and made my way down the familiar hallway to Nate's office. I was tempted to finally knock on Mr. Kordell's door, talk to him before I handled whatever it was Nate wanted. I couldn't do it, though, not if things between Nate and I were still...unfinished.

I knocked on his door.

"Come in." The words were flat.

When I walked into his office, Nate was still sitting behind his desk. He raised his head, but his eyes focused somewhere over my shoulder rather than meeting my gaze. His face was a mask of nothing. No anger. No guilt. Nothing.

"Mr. Hancock said you wanted to see me?" I moved toward the chair he'd had me kneel on last week.

"Don't bother to sit."

I stopped, wondering what he would tell me to do next and how I'd refuse him.

"This isn't going to take long," he continued. "You're fired."

FORTY-TWO

NATE

WHEN SHE CAME INTO MY OFFICE, THAT LONG, THICK hair spilling down her back and shadows under those beautiful eyes of hers, I almost asked her to close the door. I almost gave in to the temptation that was Ashlee Webb. I'd never wanted to do that before. When I was done with a woman, it was because I had no interest left in her, which meant there was nothing for me to be tempted by.

Ending things with Ashlee shouldn't have been different, no matter what the circumstances had been that had brought us here. She betrayed me. Lied to me. At least the women like Roma had been honest about being selfish. They'd told me what they wanted, and I'd told them what I wanted. Straightforward. No hiding secrets or pretending.

I'd known from the start that Ashlee was different, but I'd never imagined it meant she would be the one to hurt me.

No. No one hurt me. I'd just had an important reminder of where I stood.

I used that knowledge like a shield as I spoke, telling her

not to bother to sit down. I needed to make this fast, like ripping off a bandage. Once I told her that she was fired, I wouldn't need to worry about how tempted I was or wasn't. Terminating her employment would end things forever. It would be blurring the line between personal and professional in a way that neither of us could take back.

"You're fired."

The blood drained from her face, then rushed back, leaving her fair skin mottled. Even from this distance, I could see her lips tremble, and I knew I'd hurt her. A part of me was glad, that she'd been hurt as much as I had been when I'd found that clipping.

I waited for her to say something. Anything. Yell at me. Scream. Tell me that I was an asshole. Tell me I couldn't do this because I didn't have cause. Threaten to go to HR and tell them that we'd been fucking for the last couple weeks. That I'd fucked her here in my office.

She wasn't a dramatic person, but she wasn't a shirking violet either. She had no problem telling me when I was out of line.

Except...this time she didn't say a word. She simply turned around and walked back out the door.

I watched her go and ignored the twinge I felt when she disappeared. Now, things could get back to normal. Women were for fucking and forgetting. Work was more important than anything else.

It was only mid-morning, but I was ready for a drink.

I promised myself two fingers of my best Scotch with lunch and then turned my attention to my email. A few needed personal responses, so I tackled them first, reading through each message a couple times to ensure that I understood what was being asked. Then I took extra time to compose my responses, far more time than I'd ever spent writing an email before. My correspondence was generally succinct and to the point. That was the same, but it took me longer to put things together. I could've lied to myself about wanting things to be perfect, but I knew it was because laser focus on words kept me from going after Ashlee.

I didn't chase women. Especially not women who didn't want anything to do with me.

"You look hard at work."

Finley shut the office door behind him and came over to sit across from me. If he didn't start smiling again, I was going to get a complex. I was supposed to be the brooding one.

"Just taking care of my email from over the weekend," I said.

"You expect me to believe that you went the entire weekend without checking your work email?"

I glared at him. "Why are you here? I know you didn't come here to criticize my work habits."

"I didn't," he admitted. "I actually came to see you because I was...concerned."

I sighed and turned away from my computer to fully face him. "Spit it out, Finley. I have work to do."

"I'm sure you do." He crossed his legs, resting his ankle on his opposite knee. "Lots of work, like upsetting employees so much that they cry at their desk?"

I gritted my teeth. Of course he was here about Ashlee. Did everyone's fucking life revolve around her?

"A lot of people cry when they get fired."

Surprise registered first on Finley's face, quickly followed by disbelief, and then confusion. "You fired Ashlee Webb?"

There was something else there too.

"Yes." I let my annoyance bleed through. "I'm writing up her termination report right now. I'll email it to you when I'm done." I paused, but Finley seemed to be waiting for me to say something more. "Did you need something else? Because I have paperwork to finish."

He leaned forward, resting his elbows on his knees, and I was suddenly reminded that he was now a year closer to fifty than he was to forty. He was such a positive, upbeat guy that I sometimes forgot that his life hadn't always been easy either.

"Nate, there are some questions I'm going to ask you, and I want you to think before you answer them."

I turned away from my computer. "What the hell are you yammering on about?"

"Did you just fire the young female employee you recently admitted to having a sexual relationship with?"

Fuck. When he put it like that, I could understand why he was acting so weird about it.

I thought through my answer while Finley waited, knowing he meant it when he said he wanted me to take my time before I answered. This wasn't two friends talking. We were business partners, and I had to approach his question the same way he was coming at things.

"The relationship – if it can be called that – between Miss Webb and myself ended with the discovery of information that also led to her termination."

Finley closed his eyes. "Am I understanding correctly

that you continued seeing Miss Webb *after* I told you to stay away from her? After I told *her* to stay away from you?"

For the first time in a long time, I was...embarrassed. Ashamed. I couldn't meet his eyes. "I did. We did."

"Dammit, Nate." He sighed. "Please tell me that you at least have proof of her stealing something or embezzling or something concrete and absolutely actionable."

"I still need to go through her work history," I lied.

Finley wasn't fooled for a minute. "No, you don't. You know as well as I do that she's never gotten so much as a reprimand. She's never been late. Never asked to leave early. Since she came to work for us, she's only taken one day off."

My stomach twisted with every word he said. He was right, and we both knew it. Her work record was exemplary. It still didn't make up for what I'd found.

"You don't understand," I said. "The reason I fired her isn't in her work file."

He rubbed his forehead, his eyes still closed. "If she goes to HR, you'll be in some serious shit."

"I was at her place Friday night–"

"I don't want to hear–"

"You need to hear it," I interrupted and then kept going, "I found a newspaper clipping of the two of us from before she started working for us. She'd written notes on it."

Finally, he raised his head. "Are you telling me that you fired her because she had an article about Manhattan Records at her place?"

"She lied about why she was here," I said, knowing how defensive I sounded. "She found this article, studied it, came here and seduced me–"

Finley's laugh cut off the rest of what I planned to say. It was a deep, rich laugh, and normally, I would've had to laugh with him because it was impossible *not* to laugh. But there wasn't anything *normal* about this moment.

"I've known you for a decade," he said, "and I've never seen a woman seduce *you*. There's no way that meek little thing was the first."

I scowled at him. "It doesn't change the fact that she's been lying to us and she came here to get something from us."

"What?" he asked. "What did she ask for?"

"Well...nothing, yet. I fired her before she could."

Finley's eyes finally met mine. "I really hope you know what you're doing, Nate. Because if you're off about this at all, she could have a wrongful termination suit and a sexual harassment suit." He stood. "We could lose everything."

FORTY-THREE

ASHLEE

I CONSIDERED GOING STRAIGHT TO MY DESK, BUT A FEW stray tears had slipped out unintentionally as I'd left Nate's office, so I ducked into the restroom that was thankfully between the two. I didn't stay long in there, just enough to wipe my eyes and blow my nose. I didn't need to look good, only presentable, and only long enough to get my things together.

I doubted that anyone had heard about my dismissal since it'd happened less than five minutes ago, which meant I needed to leave as quickly and quietly as possible or I'd be right in the middle of it when things exploded. And they would explode. Of that I had no doubt. People had been talking about me too much too recently for me to hope no one would notice what was going on.

At least I wouldn't have to be here to hear all of the shit people would be saying about me until something more exciting came along.

I hadn't expected to be going home for good today, which meant I didn't have a box or big bag, but I had little of my own here. Honestly, I hadn't had the time to get used to having a desk of my own. As an intern and a runner, I'd had a small locker in the breakroom where I'd kept my meager possessions. When I'd been given a desk, I'd simply moved my purse to the desk drawer. It hadn't been until Flora had commented about my lack of personal items that I'd brought some things from home.

A picture of my mother and me, taken after she'd gotten her first all-clear from the cancer that had almost made me an orphan. Well, *almost* an orphan. Next to the photo was a short line of little mementos that Mom and I had gotten each time she'd had another test saying she was in remission. We hadn't been able to go on vacations, but we'd always done something special, even if it was going to a movie or seeing an exhibit at a museum.

I half-expected Mr. Hancock or Ms. Lamas to come talk to me, find out what was happening. A part of me even thought they might come to the rescue, tell me that they'd speak to Nate, that I was too good of an employee to lose, especially since they hadn't replaced Flora yet.

But no one came.

It took me only a few minutes to put my things in my purse and double-check that I hadn't forgotten anything. I heard the low murmur of voices as I walked past the others on my way to the elevator, but I didn't feel anyone looking at me. I hoped that meant I still had time.

I was a little surprised that Nate hadn't made security escort me out, especially since it seemed like he had serious trust issues. Granted, he'd been right that I hadn't been entirely forthcoming about my reasons for choosing to work at Manhattan Records, but I hadn't done any of the other things he'd accused me of. Whatever the reason, though, I was grateful for the chance to leave without glaring fanfare.

I considered taking a cab home, but then I remembered that I no longer had income and should probably save my money. I couldn't bring myself to walk, though. Not today. Not even though it was turning out to be a truly beautiful spring day. I didn't think my legs would hold me the whole way home. They barely got me onto the subway.

I clutched my purse on my lap and watched for my stop, repeating the information over and over, as if I was some first-time New Yorker who had to worry about getting lost. As if I hadn't made my way from home to school to doctor appointments and chemotherapy when I was still in school. Losing a job shouldn't have struck me this hard, especially not a job I hadn't really wanted to begin with.

To my relief, I got home without incident and without crying, both of which had been real possibilities, but as soon as the door to my apartment closed behind me, I stopped holding them back. Within seconds, I could barely see. Blindly, I stumbled to the couch, my fingers fumbling as I dug my phone from my purse. There was only one person I wanted to talk to right now.

She answered on the second ring. "Ashlee?"

"Mom." I swallowed a sob. It was one thing to call her upset, and it was something else entirely to lose it on the phone. I couldn't do that to her.

"What's wrong?"

The story spilled out of me, and by the time I was done, my nose was stuffed, my throat sore, and my eyes felt like I'd rubbed sand in them...but I felt better. Sort of.

"Are you going to call that son of a bitch who doesn't deserve you?"

Leave it to my mother to say exactly what I needed to hear even when she was making sure I wasn't going to do something inanely stupid. Well, *more* inanely stupid than what I'd already done.

"No, Mom," I assured her. "I won't call him. I plan on never seeing him again, and hopefully never even hearing his name again."

"You're an amazing woman, Ashlee." Mom's voice was soft. "Don't let some bastard make you feel like you're anything but that."

I smiled, even though she couldn't see me. "Thanks."

"Let's play our game. What can we do now?"

Those four words soothed me the same way they always had. We'd come up with the game when I was a kid. When something bad happened, we'd ask what we could do now that this event had turned our lives upside-down. Like when Mom first got her cancer diagnosis, we'd said that we could go on a cross-country trip, fly to the moon, search for the lost city of Atlantis, and then we'd decided that taking a trip to the zoo would be our little detour from reality.

I went first. "Well, I could go back to college and get a degree in veterinary medicine so I could deal with actual dogs."

She laughed. "You could come visit me, and we could have a tea party like we used to when you were younger."

"I never played tea party," I reminded her.

"That's right," she said. "You preferred playing Congress with your stuffed animals. Bored the hell out of me."

"That's what you get for raising me on CSPAN."

"Touché."

"Can we go back to the game?" I asked, needing the distraction.

"We could go on vacation."

I paused, "That sounds like a good idea. Some time away to clear my head. You could use it too. It's not like we ever really went on vacation before. Something was always in the way."

"All right. Vacation then. Where are we going?"

That was step two to our game. "Paris."

"The moon," she countered.

"Miami."

"Virginia Beach."

"That could be doable," I said. "And since I'm newly unemployed, I can be ready to go in twenty minutes and have no specific time I need to be back."

"Great! I'll call you before I leave. Pack as much as you can."

Mom ended the call before I could agree, and that was when I realized that she was actually serious about us going on a vacation. I wasn't normally this spontaneous, but I was starting to think that my normal way of doing things wasn't working for me, so maybe it was time for me to try something new.

Like suddenly joining my mom on a trip to Virginia

Beach to get away from my asshole boss who'd fucked me and then fired me without letting me defend myself.

I'd earned this vacation.

FORTY-FOUR

NATE

"WHAT DO YOU WANT?" I BARKED WITHOUT TAKING MY eyes off my computer screen.

How the fuck was I supposed to get any work done if people kept interrupting me?

"An assistant or two would be nice."

Stu's mild voice from the doorway almost made me regret snapping at him, but his comment buried any hint of guilt I felt.

"Considering how the last two assistants were fired, I think we need to take a little more time vetting our people." I kept my tone even but still didn't look at him. "Talk to Carole in HR." Silence for a moment, but I could feel his eyes on me. "Is there something else, Stu?"

"Are you okay?"

"I'm working, and apparently, I'm the only one." I clicked send and finally turned toward him. "Believe it or not, being the CEO doesn't mean I get to sit on my ass all day and screw around."

"Can I speak frankly?"

I turned back to my computer screen. "No."

When I didn't hear anything for half a minute, I risked a glance at the doorway and saw that Stu was gone. The way my office was set up, I couldn't see down the hall, but I doubted anyone else was coming. I'd spent Monday snapping at anyone who spoke to me, and a couple people who'd only looked my way. Yesterday, no one had talked to me at all, which should have made me grateful, but instead just pissed me off even more. Nothing anyone did would be the right thing.

I pulled up the email I'd sent to Stu and Suzie on Monday, letting them know that they would need to borrow runners or interns from other departments to do various tasks until a new assistant or assistants could be hired. I felt a minor twinge of guilt that I hadn't told them about Ashlee face-to-face, but as I'd done when I first decided to handle the situation this way, I reminded myself that if they hadn't hired Flora and Ashlee in the first place, none of this would've happened. Technically, they hadn't hired either of the women for the company, but they had been the ones who'd selected them both for their assistant positions.

While I was brooding for the hundredth time, a new email popped up. I saw the subject line first – "Ashlee Webb" – and my heart gave a funny leap. Then I saw the email address it'd come from and scowled. Stu. He couldn't have just talked to me like a man about the reasons why I'd fired Ashlee? All I'd told him and Suzie was that I'd found a couple discrepancies in her original application. Neither one of them had asked for details so I'd assumed the subject was closed.

I was tempted to trash the email without reading it, but it was a business document, and I needed to maintain at least some semblance of professionalism. Once I opened the email, I was glad I had. It wasn't about Ashlee's termination, at least not directly. It was, however, about a problem that we had because she'd been fired without warning.

On Monday, she'd left the building immediately after gathering her personal items from her desk. I'd had security watching even though I hadn't asked them to escort her out. Almost immediately after she'd left, I'd had IT wipe her computer and HR deactivate her accounts. It'd been a clean break all the way across. No second-guessing, no dragging out things.

I hadn't considered any negative repercussions from that until right now.

Stu's email was professional and polite, but I knew him well enough to know that he wasn't happy with me at the moment.

Mr. Lexington,

It has come to the attention of the A&R department that access to all of Ashlee Webb's systems has been cut off, and her computer has been wiped clean. After two days of searching for hard copies and speaking to IT about retrieving data files, we regret to inform you that two of our upcoming projects must be started over from scratch as Miss Webb had been in possession of that information when her position was termi-nated. Several other projects have lost work as well.

Due to the company's policy on electronic copies versus

hard copies as well as recent concern regarding leaks to the media, we had instructed Miss Webb to keep everything on her desktop for the time being. We attempted to contact Miss Webb to inquire if she had a thumb drive, notes, or anything else we could use to reconstruct at least some of what had been lost. Unfortunately, we have been unable to reach her.

Below are the affected projects as well as an estimate of how much time it will take to reconstruct Miss Webb's work without full-time assistants.

I stopped reading before I got to the list. Fuck! I slapped my hand against the top of my desk, and the only thing I got out of it was a stinging palm.

Firing Ashlee should have meant that I didn't have to deal with her anymore, but it appeared that my haste to get everything to do with her expunged from the company, I'd inadvertently led to her absence being more disruptive than her presence. Maybe I should have talked to Stu and Suzie before I'd fired Ashlee. That way, they could have told me that she had work they needed to access before IT came in.

I wanted to blame them for letting her keep her work entirely on one computer, but what Stu had said was correct. I'd wanted to make us a paperless company, and we had recently had some security issues with things on our servers. Since Ashlee worked for A&R, a leak about perks we were giving to various artists could start in-fighting over some of the differences, or it could ruin an event in numerous ways, including sabotage or paparazzi showing up.

Still, I couldn't believe that Ashlee was irresponsible enough to have only one copy of the work she'd done. Her having a thumb drive back-up made the most sense because, no matter what I thought of Ashlee's deceit, she had always worked hard and produced quality work. I didn't know why she hadn't responded to Stu or Suzie, unless she thought they were a part of her termination. Regardless of the reasons, we needed that information back.

I hated to even think it, but the fact that she'd taken the back-up with her when she left made me wonder if she'd been playing a long game to scam Manhattan Records. When I fired her, I'd cut her off from whatever she was trying to steal so she'd taken the only thing she could manage to smuggle out.

If that was the case, I would need to get the police involved. It was, however, possible that she'd had the thumb drive in her purse and had forgotten about it. I hoped that was what'd happened. Either way, I needed to reach out. I could have asked Finley to go since she'd most likely be more receptive to him than to me, but it had been my fault we'd lost that information in the first place. No matter how justified her termination was, the things I'd rushed through had caused this problem, and I needed to fix it.

I didn't bother calling. If she wouldn't pick up for Stu or Suzie, she definitely wouldn't for me. I'd have to go to her place. My gut churned at the thought of seeing her again, but I couldn't tell if it was excitement or dread. By the time I stood outside her door, knocking for the third time, whatever that emotion had been had turned into frustration that was rapidly becoming anger.

"She's not there."

I turned to see the door across the hall cracked open just

enough for me to see a lined, tanned face and white corkscrew curls.

"Ashlee Webb?" I asked as I turned toward the neighbor. I gave her my most charming smile, even though I wasn't feeling it. "She's not here?"

"No." The elderly woman looked me up and down. "Who are you?"

"I'm her boss," I replied promptly. It was the simplest explanation. "Do you know when she'll be back?"

"No." Her eyes narrowed. "If you're her boss, why are you at her apartment?"

"She has something I need." Shit. I hurried to clarify. "Some information at work was wiped from her computer, and we can't find her back-up. I just need to talk to her."

"There's this new-fangled invention called a phone," the woman said.

I bit back the curse hovering behind my lips. "She's not picking up."

"She's not picking up any of her calls, or just the ones from you? I saw you coming in and out of her apartment. You were drunk at least one of those times. I've seen it enough times to know, haven't I? I look out for Ashlee. She's a good girl."

I wasn't dumb enough to argue that point. "Mrs..."

"Posner."

"Mrs. Posner, I promise you that I don't intend to harm Ashlee. I just need to talk to her. Do you know where she is? Did she get another job?"

"Thought you said you were her boss."

"I was. I mean...dammit." I sighed and ran a hand down my face.

Mrs. Posner unlatched her door and opened it. "Come on in. If I like what you tell me, I may give you what you want."

Something bloomed in my chest. Hope, I realized. An emotion I'd have to consider later. "So, you do know where she is?"

"I do."

"Then what do you want me to tell you?"

She gave me a hard look and then nodded as if she'd come to some sort of decision. "Come in and find out."

FORTY-FIVE

ASHLEE

I'd never been to Virginia Beach before. It was nice, especially since Mom and I had gotten here before the inevitable flood of college kids, eager to spend their spring break on a beach. We'd driven here on Monday, not arriving until late at night, but I'd been glad that we hadn't waited. Mom hadn't pushed me for more about what had happened, instead sticking with more mundane topics, the sorts of things that we'd always talked about over lunch or the occasional glass of wine.

Yesterday, it'd been cloudy and a bit chilly, so we'd gone shopping. Mostly window shopping since we'd splurged on a nice hotel, but I'd picked up a couple things as souvenirs. Today, the sun was bright, the sky cloudless, making it warmer than I'd expected and just the right temperature to wear my new two-piece and matching sarong. Everything was absolutely perfect for sitting on the hotel's private beach and reading.

If I hadn't been so miserable, I might've enjoyed it. I *should* have enjoyed it. I'd always wanted to go to the beach and having a few days for uninterrupted reading was always good. And I never said no to spending time with my mother. One of the many things my mom's cancer had taught me was to not take any second with her for granted. Not the way Mona Wadsworth had.

I didn't like thinking about my mom's former lover, and most of the time, it was easy not to, but when something upsetting happened, I found her haunting my thoughts. For all I knew, haunting was all she could do now. I hadn't heard from her in a decade, and I'd never had the desire to find her, alive or dead.

For thirteen years, Mona had been my second mom, but I'd always called her by her first name. The day she'd left, like most kids in that situation, I'd wondered if it was my fault. As days had passed and she'd never called or come to see me, I'd gotten more and more depressed, thinking I'd done something that made her hate me.

Finally, Mom told me that Mona had lied to her about wanting a kid, that all those years Mona had given excuses for this thing and that one, that's all they'd been. Excuses. Mona hadn't wanted to come to my choir concerts or swim meets because she hadn't wanted a kid and the responsibilities that came along with one.

I pushed thoughts of Mona out of my mind, and for a few minutes, I was able to lose myself in the book I'd brought with me. Mom was reading, too, a magazine on her tablet. I wasn't sure what it was, but she was using one of those special pens to make notes, so she was probably working on something for one professor or another. The part-time researcher position her former advisor at NYU had made for her years ago was now a full-time job.

Sometimes, I wondered if her love for history had grown because she wanted to find family. Not necessarily anyone living, but family who were worth something. Even though she'd never come out and said it, we both knew that her immediate biological family wasn't worth shit. Delving into her own history, she'd found suffragettes and abolitionists, one of Broadway's first costume designers, and a record-holding triathlete. Those were my ancestors, too, and I was proud of that.

I was proud of her.

I knew that, sometimes, she felt like she'd failed me, that she wasn't a good mother because we only had each other. I'd told her more than once that I'd rather have one good family member than a huge family of assholes. We'd both talked that way a lot after Mona had left. Mom hadn't dated anyone since.

One thing we never spoke of, though, was my father. I never brought it up because I knew it would hurt her if she thought I felt slighted for not knowing him. She'd never lied to me about how I'd come to be. How, instead of asking a male friend who might have contested custody at some point, she and Mona had decided on an anonymous sperm donor. After Mona left, I'd been old enough to figure out that Mom had been the one to make that decision on her own.

"You're doing it again."

Mom's voice drew my attention, and when I looked at her, she smiled.

"What am I doing?" I asked.

"You're thinking about him."

I shook my head, glad I could answer truthfully. "I'm not. I promise."

She reached out and squeezed my hand. "Well, you're thinking about something far too hard."

She gave me a searching look, and I prayed that she couldn't see what I was keeping from her.

"You're thinking about Mona." To anyone else, Mom's voice would've sounded the same as it had a minute ago, but I knew her, and because of that, I saw the lines at the corners of her eyes tighten and heard the minute tremble in those words.

I shrugged. "Not exactly. I was just thinking about family." She winced, and it was my turn to squeeze her hand. "I was thinking how you and I don't need anyone else. We're all the family we need."

We sat in silence for a moment, letting that truth hang in the air between us, then we each turned back to what we'd been reading. I wasn't sure if she was concentrating better than I was, but I'd pretend as long as she did. Sometimes, the best way to relax was just to sit and not think about anything at all. I'd never been much good at doing that, but today might be an exception.

"How's your book?"

I froze, my mind telling me that I couldn't possibly have heard the voice I thought I heard, but the adrenaline that dumped into my veins the moment he spoke was all I truly needed.

I raised my head slowly, as if the speed made a difference to what I would see, *who* I would see.

"Nate."

FORTY-SIX

NATE

I'd never realized how helpful nosy neighbors could be until I sat down for coffee and cookies with Mrs. Posner. She'd nearly talked my ear off, but I'd gotten the information I'd needed. Ashlee was with her mom in Virginia Beach.

I'd also learned some information that I hadn't been after, but I'd paid attention to it all the same.

Ashlee's mother, Roberta Webb, had raised Ashlee on her own. As far as Mrs. Posner knew, Roberta didn't date, and there'd been no mention of any sort of father. Ashlee dated some, but no man had stayed overnight. I'd already known that.

While Mrs. Posner had been talking, I'd managed to surreptitiously get a private jet ready and waiting. I'd considered going straight from the apartment to the airport, but I needed clothes. I didn't know how long I'd be staying in Virginia Beach, or how long it would take me to find Ashlee once I was there. I didn't want to waste time by having to buy clothes.

The flight landed late, but I was tempted to start searching right away. However, Ashlee was with her mom. I had a feeling that waking up her mom in the middle of the night because I was impatient wouldn't be the best way to start an already rocky relationship. I couldn't sleep, though, so I spent the time making contact with every hotel, calling in favors, and promising a few of my own. It still took me until after noon to find them.

The guy at the check-in desk took fifty bucks and directed me to the beach. As I walked the direction he'd pointed, I reminded myself that I was just here to get the information I needed to get A&R back on track. Nothing else.

I came up behind the two women and took a moment to gather myself before stepping around and saying the first thing that popped into my head.

"How's your book?"

It took her a moment to look at me, and when she did, she said my name.

"Wait, Nate? As in the Nate you told me about?" The white-haired woman next to her sat up straight. Her hair might've been white, but her face was still young, and the resemblance between her and Ashlee left no doubt as to her identity.

"What are you doing here?" Ashlee nearly stumbled getting to her feet, her book falling to the sand. "And how the hell did you find me?"

I had a moment to register how absolutely fuckable she looked in a bikini that matched her eyes and showed off all of her curves in a way that made me want to forget why I'd come here in the first place. My voice was rougher than I intended as I answered her first question and ignored the second. "You left with Manhattan Records proprietary information."

She blinked at me, as if she didn't understand what I'd just said. "I did what?"

"There were several projects you were working on that have fallen apart since you...left." I clasped my hands behind my back, unable to stop from fidgeting with my fingers. I hated that I felt so rattled.

"If you remember correctly, I didn't leave voluntarily," she countered, her face flushed with anger.

"I need that information so Stu and Suzie can complete the projects in a timely manner." I couldn't look at her.

"Why did you come all this way to ask me for something you already have?"

"I don't have it." It was painful to admit, but she knew it didn't make sense for me to be here.

"I don't give a fuck." She sighed. "Sorry, Mom."

"Don't apologize to me." Roberta Webb's voice was cold. "Anything you want to say to that bastard seems appropriate."

Damn. She'd told her mom about what'd happened between us.

"Look," I said, "your computer was wiped and your accounts deleted."

"Again, I don't give a fuck. I don't work for you anymore. I didn't steal anything from your company, so you have no right to be here, where my mother and I are on vacation, demanding I give you something that you foolishly threw away."

I looked at her now and nearly flinched at the fury on her face. My reaction pissed me off, and I took a step toward her. "No, this is not on me. You falsifying information on your job application is why you were fired. That's on you. As per policy, you should have backed up everything somewhere, which means you either stole the backup or didn't make one. Both of which means it's on you."

"I didn't falsify shit." She pointed at me.

"You had research on me," I shot back.

"No, I had research on Finley Kordell!"

I didn't quite know how to take that. "It's the same thing."

"No, it's not." She shook her head. "He's my father."

FORTY-SEVEN
ASHLEE

As soon as the words left my mouth, I wished I could take them back. For four years I'd kept this secret close, never wanting my mother to know that I'd gone looking for the man who'd contributed to half my genetic makeup.

Tears flooded my eyes as anger and shame battled for control. Anger quickly won, and I stepped forward, planting my hands on Nate's chest and shoving him with every ounce of strength I had. He stumbled back, almost falling, the look on his face so comical that, had circumstances been different, I would have laughed.

"Go away!" My voice cracked, but I didn't care if he knew how pissed I was at him. He didn't matter. Only my mom did.

"Ashlee, I–"

"No!" I snapped. "Whatever you have to say, I don't want to hear it."

He held up his hands, palms out in the universal sign of surrender, and began walking backward, his expression stricken. I didn't wait to see how far he'd go or even for him to turn around. I needed to talk to my mom before things got any worse.

"I can explain," I said as I turned toward her. "Please."

Her face was pale, lips pressed into a flat line that I recognized all too well. As a child, I'd seen it when she and Mona had fought, only realizing later that it meant she'd been hurting.

I sat back down and moved my chair until I was facing her. I reached out, half-expecting her to refuse to let me touch her, but she didn't. I took her hands, hating how cold her fingers were, hating that I'd hurt the only person who'd always loved me, always been there for me. Even when she'd been fighting for her life, she'd made sure I didn't lose myself while helping take care of her.

"I'm so sorry, Mom. I never meant..." My words trailed off, my chest tightening.

"How long?" she asked softly, her eyes wet.

Maybe it made me a coward, but I avoided answering her question. "Finding my dad doesn't mean you're not an amazing parent or that I felt like something was missing in my life. It's just—"

She cut me off. "You think I'm upset because you looked for your father?"

I frowned, confused. "Aren't you?"

Mom sighed. "Ashlee, what was the one thing I always said was worse than any rule you broke?"

That was when it clicked. Shit. "Lying about it."

The two of us had never really butted heads like a lot of mothers and daughters, mostly because I was generally a good kid and she was an awesome mother. I'd never been a fan of parties or just hanging out, so there'd never really been a need for a curfew or grounding or anything like that. Despite that, I'd always known that if I broke a rule, it was better to confess than to try to hide it. Getting caught in a lie meant a punishment twice as harsh.

"I'm upset that you didn't feel like you could come to me about this," Mom said. "I could have helped you, or at the very least, listened when you needed to talk. You shouldn't have had to go through this alone. You could have trusted me."

Tears spilled down my cheeks. "I'm sorry, Mom. I'm so sorry. You're right. I should have come to you. I thought I was protecting you, but I should have trusted in you and our relationship."

She freed one hand and put it on my cheek, wiping my tears away with her thumb. "I love you, Ashlee. More than anything in this world, I love you."

"I love you, too," I sniffled. "Can you forgive me for lying to you about this?"

She leaned forward and kissed my forehead. "Of course. Forgiven and forgotten."

We leaned against each other and didn't say anything for several minutes. I knew that, eventually, I'd need to tell her the whole story, and I'd have to deal with whatever issues Nate had brought with him, but for a few minutes, I was content to sit right here with her.

Before I was ready, Mom pulled back, settling in a more comfortable position. I knew what she was going to say, but I waited for her anyway. I needed to be completely sure that this was what she wanted. I didn't want to lie or tell half-truths, but I also didn't want to give her too much information. Guilt and worry knotted my stomach. She had forgiven me, but I didn't know if I could forgive myself.

"Tell me everything."

She was the bravest woman I knew. After losing Mona, Mom could've been so frightened of losing me too, she could have held me back from the world. Now, she could have used my guilt against me to keep me from knowing my father. Instead, she wanted me to talk.

"When you were first diagnosed with cancer, it hit me that if you died, I'd be alone." I hated how blunt that was, but Mom had never liked sugar-coating, and if I was going to do this, I'd do it right. "I was seventeen, had only one parent and no extended family. I had a couple friends, but no one close to me except you."

"Ash, sweetie." Mom's eyes shone with tears. "I didn't know."

"I know, Mom." I gave her a watery smile. After a moment, I continued, "At some point, I started thinking that if I found out who my father was, maybe I would have someone if you died. I knew that it would be nearly impossible, but it was something I could think about when everything got to be too much."

"Was that what you did those times I was in the hospital, and you were home alone?"

"It was." My cheeks flushed. "I'm ashamed to say that I did some snooping. I had to find out where you'd gone for the insemination."

It was Mom's turn to frown. "I don't really have anything

that I'd worry about you finding, but I didn't think that I kept anything that would tell you about the sperm bank I used."

"It took me the better part of a year to finally find it. A charge on a credit card bill from the early nineties. It was stuffed in the back of a box in the back of your closet." I hesitated, then added, "There were some of Mona's things in there too."

A shadow of pain crossed her face, and I hated that there wasn't anything I could do about it. I'd often wondered if a part of her still loved Mona, and now, I was fairly certain of it.

"I put her things in an old box after she left," Mom said. "That statement must have gotten stuck from when I used the box for receipts."

"That makes sense," I said before going on with my story. "I was so excited when I found it. I don't know why I thought it'd be easy after that. I never thought of myself as foolish until I called the sperm bank and asked them to tell me who my father was. The receptionist was nicer than she had to be, but I knew it was because she felt sorry for me."

Mom reached out and touched my arm. A gentle reminder that I wasn't alone.

"I called pretty much every law firm in the city, trying to find someone who would try to get that name for me." The memories of those calls washed over me. The hope I'd felt every time I'd dialed a number, dashed the moment I was informed that they couldn't possibly take on such a case. Some of them were honest enough to say that it was about money. "Needless to say, no one would even try to help me without a sizable deposit and an insane hourly rate."

I didn't need to tell her what our finances had been like back then.

"Finally, just before I turned nineteen, I decided to go to the clinic myself, see if I could get answers if I made them look me in the eye. Of course, they still refused. So I went back the next day, and the next. Two weeks, and I didn't get answers. But I did manage to get someone to have a little sympathy for me. Laurie, her name was. I never got her last name." I looked down at my hands. "One day, while we were talking, she pulled up some information on her computer, and then walked away. Mid-sentence. Gave the screen a not-so-subtle look. I only had a minute, but I got the most important information. A name. Finley Kordell."

I could still remember how I'd walked out of the clinic, repeating his name like some sort of mantra. I didn't know where he was from or how old he was or anything like that, but I'd known that, with a name, I could find him.

"Finley Kordell isn't exactly a common name, so it didn't take me long to find out that a man with that name was co-owner of Manhattan Records. The newspaper clipping that Nate found, that's what led me to him. To Finley, I mean." I stopped myself from looking over my shoulder to see where Nate had gone.

"You changed your major to communications your sophomore year. Was it because of him?"

I nodded. "I didn't know how to talk to him, how to approach him. I didn't know what sort of man he was. If he'd been someone awful, I would've walked away, but I had to find out for myself what he was like. I couldn't trust an article in a newspaper. Not to tell me the sort of things I needed to know. I had to see him with my own eyes."

"So, you applied to be an intern?"

I shrugged. "It seemed like a good way to see how he treated everyone in the company, not just the ones at the top. Besides, it wasn't like I had some career planned out. It was as good a business as any."

"And what did you find?" Mom sounded curious, and for the first time, I wondered what it would be like to have her meet Finley.

Well, after I told him.

"He's a good man," I said. "Everyone speaks highly of him, and he's always been kind when I've seen him."

"You haven't talked to him yet?"

"Not exactly. He's a good man, but I don't know how he might react to finding out about me. He most likely has no idea that I exist. Hell, he could've even forgotten he'd made a deposit."

"If he doesn't immediately see that you're everything a father could want in a daughter, then he's an idiot."

I smiled at her. "That's only part of it. It's more about how I have no idea how to have that conversation. Just walk up and say it? Schedule an appointment?"

"That does present a dilemma," she said. "But I know you'll make the right choice, in the right time. And if you need me, I'll be there."

It was strange. I'd been so worried about telling Mom, and now that I had, it was as if a weight had lifted from my shoulders. Everything was perfect.

Almost.

"Now that you've explained things to me, you need to explain things to him." Mom gestured behind me, but I didn't need her to point. I knew who she meant and knew that he was still here because I could feel him watching me.

"I don't owe him an explanation," I said. "I'd tried to give him one before, but he didn't want it then. He can't suddenly decide to come after me, make accusations, and then get angry when I don't do what he wants."

"You don't see it, do you?"

"See what?" I asked, my insides squirming.

"He didn't come here for work. He came here for *you*. And I see it on your face, too." She was smiling, but her eyes were serious. "Go see if you can fix what's broken between you two. I'll be fine here."

FORTY-EIGHT

NATE

I COULDN'T SEEM TO STOP FUCKING THINGS UP WITH Ashlee. I'd kept telling myself that I was only coming down here for work, but as I walked away from her, I had to admit that I'd come for her. Despite everything, I still wanted her. And not just for sex either. I couldn't – or wouldn't – give it a name, but it was something I hadn't had before. Not with anyone. I wouldn't have come all this way for a little bit of information, no matter how much I'd tried to convince myself otherwise.

I needed more time with her to figure it all out.

I glanced back to where she was sitting with her mom and wondered what they were talking about. Yes, I knew they were talking about her bizarre statement that Finley was her father – and I was still trying to wrap my head around that – but I wondered about the details. Wondered how Finley could have had a child I'd never heard of before.

I didn't doubt she was telling the truth, or at least what

she believed the truth to be. The expression on her face when she'd blurted it out had been nothing but honest. Whatever the proof or story, she whole-heartedly believed that Finley Kordell was her father.

And I now felt more like an asshole than ever.

I hadn't let her explain. I'd just jumped to the worst conclusion, and that was it. If it'd been anyone else, I didn't know if I'd care as much. Maybe that made me a dick – okay, it definitely made me a dick – but I didn't care about people in general. She was different.

I wasn't sure how long I'd been standing there on the beach, hands in my pockets, sand in my shoes, when I heard footsteps behind me. I turned, not daring to hope that it was Ashlee and that she wasn't coming to tell me off for not going farther away.

I had an apology to make.

"Nate." Her voice was softer than I'd ever heard it. "We need to talk."

I let out the breath I'd been holding. "We do. But first, I need to tell you that I'm sorry for how I handled everything. I was wrong. I handled all of this the wrong way."

"That's definitely true," she said with the softest of smiles. "But I did hide things from you, including why I applied for a job at your record label."

"Finley's really your dad?"

"I'm as sure as I can be without a paternity test," she said. "The short version is that my mom used an anonymous sperm donor to have me. A few years back, I decided I wanted to find my father. I had the opportunity to see the name of my donor, and there aren't a lot of Finley Kordells, not even in New York City."

It didn't take much to connect the dots. "And an internet search brought you to the article I found."

She nodded. "I didn't know how to approach him or even if I wanted to get to know him."

"Finley's a great guy," I cut in.

"He is," she agreed. "And I know that now, but I didn't know that then. How could I? I didn't know him, and I'm not naïve enough to trust what the media has to say. Who knows what their biases and intentions are?"

My eyebrows went up at that. A lot of people believed what they read in magazines, and I'd naturally assumed she was one of them.

Me and my asinine assumptions.

"Maybe it wasn't the brightest way to go about it," she said, "but it's the path I chose."

I reached out and took her hand, waiting for her to pull away. When she didn't, I felt a flicker of hope and didn't squash it.

"Can we start over again?" I asked. "Go into things with our eyes wide open this time?"

"Does that mean we have to go the traditional route?" she asked, a smile playing on her lips.

"What?"

"Does starting over mean that we have to go on a certain number of regular dates before we have sex again?" She glanced over her shoulder at her mom, who smiled and nodded at us like she knew what we were talking about and approved.

"Ashlee..."

"Do you have a hotel room?"

My eyes met hers, and the confidence in them made me nod.

"Take me there."

She didn't have to tell me twice.

FORTY-NINE
ASHLEE

THE SMART THING TO DO WOULD'VE BEEN TO ASK HIM TO dinner, well-chaperoned by my mother, and make sure she knew not to let me go anywhere alone with Nate. The smart thing would've been to slow things down to a glacial pace, complete with chaste first kisses in this 'do-over.'

I'd done the smart thing most of my life. Taken the safe route. Hell, that was why I'd been working at the same place as my father for years and hadn't approached him with the truth.

Nate, it seemed, was the one person who short-circuited that part of my brain and made me behave impulsively. Recklessly.

When I told Mom that I was going somewhere more private with Nate, I almost expected her to tell me it was a bad idea. Common sense said it was a bad idea. *Everything* said it was a bad idea. Instead, she told me to have fun and double-checked that I had my room key in case I was 'out late.'

She would've made a great wingman if that hadn't been weird.

Mom and I hadn't skimped on our accommodations, but Nate took me to the sort of hotel where I'd never even imagined staying.

"How did you manage to get a room here on such short notice?" I asked as he led me through the opulent lobby to the elevators.

"I've been looking into buying a hotel or two in various vacation spots," he explained. "I just used it to my advantage. Besides, places like this usually keep a room or two open in case someone like me gets the sudden urge to go on a vacation." He glanced down at me, dark eyes sparkling with rare humor. "Or they need to go after a rogue employee."

Another couple got onto the elevator with us, and Nate surprised me by putting his arm around my waist and pulling me back against him, his palm hot against my bare skin. He kissed the top of my head before putting his mouth to my ear.

"If we were alone right now, *le soleil*, I'd slide my hand down the front of those tiny bikini bottoms you're wearing under that sarong. While my fingers were exploring that slippery, sensitive skin, my other hand would play with your nipples. Over your clothes, of course. I don't want anyone else seeing what's mine." His fingers flexed on my side. "I'd make you come before we reached our floor."

Fuck. Me.

I barely bit back a whimper and prayed my nipples weren't as visible under my top as I expected they were. I was trapped by his arm, by the fact that we weren't alone, and all I wanted to do was press my thighs together to relieve some of the ache between my legs.

The other couple exited one floor below our destination, and the tension radiating from Nate made me wonder if we'd even make it to his room before he gave in and kissed me. To my surprise, we left the elevator a few seconds later, without him having made a move of any kind. If it hadn't been for what he'd whispered in my ear, I might've thought his objective wasn't the same as mine.

Without losing hold of me, he unlocked the door and took me inside. I barely had time to register anything about his room before he spun us around, my back thudding against the door as he trapped me between it and his body. Again, I was reminded of the sheer size difference between the two of us.

His eyes locked on mine, and my heart leaped into my throat. The intensity I saw there was almost too much for me to handle, but I didn't look away. Despite everything that had happened between us, and everything we still had to work through, here, like this, I was safe. Safe to drop the walls I'd built up. Safe to be who I was and want what I wanted.

Long fingers wrapped around each of my wrists, then moved my arms up above my head, holding them there with one hand. His grip was tight enough to make things in my stomach go all fluttery, but not so much so that it hurt. It was different than when he'd restrained me before. The feel of his skin on mine. The knowledge that it was his fingers keeping me bound. He stared at me for another moment before crashing his mouth into mine.

I arched away from the door, desperate for more contact as his tongue teased my lips apart, then slipped inside, exploring as if it was our first kiss. His free hand untied my sarong before moving up to squeeze my breast. Talented digits pinched and teased my nipple through the thin material before pulling my top down. I tried to reach for him, to feel skin over hard muscles, run my nails across his shoulders and down his back, but he held me tight.

I squirmed, half-frustrated, half-aroused. He used his knee to move my legs apart, rocking his thigh against my now-damp bottoms. I moaned, and he chuckled, a rich, deep sound that vibrated through me. The sound turned into a growl as I nipped his bottom lip and he pinched my nipple in retaliation. My yelp sounded loud in my ears as he broke our kiss to bite his way down my jaw and neck. Dimly, I was aware that I should tell him not to mark me anywhere people could see, but it was a faint concern, pushed to the back of my mind with everything else that we'd eventually need to discuss.

His fingers moved beneath my bikini bottoms, and my head fell back against the door with a thud. Two strokes across my clit had me writhing, unsure if I wanted him to continue or stop until we made it to a bed.

"Do you want me to take you here, like this?" He broke the silence with an impossible question. "Up against the door, clothes mostly on, neither of us patient enough to go a few extra feet or take the time to undress."

His tone was leisurely, as if I couldn't feel how hard he was, as if I was the only one being teased.

"Yes," I whispered, desperate for something more than his fingers. He could make me come like this, I knew, but I wanted him inside me when I got there.

"Yes, what?" He palmed my sex, fingertips teasing my entrance without actually penetrating. "Say what you want. Look at me and tell me."

I met his gaze. "Fuck me like this. Here. Now."

His hand moved between us, and then he was there, thick shaft sinking into me even as he pulled my leg up around his waist. My eyelids fluttered, then closed, blocking out visual stimuli as my body and brain fought to cope with the new sensations coursing through me. His thrusts were short and fast, the base of his cock rubbing against my clit until I cried out, my climax taking me off-guard.

He was still inside me, hard and throbbing, as he released my arms and picked me up. I wrapped arms and legs around him, burying my face in his neck as he moved us over to the bed. I made a nonsense sound to protest him pulling out, but then I saw him undressing and settled back down, content to watch. He removed my clothes with the same efficiency, and then reached into his pants for a condom.

It wasn't until that moment that I realized he hadn't been wearing one before. I filed that away under more things we needed to talk about. After. Right now, I needed him back inside me.

He knelt on the bed between my legs, running his hands from my hips to my knees before lifting my legs to go around his waist. I automatically crossed my ankles and waited to see what he'd do next. His hands went to my breasts, palms rubbing over my hard nipples.

"There's so much I'm going to teach you, *le soleil*," he said, flicking my nipples hard enough to give me a little jolt of pain.

Before I could ask for an example, he gripped my hips and buried himself inside me. I gasped as he went deeper than before. I reached for him, but he pulled my ass higher, leaving all my weight on my upper back and shoulders. It would be a painful angle to maintain for a long time, but he didn't give me time to think about it for more than a fleeting second. He drove into me hard enough to make spots dance in front of my eyes, then did it again. And again. And again. Each stroke pushed the air from my lungs and stoked a fire in me that quickly had me calling out his name.

I couldn't reach him, couldn't feel him anywhere but the place where we were joined and the two places we held on to each other, but his presence surrounded me, consumed me until I wasn't sure I could survive much more. Just as it became too much, he pressed his thumb against my clit, pain and ecstasy impossibly mixing. I felt him jerk against me, say my name, pulse inside me...and then I was floating.

I'd have to come down eventually. Clean up. Dress. Talk. Things weren't settled between us, not by a long shot, but for these few moments, I let everything else go and enjoyed the part that was easiest for us. The part that made the world go away for at least a little while.

We'd work through the rest.

THE END

There's more to Nate and Ashlee's story in *The Dom (Manhattan Royals 2)*.
Don't miss Nate's brother, Joshua Lexington's book, *His Inspiration*. Turn the page for a free preview.

HIS INSPIRATION: PREVIEW

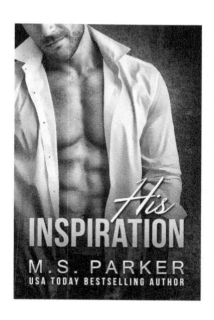

ONE

TRISSA

"I don't know why this surprises you. You've known me for, what, ten years now?"

I raised an eyebrow at Bevyan Kelly, my roommate and best friend. She had one of those poker faces that made it virtually impossible for me to tell if she was joking or serious. The fact that she was one of the smartest people I knew didn't even factor into the equation since I'd once watched her search for her phone while holding a conversation on said phone.

"Five, Bevyan," I said finally. "Ten years ago, we were both fifteen and living on opposite sides of the country."

She frowned, a slight crease appearing between her eyebrows. "Huh. I guess you're right."

"I have to ask. Were you forgetting how long it'd been since we were in college, making us older than we actually are, or were you forgetting that we'd met in college?"

"I'm not sure." She smiled, her pewter gray eyes lighting

up. "But at least we're at an age where it's always nice to remember we're not as old as we think we are."

One of the things I loved the most about her was her inability to stay down for more than a few minutes before her naturally bubbly personality chased the darkness away. It wasn't that she didn't know how to take things seriously, but rather that she always looked for the silver lining. She was so genuine about it that I never managed to stay annoyed when she did it to me.

"I always assumed that you didn't know how to drive because a lot of native New Yorkers don't bother learning since there's so many public transportation options." I stood as the timer on the washer reached one minute. It was all too easy to get distracted when talking to Bevyan, and I didn't want to spend the entire night at the laundromat.

Bevyan reached for a strand of hair to twist around her finger, then scowled when she remembered that she'd cut her dark blonde locks short to break this exact habit. I would've thought it was a bit drastic a move simply to prevent playing with hair, but I was the one who'd had to help her two weeks ago when she'd cut off circulation in her finger and hadn't been able to free herself.

"My parents wanted me to learn how to drive, even if I didn't need to." She hopped off the out-of-order dryer and came over to join me. We folded our clothes as she continued her story. "I told them I didn't think it was a good idea, but Mom said I needed to know how to drive, in case I was ever kidnapped."

I wished I could say that particular bit of information shocked me, but I'd met Bevyan's parents. Francie Kelly had come from the sort of old money, high society family where kidnapping had been an actual threat. Add in the fact that Bevyan's father was one of the top television producers in New York and neither of the Kellys was overreacting when it came to their daughter's safety.

"Anyway, she and Dad hired this bodyguard to teach me defensive driving. The kind you'd use when being chased, all that."

Bevyan's voice, as usual, carried, and I watched the two older women at the far end of the washer row turn in our direction. I gave them a sheepish, embarrassed smile, but didn't bother trying to quiet my friend. It wouldn't do any good. At least this way, everyone got to hear what was sure to be an entertaining story.

"No one bothered to tell Harris that I also needed to know basic driving skills. I'd never been behind a wheel until I went for my first lesson, and I spent almost two months with Harris teaching me all these maneuvers and tricks." Bevyan held up my black cotton bra, a disapproving expression on her face. "This should be hand-washed and hung to dry."

It wasn't the first time she'd told me that. I snatched the bra from her and dropped it in the basket with the other clean clothes. "I would do that if there was a space anywhere in our apartment that wasn't already being used for your lingerie."

She grinned at me and went back to her story. "Anyway, my parents sent me out to take my driver's test without bothering to ask if any of the hours I'd put in had been regular driving. So the license person got into the car and told me to pull out of the parking space." She shrugged. "Let's just say I'd never heard the phrase 'flunked with flying colors' before."

"How have I never heard that story before?" I asked. "I mean, you'd think it would've come up at some point."

"And when, exactly, would it have come up?" she countered. "When we were being chased by assassins through Beverly Hills?"

I pointed at her. "Your sarcasm, my friend, is much appreciated."

"You'll appreciate my driving if we're ever caught in a car chase."

"I'm sure I will."

The bell over the door dinged as the two older women carried their baskets out. For a moment, I wondered if that would be me and Bevyan in the future. Then I remembered that she and her boyfriend, CB, had been talking about moving in together. And that wasn't even considering the fact that she might just decide to go back to New York and leave both me and CB behind.

I pushed those thoughts aside. Planning for the future was one thing. Worrying about what things may or may not happen due to circumstances I had absolutely no control over was pointless. I'd learned that as a kid.

"Does this mean you're going to teach me to drive?" Bevyan picked up one of her shirts and folded it in half before dropping it into our basket.

I watched it fall and then looked at her. "Will me teaching you to drive have better results than when I tried to teach you how to fold your clothes?"

"I already knew how to fold my clothes," Bevyan countered. "I've just always sucked at it."

"Your parents didn't hire someone to teach you how to

properly fold garments?" I laughed as I said it, but I wasn't entirely joking.

She shook her head. "We had a housekeeper who did the laundry, but I had to fold and put away my own since I was a kid. That and cleaning my room were always my responsibilities. I had other chores growing up, but those two things were always mine."

"Is that why your room is such a disaster?" I asked. "You had to spend your childhood cleaning up after yourself, so now you don't want to?"

"Exactly."

My phone buzzed with a text alert, and I fished it out of my pocket.

Thank you for the model heart. It was exactly what I wanted. Love Meg.

I smiled as I hit reply. *I'm glad to hear it, but I can't take all the credit. Kevin told me you'd asked for it.*

"Meg?" Bevyan asked.

I nodded. "I have to remember to give Kevin something extra nice for his birthday. He was exactly right."

"Meg's a little scientist," Bevyan said. "Not surprising. You said she was smart."

"She is." I sent off a good night text and put my phone back in my pocket. "Is it weird that I hate what my dad did to my mom and our family, but I love Meg and Madison to pieces?"

"Not weird at all," Bevyan said. "Meg and Madison are awesome."

"You've never met either of them," I pointed out.

"Not true."

"FaceTime does not count."

"It does too count. FaceTime introductions are just as valid as face-to-face ones," she informed me. "But I still want to meet the munchkins for real. I've met everyone else in your family."

"Maybe I'll take them for a weekend in the summer," I said. "Three days and two nights with an eight-year-old and a five-year-old should cure you of ever wanting to spend time with anyone else in my family ever again."

"If your teenage brother shooting spit-balls down my shirt during dinner wasn't enough to chase me away, then I don't think two little girls would do it."

"You never did much babysitting, did you?" I asked with a laugh.

"Only child, remember?" She stuck her entire head and shoulders into the dryer and emerged with a single sock. "Dammit."

"Another deposit for the lone sock drawer," I said, plucking it from her hand. "Didn't any of your friends growing up have younger brothers or sisters?"

"Yes, but those families had nannies."

"Ah, yes, of course. Nannies. Why didn't I think of that?"

Bevyan threw a wet sock at me. I caught it and tossed it into the dryer. "We'll get pizza and ice cream and watch Disney movies."

"Meg's a vegetarian and Madison is lactose intolerant."

"Not a problem," Bevyan said. "I know how to made lactose free, vegetarian pizza."

"Bevy, I love you," I closed the dryer door, "but I've seen

you try to cook. You lost the security deposit because you blew up the microwave a month after we moved in."

"In my defense, it was the fork's fault the microwave blew up." Bevyan pointed at me. "And you've never seen me make pizza."

"True, but you did leave the fork in the popcorn bowl."

She planted her hands on her hips. "That's it. We're stopping at Whole Foods, and I'm making pizza for a late-night snack."

I was too busy explaining to her the reasons why we couldn't stop for pizza making supplies that I didn't notice a third person entering the laundromat until he grabbed my purse off the counter and ran.

"Shit!" I nearly twisted my ankle turning so fast. Bevyan shouted after me, but I was already heading to the door. She'd call the cops, but by then, the thief would be long gone with my purse.

I didn't have much cash, but it was all in there. I'd worked my ass off for every penny of it, and I'd be damned if I was going to let some jerk run off with it.

I hit the bar on the door with both my palms and it flew open. The sun had already set, but the street lights in this area were surprisingly good. I assumed that because I'd seen him turn right, I'd be able to spot him running away.

And that might have been the case if I hadn't run into something large and hard before I'd gone more than a couple steps.

I bounced off and landed on my ass, hard enough to jar my spine and clank my teeth together. I'd put my hands out too, and I knew I was going to feel it all in the morning, but I couldn't let myself feel it now. I didn't have the time. I let out a string of curses as I tried to pull my feet underneath me, but as soon as I did, white-hot pain shot through my ankle, and it buckled.

"Fuck!"

"Let me–"

I looked up at what I'd hit and found a huge man leaning over me. "What the fuck were you thinking?!"

TWO
JOSHUA

I DIDN'T REALIZE SOMEONE HAD RUN INTO ME UNTIL I'D taken two steps back and she started cursing at me from the sidewalk. I wasn't the most social of people, but I'd always assumed that I had basic conversational skills for situations such as this. Knock someone down, help them up and apologize.

I stared at her, completely at a loss for words. I couldn't tell how tall she was, but she looked delicate from where I was standing. Shoulder-length jet-black hair and porcelain skin made me think of Snow White, but her mouth was definitely not Disney-rated.

To my embarrassment, my mind instantly went to other non-Disney things she could do with her mouth, and blood rushed south. I clamped down on those wayward thoughts and started mentally singing the Fluffy Bottom jingle. No better way to kill an erection than singing about toilet paper.

She tried to stand before I could offer her a hand but

swore again as her leg buckled. A new wave of guilt washed over me as I realized she was hurt. Not just guilt, I realized. An unfamiliar wave of protectiveness hit me too.

"Let me—"

"What the fuck were you thinking?!" she snapped, her dark eyes angry.

My eyebrows shot up. I had no problem taking part of the blame for the collision, but she hadn't been paying attention to where she was going any more than I had been.

"I didn't see you," I said as I held out my hand.

"Are you blind as well as rude?" She glared at my hand. "I was right behind the thief who stole my purse. You managed to not run into him."

I remembered seeing a guy running across the street about half a minute before she hit me, and I turned to look, but he was already gone. He could've been anywhere. I knew of at least half a dozen alleyways he could've used to get to the next street over where he had too many escape possibilities to count.

"I would've caught him if you hadn't gotten in my way."

I turned my attention back to the girl who was now gingerly touching her ankle. I'd first put her age around nineteen or twenty, but now that I studied her a bit more closely, I added a few years to put her closer to twenty-five than twenty.

And I noticed something else. She wasn't being bitchy because she was some self-absorbed teenager. She was angry at the situation, including the fact that she was hurt and vulnerable in front of a stranger.

"He went across the street," I said as I leaned down to put a hand under her elbow. "I didn't see where he went from there. It's too easy to disappear in this damned city."

She jerked her arm away the moment we made contact, and I mentally smacked myself as I realized that my previous statement wasn't very supportive.

I took in a deep breath and tried again. "My name's Joshua Lexington. I just want to help you up, I swear."

Her eyes narrowed, but she let me set her on her feet, her hand tightening on my arm momentarily as she tested her injured ankle. When she released me, I felt the strangest urge to tell her she could lean on me as long as she wanted.

"Let's go inside, and I'll call the cops while you get off that ankle."

The look she sent my way said that my suggestion wasn't a welcome one.

"I have my phone," she said, her voice softening a little. "Besides, my friend should have called them all ready."

I was surprised at how curious I was about this 'friend' of hers. Was she saying that as a protective measure, something to chase me away if I'd been looking to prey on a lone woman? Or did she have an actual friend waiting for her? A guy who might want something more? A girlfriend, maybe?

What the hell was I thinking?

I shook my head as she turned back the way she'd come. The laundromat she'd come out of was only a couple yards away, but I'd seen the pain on her face when she tried to put down her full weight. A part of me doubted she'd be able to make it even that far without help, but a larger part thought that she'd do it just to prove she could. Whether she'd be proving it to me or to herself, I hadn't yet figured out.

I followed a few steps behind her, wondering if at any time she'd turn around and tell me to get lost or she'd be calling the cops on me too, but she didn't. She stayed focused on her goal, and the reflection in the glass front of the laundromat showed me the determined look on her face.

I had to admit, I was impressed. She'd charged after a thief, but even after she knew she wouldn't be able to continue giving chase, she hadn't called for help. She said she had her phone still, so she could have called her friend. No one would have thought any less of her.

"Trissa!" A slender blonde came running the moment the girl – Trissa – stepped inside. "What happened?"

"Ask him." Trissa jerked her thumb over her shoulder. "Gigantor back there got in my way."

"Gigantor? Really?" I wanted to laugh, but this didn't seem like the best time or place.

She turned toward me as she leaned against a washer, and I saw that her eyes weren't brown or black like I'd assumed, but rather a deep purplish-blue that I'd never seen before. Not in someone's eyes anyway. Her fingers snapped in front of my eyes, and I realized I'd been staring again.

"I said you can go. Bevyan already called the cops so we'll wait for them here."

"What if he comes back?" I countered. No decent guy would've let two young women wait alone in a laundromat after they'd been robbed. I could be a jerk sometimes, but I was close enough to my mother to hate thinking about what sort of guy would do that to her.

"Why would he?" Bevyan asked. "He knows that Trissa was chasing him and that we'd call the cops. If he got away free and clear with one of our purses, why would he risk getting caught?"

Logically, that made sense, but I knew criminals didn't always think logically. "Maybe he'll think that if he gets to you, he can keep you from pressing charges."

"Shit." Trissa's eyes went wide. "My license and my key were in there."

"That settles it," I said. "You two can stay at my place tonight."

"Excuse me?" Trissa's expressive face told me exactly what she was about to say. "You're just a stranger I *literally* just ran into. Why are you any safer than the punk who took my purse?"

I opened my mouth to give her a list of reasons and then realized that those reasons didn't mean anything if she didn't know that they were true. For all these two knew, I was working with the thief, or I was someone worse than a purse snatcher.

"You're right," I said. When both girls tensed, I quickly clarified. "You don't know me. *I* know I'm trustworthy, but you don't know that. But you two shouldn't be alone tonight."

Why was I pushing this so hard? I didn't know these women. Sure, one of them had run into me, and as a result, had lost the person she was chasing, but I didn't owe her anything for that. I might not have been paying as much attention as I should have been, but neither had she. The only reason she'd been the one of us to get knocked down was the difference in our sizes.

"We won't be," Bevyan said, putting her arm around her friend's shoulders. "We'll stay with my boyfriend."

If I hadn't been looking at Trissa, I might've missed the annoyance crossing her face. Something told me that Trissa wasn't a fan of Bevyan's boyfriend, and Bevyan didn't know it.

"Is he on his way?" As soon as I asked it, I wanted to take it back. Everything I said was coming out wrong, making me seem like I was one of those creepy stalkers or serial killers who lurked in the dark, searching for single women to assault or kill.

"He's working, actually," Bevyan said. She yelped as Trissa dug an elbow into her side. "What? If this guy was going to turn us into lampshades, he would've done it by now."

Fortunately for both Trissa and me, the sound of police sirens filled the laundromat, and we all turned toward the door to watch the blue and red lights flash as a cop car pulled up front. I stepped back, my hands hanging open at my side. I didn't want to get mistaken for a criminal simply because I was a big guy in a room with two women more than a foot shorter than me.

The first cop rushed through the door, eyes wide in a way that made me think this was his first crime-in-progress. The way his hand hovered over his gun worried me as much as the fact that the kid nearly tripped over his own feet as he skidded to a stop. Then his gaze zeroed in on me, and he swallowed hard.

"What...who...I mean..."

The door opened again, and the other police officer came

in. I wondered if the exhaustion on his face was from all the nervous energy his partner was putting out or something else.

"I called," Bevyan announced. "Some guy stole my friend's purse."

"Wait, a purse?" The younger guy's eyes darted from me to the girls and then back again. "I thought it was a robbery in progress."

Bevyan put her hands on her hips and sighed. "It was when I called. This guy came in here, grabbed my friend's purse and ran with it. She chased him but had a little...accident."

"*He's* not a little accident," Trissa muttered, glaring at me. But I didn't feel the heat of anger in the look this time. When her gaze met mine, pink crept into her cheeks.

No, not anger. Maybe interest? Something else?

"What did you do to her?" The younger cop stepped between me and the girls, cutting off my crazy thoughts. The action made me respect him a little more since I was several inches taller and definitely outweighed him.

I held up my hands, palms out. "I was out running, and when she ran out to follow the thief, we collided."

"And then you followed her?" Now, the older cop was giving me funny looks.

"She hurt her ankle," I explained, trying to keep the exasperation from my voice, "and I didn't think it was safe for the two of them to wait here alone. In case the guy came back."

"If we take you in, are they going to say the same story?"

How had I ended up a suspect? I'd just been trying to help.

"He didn't steal my purse," Trissa cut in. "He's annoying, but not a thief."

I huffed out a breath. "Thank you?" I turned my attention from Trissa back to the older cop. "Before she and I ran into each other, I saw someone in a hoodie run across the street. I didn't get a good look, but he was probably a little under six feet tall and skinny. Fast."

"Are you sure it was a man?"

"I'm sure," Bevyan interjected. "I looked over when he first came in. The hoodie was dark gray, and he was wearing blue jeans and sneakers."

"I saw his hands when he grabbed my purse. He had light brown skin," Trissa said. "Like a really good summer tan."

"Anything else? Identifying features?" The younger guy jotted down notes as we answered the questions he and his partner asked.

Now that I'd given them all that I had to offer and they knew I wasn't involved in the theft, it'd be easy to leave. The cops wouldn't keep me here, and the women were safe.

Once they were done here, they'd go to Bevyan's boyfriend's house for the night and then deal with changing the locks and canceling credit cards...and why was I even going through a mental checklist of the things they'd need to do? I'd already made this too much of a thing. I had my own life and my own problems. I needed to get back to them.

"Do you need me for anything else?" I asked during a pause in the interview. "I only wanted to make sure that the ladies were safe."

"Can you give me a number where you can be reached if we think of any additional questions?" the older cop asked.

I rattled off my cell number and then headed for the door. I could feel eyes on me as I left, but I didn't turn around. I just wanted to finish my run and go home. It wasn't late, but I'd had a long day already.

I'd cooled down while waiting, so I walked a few feet down the sidewalk and stretched my muscles back out, then bounced on my toes...but didn't take the next step and start jogging.

Dammit.

I couldn't do it. I couldn't walk away and not know they at least made it safely from here to where they'd go next. The cops probably wouldn't escort the pair home unless they asked, and my gut said that they'd tell the cops they needed to finish their laundry or something like that.

Mind made up, I jogged up and down the sidewalk, never going far enough that I couldn't keep an eye on the doors. When I saw the cops drive away after another five minutes, and no sign of the girls, I knew I'd been right.

How had those two survived in LA as naïve as they were? Maybe I was misjudging them, and maybe I was being a little chauvinistic, wanting to protect two young women, but I wasn't going to apologize for it. Not when all I wanted to do was keep them safe. I couldn't explain why I felt so strongly that I needed to do it, but I did. Once I knew they were safe in the boyfriend's place, then I'd go home.

END OF PREVIEW

The story continues in His Inspiration, coming on Amazon at

the end of the year. But you can read it now! Become a M.S. Parker VIP.

CLICK HERE to sign up and get your copy today. All my newsletter subscribers have already received the pre-release ebook AND audiobook for free.

OFFICE ROMANCES BY M. S. PARKER

Chasing Perfection

Unlawful Attraction

A Legal Affair

The Pleasure Series

Serving HIM

The Billionaire's Muse

Bound

One Night Only

Damage Control

Pure Lust Box Set

Made in the USA
Monee, IL
31 January 2021

59280867R00193